CW00408537

London Calling

2nd Edition

MARK DAYDY

Cover design by MIKE DAYDY

CONTENTS

1. NOW

London – the present day

Approaching Broadcasting House from Oxford Circus, Erin Goodleigh felt the memories gathering. So much had happened here all those years ago, when life revolved around the old place.

Slaloming through the oncoming human traffic, past the busy shops and restaurants, with All Souls Church partially concealing the ultimate destination... how many years had it been?

Too many.

As she rounded the church, her eyes rose to greet the statue of Prospero and Ariel, mounted over the entrance of the old building.

She paused before going in – her eyes drawn to the right, where the new building ran parallel to the old to form a canyon that ended in curved glass. It was a marvel of sympathetic design, with both buildings united in a horseshoe shape, one side eighty years older than the other.

Back in her time, they only had the old part, of course. The old, grimy, rundown, falling-to-bits part. Now the Portland stone looked clean and cared for.

Two men got out of a taxi and headed for the glass

curve at the end of the canyon. One was the Minister for Health. And even as she watched him making his way to the new foyer, pop star Ed Sheeran was emerging and laughing along with a couple of people.

Broadcasting House, home of radio.

It all happened here.

It always had.

She wouldn't be going into the new bit. It was the old entrance for her. The original portal into the world of broadcast.

Pushing through the art deco doors revealed...

Oh, that's different.

Ahead should have been a small desk with a receptionist waiting to greet her. Beyond the desk would be the ancient lifts to whisk her up to the top floor, or the stairs should she feel like the exercise.

Ahead though, was a glass wall. The lifts and stairs were beyond this impenetrable barrier. The reception desk was now to her left.

"I'm here to see the Head of Radio Four," she informed the receptionist, a young man with Stan Laurel hair.

"If you could sign in, I'll let them know you're here."

While she entered her details into the visitors' book, the receptionist phoned upstairs.

"Someone will be down to collect you," she was duly informed.

"No need, it's the top floor, isn't it?"

"Yes, but you have to be accompanied. They won't be long. Please do take a seat."

She took a seat and checked Facebook on her phone.

A few moments later, behind the glass, a lift door opened to let out a young man with messy hair. He pushed through the glass security door, checked with reception, and came over.

"Erin?"

"Hi, that's me."

"Great. I'm Jonathan. If you could follow me."

Erin did so, watching Jonathan use a pass to activate the door. Then they were through and waiting for a lift.

"Have you been to Broadcasting House before?"

"Yes, this is where I started over twenty years ago – as a non-commissioned writer on a light entertainment show."

"Oh great."

"Mind you, back then there wasn't security glass. A wannabe writer could walk in off the street without an invitation and talk with producers and script editors."

"Really? I didn't know that."

"Yes, straight in off the street. No ID, no questions asked."

"That wouldn't be allowed now."

"No, well… it's a different world now."

As they stepped into the lift, Erin glanced back, through the security glass, to the main entrance. Had it really been that long ago? Where had the time gone?

She could almost see herself entering, young and anxious…

2. THEN

Standing outside Broadcasting House, the home of radio, all the doubts began to surface again. What was she doing here?

Erin's gaze rose up to behold the statue of Prospero and Ariel. Impressive, if a little grimy – like the rest of the building.

No matter. This was it. She was almost thirty. It was time to get her life on track.

Not for the first time, her nerves flared, but she held them at bay with a steadying breath. Two and a half years earlier, lazy, useless Ian Crawford-Troy had walked in through this very entrance. Now it was her turn.

Pushing through the art deco doors, she entered a 1930s time-warp reception area. It was library-quiet. A woman was reading a magazine by the window to the right. To the left, a man stood by a potted plant, possibly thinking of hiding behind it.

Ahead lay a small reception desk and, just beyond it, art deco lift doors.

Erin approached the desk, staffed by a man in his forties talking in a low voice on the phone. Maybe the Head of BBC Radio was calling down to ask if Mr Bean had arrived yet. Poor choice, really, as Bean's visual comedy would be rubbish on radio.

She straightened her midnight blue power suit and puffed up her auburn bob. *London, here I am.* Okay, so power suits had gone out of fashion five years ago. So what? Just because nobody said 'dress for success' anymore didn't make it wrong. Besides, she didn't buy clothes much and the power suit had spent five years in the wardrobe waiting for its chance to get out there and be powerful. Was she overdressed? *No way!*

She thought of Ian Crawford-Troy again; one hand up her blouse, his breath smelling like a brewery, a bit of tuna stuck between his front teeth…

She snapped out of it.

Positive thoughts…

Her mum's worries came back to her.

"Watch out for IRA bombs, Erin. The Grand National had to be called off."

"Mum, the Grand National is run in Liverpool, not London."

"They bombed the London Docklands, Erin. And Downing Street. They bombed Harrods, too. Try not to shop there."

Positive thoughts…

Meditation. That was the key. Think of nothing.

Ian Crawford-Troy… in London… writing professionally. What pact with Satan had he entered into?

Erin continued fighting her nerves, although it wasn't easy with adrenalin seemingly shooting from a burst fire hydrant in her stomach.

Why didn't I fax the sketches!

But no. Ian Crawford-Troy, via his mum, had said that some producers didn't like the fax machine's flimsy paper and faint print. They wanted print quality paper that could be photocopied and distributed to performers. He also reckoned the BBC didn't have the staff to track down non-commissioned faxes. You might send in a lot of work that ended up with other faxes on the wrong desk. That's not to say someone wouldn't work out who they were intended for but whether that would happen before the show's deadline...

Also, according to Ian, they wouldn't accept e-mails as the computers were slow and tended to crash if there was too much activity.

She eyed the woman with the magazine, now tapping a number into a mobile cellular phone. Flash or what? It was only high-flying business execs and Mafioso who had those. Okay, so more people were getting them now that they weren't the size of a house brick, but they still cost a fortune.

"Rob, I'll be a few minutes late," she said into the phone. "Colin's still not here ... Okay, see you soon."

Erin checked her watch again. The meeting would be starting soon and the receptionist looked deep into a long call.

Crap.

What if she asked Woman With Phone if she could call someone inside the BBC?

"Excuse me...?"

Woman With Phone stuffed her phone into a handbag.

"The battery's dead. Had to switch it off."

"Oh. Right."

Just then, as Woman With Phone's phone began ringing, the receptionist looked up – his previous business finished.

"Can I help?"

"Hello, yes, I've come for the *It's News To Us* non-commissioned writers' meeting."

"That was yesterday."

"What?"

Erin's heart began thumping like the bass guitar in Led Zeppelin.

Chaos.

Disorder.

Death.

Indeed, whole worlds ending.

"Or was that *Newslines*?" the receptionist said absently. "No, you're probably right. First floor, Light Entertainment. If you could sign in first."

Erin had to wait for her near-death experience to pass before she could pick up the pen.

Once she had shakily signed in, she wanted to ask for specific directions, but the phone rang and the receptionist picked it up.

Beyond the desk were three options. To the right, an escalator. Ahead, the lifts. To the left, stairs. The receptionist put his hand over the phone's mouthpiece and eyed Erin.

"Stairs or lift for the first floor. The escalator goes to the second then you walk down one."

"Thanks."

It occurred to her that if Broadcasting House dated back to the 1930s, then so did its lifts. God, after sixty years, the cables holding them might be threadbare. She could see the newspaper headline now: "Writer Trapped In Basement Wreckage – Receptionist Unaware Due To Endless Phone Calls".

She opted for the stairs.

Halfway up the first flight, she looked back across the ground floor reception area. She was inside the home of radio. *In-bloody-side.*

At the top of the stairs, she turned and entered a long, grubby corridor where an electrician was wrestling with cables. A door opened farther on and a man emerged laughing. None of the signs stated Light Entertainment though.

Erin continued to the double doors at the end of the corridor. Pushing through, she found yet more corridor stretching on for miles with no sign of a portal into the world of Light Entertainment. Still, one of the door signs stated 'Ladies'. Did she have time? She checked her watch. Two minutes. No sense in wriggling during the meeting. It was a well-known fact that you couldn't wriggle and concentrate at the same time, and she hadn't come 150 miles to mess this up.

Perched on an ancient toilet, she wondered what famous bottoms had sat on this very loo. Then she pondered whether or not this was madness. No, she doing the right thing. Had she not co-written the school play back in sixth form? Had she not written sketches for a comedy troupe at university? Had she not performed at the Edinburgh Festival Fringe...?

She thought back to just before Christmas – to the soul-stewing moment Ian Crawford-Troy's mum dropped the Ian revelation at the Taunton Amateur Dramatic Society's *Cinderella* rehearsals.

"Ian's a professional writer with the BBC in London."

Her son? Ian? The laziest b—

It wasn't until January that she called the BBC to find out how one went about switching from amateur pantomime to national broadcasting. She was transferred a couple of times and ended up talking to Sarah Bryce in Light Entertainment Radio. Sarah's response was incredibly encouraging – for anyone living in London. For someone living 150 miles away in Taunton, it wasn't quite so heartening. In short, coming into the building was everything, because people making shows didn't have time to field calls and faxes from non-commissioned writers.

She checked her watch.

Bloody hell!

Hurrying, she was soon out of the cubicle, washing her hands, re-entering the corridor and rushing onward with no time to spare.

The corridor eventually brought her to another set of double doors. Above them, a large banner sign proclaimed BBC Light Entertainment Radio. Her nerves jangled. But she didn't have time for nerves. She had been heckled on stage at the Edinburgh Fringe. She could handle this.

3. THE WRITERS' ROOM

Erin pushed through into an area with comfy seats and a coffee table covered in newspapers and magazines. A dozen young men were hanging around, reading or chatting in low voices. None of them had dressed nicely. To the left and ahead were a few offices, while in the far right corner, a set of glass double doors were open and led to another, smaller corridor.

Erin weighed her options. Maybe a quick word with the broadcast assistant she had spoken to in January.

She popped her head into one of the adjoining offices.

"I'm looking for Sarah Bryce," she asked a middle-aged woman.

"Opposite the writers' room."

"Er...?"

The woman came out and indicated the open double doors. Erin thanked her and went through into a short corridor flanked by small offices. *The inner sanctum.* Seven or eight scruffy men were hanging around by a door up on the right. Stopping short of them, she popped her head into an office on the left. There was a solitary young woman inside.

"Hi, I'm looking for Sarah Bryce."

"Guilty."

"Great. I'm Erin Goodleigh. I phoned you a few

months ago?"

Sarah did what could have only been a mental check through the no-doubt four million people she had spoken to on the phone in the past three months. To her credit, she smiled.

"Have you come for *It's News To Us?*"

"Yes."

"The door with the crowd outside is the writers' room. The commissioned writers are in with the producer at the moment. Once they're done, there'll be a meeting for the non-comms."

"Great. Thanks. That's brilliant."

"They started late so you might have to wait ten minutes or so."

"Right."

"So, probably best to wait in the reception area."

"By the main entrance?" It seemed a long way to go.

"No, just out there in the LE reception."

"LE?"

"Light Entertainment. Or Light Ent. Call it LE and you'll fit right in."

Sarah's phone rang. It was Erin's prompt to leave. Did they like hordes of non-commissioned writers cluttering up the inner sanctum? She doubted it. She felt like mentioning it to the scruffy gathering but decided against it.

Back in the LE reception area, Erin smiled at the nearest faces and tried to remain calm. *I can do this.* There were a dozen non-commissioned writers here, another batch outside the writers' room, and no doubt a small army of commissioned writers inside it. Okay, so she had some competition. No problem. It just required a bit of focus.

Yes, focus…

For some reason, it occurred to her that she didn't fancy any of the writers on view. Not that she was in London for that. She had Charles, who played a lot of rugby, which meant he took plenty of showers. His job as a lawyer also meant he dressed nicely. Looking around, Erin couldn't believe how scruffy this lot were. Was it a post-student thing? The thought annoyed her. Why hadn't she known about LE when she left university back in the late-80s?

Focus.

Yes, it was all about the here and now – an opportunity to become a writer with contracts and an agent. And wouldn't it be brilliant to go to an awards ceremony as a nominee?

"Here for the *It's News To Us* meeting?" a scruffy young man asked her.

"Yes," she replied. "You?"

"Yes," he said, smiling nervously.

She had listened to the previous week's show, of course. Prior to that, she'd never heard of *It's News To Us* despite its incredibly long run. Still, having listened a few times to the cassette recording she made, she understood what was required. Sketches about the week's events.

One of the men got up and went through to the writers' room. Something in Erin, the eternal head of the sixth form, wanted to suggest waiting until they were called but the other non-commissioned writers were only half a beat behind.

Following them, Erin found the engorged throng outside the writers' room becoming talkative.

"Get anything on?" asked one.

"No," said another. "You?"

"No."

Suddenly, the writers' room door opened and out they

came – the gods, the chosen ones, the commissioned writers. There were around ten of them and they were only marginally less scruffy than the non-commissioned bunch.

"Come in, come in," said a cheery fellow wearing a purple waistcoat and gold-framed glasses.

Erin filed in with the others. It was an uninspiring room with an old upright piano, a few chairs, a couple of tables and half a dozen typewriters, a few of which were electric. The seats went fast so Erin stood by the piano.

With the arrival of some latecomers, including another female writer, there were soon around twenty-five of them crammed in. A fire hazard, surely. Oddly, one writer was laying on the floor, maybe to absorb the meeting in a Zen-like manner. Or maybe he was catching up on his sleep.

She looked down. She was treading on a foot. She looked up to its owner, a sapphire blue-eyed, dark-haired tall guy in his mid-thirties wearing a Clash t-shirt.

"Sorry," she whispered, even though it was clearly his fault for having enormous feet.

Or did he? She gauged them. Size what... nine? Not all that big after all. Obviously, he was just careless about where he put them.

"Okay," said the man in the purple waistcoat. "Most of you know I'm an escaped South American military dictator posing as Gavin Gould the script editor. If you're new, you'll have just seen the producer and commissioned writers fleeing. It's nothing personal. The producer has just gone through this week's news stories with them and they'll go off and write lots of lovely sketches. My job is to go over the same stories with you highly talented non-commissioned writers. Your job is to come up with better sketches than the commissioned mob and get your stuff on the show. Okay, any questions?"

Erin felt her hand go up a little. She pulled it down again. *Stupid hand!*

But too late. Gavin had x-ray vision.

"Yes?"

"Oh… should we avoid covering what the commissioned writers are covering? I mean the angles they might take? Sort of thing?"

"Just write brilliant sketches on the topics we cover in this meeting. Worrying about what others might do will drive you insane and you'll end up a gibbering wreck in the pub. If that happens, mine's a lager."

Erin smiled. Gavin was nice. He had a way of putting people at ease.

"Okay, we have half a dozen more shows before the summer break. If you give it a real go you'll have three months to bask in the glory of your successful sketch-writing. Trust me, there will be people hunting you down for your autograph, or if you've mocked Tony Blair, just hunting you down. So – this week we have the election looming and lots of silliness from Major, Blair and Ashdown. Now there are a few angles the producer is particularly keen on…"

Erin felt like a dinghy adrift in a sea of news stories. She had never been a fan of satire. Yes, she put topical jokes into Christmas pantomimes for TADS – the Taunton Amateur Dramatic Society but that was just a bit of fun. And yet, here she was, among a couple of dozen men – and one other woman – about to do battle on the satire front. Why had she come? What was the point?

She thought back to the previous week's show. The first time she listened to the tape she failed to understand it. A second listen was helpful and she was able to hear that there were some decent jokes in there. It was a jumble of styles though and it lacked coherence and consistency. Its producer was Leanne Fuller, although, according one of Ian's tip-offs via his mum, the show changed producers on a regular basis.

"Stop me at any point if you have a question," said Gavin.

Erin raised a hand. "Is Leanne Fuller producing the show again?"

"No, this week it's Caroline Felby."

The man next to Erin raised a finger.

"Is it okay to cover sport?"

"Only the big stories that break out of the back pages. Most producers don't care who's going to win the league."

The meeting continued with talk of John Major's Conservatives either ignoring him or plotting against him, of Tony Blair calmly confident of taking over Britain and the rest of the world, and of the Liberal Democrats hoping to be relevant. Then it was all over and Gavin was reminding people to put their name and phone number at the top of their sketches.

People were filing out of the room. Erin felt lost. What was she going to do? Foot Tread Man smiled and mock-hobbled away.

"That's my dream of playing for England shot down," he said.

Annoyingly, he was quite attractive, in a casual way.

She followed him outside.

"Erin?"

She turned to see who knew her name.

"Ian?" God, he looked so different. For instance, she had never seen him with an earring and torn jeans before. And had he bleached his blond hair blonder?

15

"Erin, you look… powerful. I never thought you'd come."

Bloody cheek.

"Ian, really, your mum wasn't going to put me off with her tales of how difficult it was for you."

"Cool. It's great to see you."

"It's great to be here." She wasn't about to let him know how news of his success had festered for months before she eventually took the plunge.

"Wait there a sec," he said. "I just need to catch someone."

He disappeared into a small office off the corridor.

Erin checked her watch and sighed. Writing the school play together at the age of eighteen seemed a lifetime ago. Even so, her memory of it was crystal clear. Ian was useless and she had to carry him. That never stopped him taking the lion's share of the credit though.

He returned.

"Mum said you still work in that box factory. I'm assuming your parents still own it?"

"Yes, and it's a great modern company to work for. We've had computers since 1992 and we regularly send e-mails."

"Right, so… you don't do Edinburgh shows any more, do you?"

"No, not for a long while. I have plays performed locally nowadays. Mind you, I've got high hopes of doing something with the Royal Court in London."

If you ignore their recent rejection letter.

"Cool. Um, did you fancy lunch and a catch-up? We haven't met like this in years."

"Sorry, I can't. I'm only in London for a short visit and I want to get some sketches written up for tomorrow. There's a deadline at one."

"I know. I did *It's News To Us* for two years. I'm doing a non-satirical sketch show now and I'm also developing a sitcom with a female lead."

"Nice work if you can get it. Any tips?"

"Just do your best and keep those fingers crossed."

Bloody cheek. I carried you, Ian Crawford-Troy.

"Ian. Yoo-hoo!"

It was a woman calling – a woman in jeans, white trainers and a baggy blue jumper.

"My producer," said Ian. "Look, if I don't see you tomorrow, good luck."

"And you, Ian."

Erin looked down at her five-years-out-of-date *Working Girl* power suit.

Definitely overdressed.

As Ian disappeared into an office, it occurred to her that he was probably the best person in the world to advise her on cracking the system. Why hadn't she taken him up on his lunch offer? It wasn't as if he'd ever get his hand up her blouse again.

4. A PLACE TO STAY

Having wandered around Oxford Street for a couple of hours, mainly because teaching assistant Trish wouldn't be home from work until four, Erin eventually hopped off a Bakerloo Line train at Kilburn Park. Next, it was a simple case of reading Trish's written directions for the five-minute walk to Prince Road – only it was hard to think straight with Duck Voice Man performing 'Wonderwall' on an acoustic guitar just outside the station.

Dropping 10p into his tin, she set off on what was a straightforward case of turn right, go straight, then right. Only, there were three roads and the straight-ish one looked more of a veer right. Oh well…

She was looking forward to seeing Trish again. They had spent three years together at Exeter University – two of them sharing a house with three others in the town. Now, at the other end of their twenties, Trish shared a house with four others in London, which surely had to rank her as one of the most tolerant people in the Northern Hemisphere. When Erin phoned to ask if she knew of any cheap hotels that weren't given over to 'professional night-time activities', Trish informed her that a housemate would be away in Scotland this week and that she would arrange an overnight stay. Typically,

Trish had found the whole thing a hoot and looked forward to having a laugh over drinks – until Erin explained how she would only be in London for sketch writing.

Writing in London…

Not for the first time, she thought back to TADS and the moment before Christmas, standing between cut-outs of Ginger Spice and Posh Spice on the stage at All Hallows church hall, and Liz Crawford-Troy turning up out of the blue seeking to join the troupe.

Okay, no problem, it was just a woman she hadn't spoken to in a couple of years, a woman whose son Ian co-wrote the school play with Erin – although his laziness and ineptitude stretched his co-credit to breaking point.

Next thing, there's Erin, the amateur scriptwriter, listening to Liz boast how her precious Ian was now a professional television and radio writer with the BBC. Even as Erin choked on the news, she learned he'd started by writing sketches for a radio show that welcomed non-commissioned amateurs. In that moment, Erin's mind switched from how Prince Charles was trying to sell Cinderella a secondhand royal carriage to a party after a school play many years earlier where she and Ian clinked glasses of cheap cider and made a solemn vow that, one day, they would both make it as successful writers.

With the five-minute walk to Trish's now in its fifteenth minute, everywhere seemed to be rows of 19th Century houses bearing the wrong street name. Keen to avoid having it turn into a Michael Palin TV trek, she asked a woman who looked like Princess Anne for directions. Somewhat unhelpfully, Princess Anne pointed the way

Erin had just come.

Erin ignored her advice and eventually found herself in Elgin Avenue. Further up was the station. At least she could start again. Only, it wasn't Kilburn Park Station. It was Maida Vale Station.

Yikes.

Inside, she studied the London Tube map. Handily, Maida Vale was on the same line as Kilburn Park, so she paid the fare again, boarded a train and got off at Kilburn Park.

Right…

She donated another 10p to Duck Voice Man, who was still entertaining passers-by with 'Wonderwall' and asked him for directions.

Three minutes later, she was ringing a doorbell.

Trish answered – and for a second Erin took in the shiny copper hair, sparkling green eyes and welcoming smile. Then they hugged.

"Welcome to the grotto," said Trish, finally pulling away. "Did you find it okay?"

"Easy-peasy," said Erin.

"Brilliant. Most people get lost."

Trish ushered her in, took her coat and showed her the room between the lounge and kitchen where she'd be sleeping.

"So what does Phil think of all this?" asked Trish, showing Erin to a brown suede sofa in the lounge.

"We split up."

"What?"

Erin sat down and sank into the old fabric.

"Sorry I didn't tell you on the phone, but…"

"You and Phil – *finito*?"

"Before Christmas."

"Arghh. No wedding then?"

"Well, no. I'm not marrying someone I've split up with."

She recalled sipping sparkling water at All Hallows church hall. Had things gone differently, it might have been champagne.

It had been a simple plan: 1) *Cinderella* rehearsals at the hall until six p.m. and 2) return to the hall at eight for a party to celebrate her engagement to Phil Collins – no, not *that* one.

Well, it didn't really matter which one – the second part of the plan never went ahead. She'd never before kneed a man in the groin, and was generally against attacking a person's squidgy bits, but he'd asked for it by being naked in their bed with Theresa with the big hair.

"So, all alone then," said Trish.

"No, I managed to land this strapping fella called Charles on New Year's Eve."

"Jeez, you didn't hang around."

"Nor would you if you met Charles. Rugby-playing lawyer who wears nice suits."

"Who would have thought it – the love of your life is a rugby player. Don't footballers earn more?"

"I don't follow football." A cheeky writer feigning a football injury popped into her head. She used Charles' bulky image to push him out again.

"Good sex?"

"Trish, please. Let's just say Charles is very adept between the sheets. You can use your imagine to fill in the details."

"So, he's classy, is he?"

"Absolutely." She decided to leave out the recent rugby club party where Charles lit one of his farts.

"God, I am so jealous. Haven't had a boyfriend in ages."

"I find that hard to believe."

"Erin, I smell of five-year-olds."

"Exciting times though – what with the course coming up."

"You're right there. I can't wait."

Teaching assistant Trish had signed up for a year's training from September to become a fully qualified teacher. A bloody good one, if Erin was any judge.

"Right, where are my manners?" said Trish. "Tea? Coffee? Water?"

"Tea would be great, thanks."

"Actually, I'm out of tea and I don't want to nick Wayne's last few PG Tips."

Typical Trish.

"Coffee then, thanks."

While Trish disappeared into the kitchen, Erin took in the lounge's décor – purple and hideously so, from the peeling wallpaper to the cracked paintwork. Still, it was just a one-night stopover so there was no need to suggest a make-over.

"Fancy a custard cream with it?" called Trish.

"Definitely, thanks."

Erin and Trish's friendship began on their first day at Exeter. They quickly gravitated to each other to form an invincible duo, capable of repelling all men – unless they were in the mood for a spot of non-repelling. Together, they rode out the storms of being young and away from home, and looked out for each other. Like the time they were in a pub and Erin spotted a suave guy dropping a tab into Trish's drink. Trish was really touched by Erin's vigilance and forgave her the fact that it wasn't her glass; it was the suave guy's own, and that he was perfectly entitled to drop a vitamin C pill into his non-alcoholic cider and didn't technically deserve to have it poured over his head. Since university, there had been long stretches when they might not see each other, but even now, after a two-year gap, it was as if they had never been apart.

Trish returned with two steaming mugs, one of which she placed in front of Erin.

"So... you're a top-flight writer then."

"Hardly. Obviously, if I write some brilliant sketches the producer will have no choice but to broadcast them to a grateful nation."

"So what's Broadcasting House like?"

"Old and tired, but with a sense of magic."

"Meet anyone famous?"

"Sadly no."

"You didn't bump into Noel Gallagher and get a date then."

"No chance."

"Damon Albarn?"

"No."

"Don't say you had to settle for a Radio 3 announcer?"

"It's not like that in LE. It's just lots of behind-the-scenes types making radio shows."

"LE?"

"Light Entertainment. It's where they make *It's News To Us*. Speaking of which – you mentioned a typewriter?"

Trish indicated an old model on the sideboard.

"It's been here longer than any of us."

Erin eyed a typewriter that Charles Dickens would have considered ancient.

"So, how's the family?" asked Trish.

"All well. Jonathan moved to Bristol last autumn. He's working in shipping."

"What? You mean your brother was allowed to leave the family firm? I thought they manacled you for life."

Erin smiled. Her older brother had been threatening to leave for years. Would she follow him out of the door? That was the big question.

"So, who are you living with, Trish?"

"Right, so there's junior marketing man Wayne, Selfridges assistant Frances, admin girl Anthea who's in Scotland, post-grad psychology student Mitch and me. It's a pretty good mix at the moment, although, as you know, house-sharing can be a bit of a lottery."

After their coffee, Erin changed into a blouse and cardigan over jeans, and wondered how to start writing for *It's News To Us*. All she had was a short list of sketch topics, none of which inspired her.

"If you fancy a drink later," said Trish, "there's a nice pub just up the road. We could have a proper catch-up."

"Sorry, Trish. Writing comes first. There's no way I'm ending up in a pub tonight."

"You *are* Erin Goodleigh? You're not an alien clone?"

"Sorry, Trish."

Trish left her to it. But to what? Sitting at the typewriter in the kitchen, Erin stared at her list.

Come on, imagination. Fire up.

She made another coffee. That would do it. Coffee never failed. Coffee meant business. This was it. The big push. All she had to do was think of something to write.

A biscuit would be nice.

No, this was a mission and she just needed to focus on it.

Yes, focus!

No doubt Ian Crawford-Troy had focused when he started out on the road to success. God, with his minuscule talent, he must have focused like the Hubble telescope.

Maybe she could write something about the Liberal

Democrats. Their leader Paddy Ashdown was going to lose the election. What about him being defeatist? He could be with his Number Two, Charles Kennedy. Perhaps Kennedy could play the optimist?

She typed.

> KENNEDY:
> (Very positive) Look Paddy, we're going to occupy a very large part of the moral high ground.
>
> ASHDOWN:
> And a very small part of the House of Commons... sob!

Was that the kind of thing the producer would be looking for?

Trish's head popped round the kitchen door.

"So, basically, you're saying sketch-writing, early night, back to Broadcasting House to submit, then a train back to Taunton?"

"You left out a morning of sketch polishing."

"What about lunch tomorrow? Before you go back?"

"You're on."

Just before nine p.m., Erin stretched her arms above her head and let out a yawn. She had been writing for four hours. The only stop had come at half-six when Trish slid a plate of beans on toast and a coffee in front of her and introduced Wayne, who lived in the loft room.

Erin went into the lounge where Trish and Wayne were watching the end of a nature documentary.

"How's it going?" asked Trish.

"I'm knackered."

"Take a break then. Come on, I'll buy you a pint of cider in the King's Arms."

"I can't."

"A glass of wine then. Come on, you need to step away from it so you can come back with fresh eyes. Wayne, tell her."

"You need to step away from it so you can come back with fresh eyes," said Wayne without looking away from the TV.

"See?" said Trish. "Wayne has spoken."

5. A SHORT BREAK

The interior of the King's Arms pub probably hadn't changed much since the War. Somewhat at odds with that look was the sound of Oasis on the CD player competing with a couple of excitable fruit machines.

"Here she is, Liam. The next big thing in television." Trish knew the barman; a young man with a ponytail who looked like a student.

"Radio," corrected Erin. "And I can't believe you've been telling people."

Liam smiled. "She was in last night, telling everyone where her friend's going to be working. See anyone famous?"

"Yes, I had a mad, passionate fling with the bloke who reads the shipping forecast."

"While he was on air," Trish added.

Erin giggled. Trish was right. It was good to relax a bit. She would go back to those sketches with a fresh perspective.

"Now, Liam, I dare you to force two small chardonnays on us. Go on, I dare you."

Liam saluted and set about getting their drinks.

A moment later, armed with glasses of wine, they adjourned to a table in the corner.

Trish took a slurp.

"Mmmm… So what's it like to be famous?"

"Hardly famous."

"There's a barman in London who knows who you are. I can't believe you didn't give him an autograph. Knowing Liam, he'd let you sign his bum."

"Really? We should have asked him for free drinks then."

"You're not kidding. The price of drinks in London is getting ridiculous."

"Taunton's not exactly cheap. Half a lager's nearly a quid."

Trish took another swig of wine.

"Shame about Phil," she said. "Still, you've got classy Charles now. You can marry him instead."

"Yes, well…"

"When you're ready, I mean."

"Yes. As you say, when I'm ready."

"Seeing as he's nicely suited to you."

"I said he wears nice suits."

"Am I detecting a lack of enthusiasm? He's not a caveman, is he?"

"That's a bit unfair. He's a lawyer."

"A caveman in a suit?"

"No, he's civilized, obviously. Oh, he's lovely really. I shouldn't complain."

"But something's missing?"

"As I said, I shouldn't complain."

"What is it with men? They're like a jigsaw puzzle. You spend ages on the bloody thing only to find there's a piece missing. Take my last boyfriend. His missing bit was the emotional side. It was all too functional. Oh, I'm assuming it's the emotional side with Charles. It's not physical, is it?"

"The eyes," said Erin.

"They're missing?"

"No, he can't stare into mine and tell me I mean the world to him."

"Ah well… maybe you don't."

"That's what bugs me."

"Here's an idea – have fun. There's a lot to be said for unpeeling a rugby kit and enjoying the contents. I bet he's huge, isn't he. God, I can feel him sliding up me as we speak."

"Trish! You are appalling."

"Tell me how you met him then. Was it lust at first sight?"

"I was at a New Year's Eve pub do with Cat and Rose from work. The idea was to drink ourselves senseless as a snub to the rubbish old year."

"Only, you clapped eyes on Charles."

"No, I clapped eyes on Terry, one of love rat Phil's best mates. He was there with his girlfriend. I almost left but then I bumped into this mountain at the bar."

"Mount Charles. And you did."

"Not straight away. Well, not for a few hours."

"You randy little mare."

"I know it's a cliché, but I really couldn't let Terry tell Phil how tragically single I was on New Year's Eve. Anyway, Charles was the perfect gent."

"Well, it's all worked out perfectly. What does Charles think about you coming to London to write?"

"Well, it's only an overnighter. It's not like we'll forget each other."

"But what if you catch the bug and want to stay. Would he support you then?"

"I think we're getting into the realms of fantasy now, Trish."

"Fair enough. But I know you. I know what you're like

when you want to achieve something."

Later, walking back to the grotto in Prince Road, something obvious occurred to Erin.

"Forty," she said.

"Forty?"

"The age by which a woman will have her life in some kind of order. You'll either have children or not, you'll either be married or not, you'll either have a great career or not…"

"That doesn't sound very definite," said Trish.

"Fifty then. Although that leaves us with a twenty-year gap where things can continue to go wrong."

"Which is why you should use your new-found fame to have fun. You'll soon be fifty and juggling a family and a career. You said so yourself."

"I hope it doesn't go too fast. I'd at least like to spend some time taking a good look around."

"If you do, you'll see other people with a modicum of fame having fun."

"Fame's not all it's cracked up to be, Trish. I'd settle for a fireside with Charles and watching a sitcom – one I've written myself, obviously."

"Charles doesn't sound too bad. Stick with him. He could grow on you. Like a fungus. Charles the sexy fungus. Who needs Mr Right?"

Erin agreed. Besides, ending a relationship was hard. Prior to Phil's instant dismissal she was with Jason for a year. The first six months had been good, but then came the not so good part. Before that, Anton lasted ten months which had begun to go sour after four. And before that, Tony at university – two years that included only twelve good months. And prior to all that, her first real boyfriend, Ian Crawford-Troy. Three good-ish weeks followed by four hell-ish months.

Ian Crawford-Troy...

At seventeen, she'd been obsessed with the idea of falling in love with a hopeless romantic. But Ian was just hopeless. His assertion that Valentine's Day was 'for mugs who bought in to corporate romance' meant her spending the evening with her parents watching TV. He'd tried to be clever, getting her into a vibe that parents were oppressors and that it was every teen's duty to rebel against their values. Then, during the summer, he got her into the idea that wearing a bra was a restriction imposed by society. That was followed by exploring more ways a teen could be a complete and utter rebel. Having sex, for example. That's how she ended up with his hand up her blouse, tongue down her throat and erection pressing through his chinos against her pelvis. Poor Ian. He saw himself as a bit of a dude. But he was more dud than dude. In the end, she just hadn't fancied him enough to go all the way and he'd failed to ply her with enough cider to overcome that important detail.

In the grotto's lounge, after coffee and toast, Trish yawned.

"I'd better turn in, Erin. I have to be up at seven."

"Night-night then. And thanks for everything."

"That's what friends are for."

"No dreaming about Charles, okay? He's mine."

"I don't know how to break this to you, but he's going to be unfaithful. In about two minutes, to be exact."

"Well, you be gentle with him. He's only six-foot-two."

"Ooh, any other vital statistics you want to share?"

31

"Certainly not."

Erin went to her room and wondered – should she take a look at those comedy sketches again or get a good night's sleep?

Sleep. That was the thing. Eight refreshing hours then she'd leap out of bed, have some coffee and read through her sketches. Any tweaks would be immediately obvious, along with any brilliant fixes they required.

She got into her nightie and slipped beneath the duvet.

Yes, sleep…

Two minutes later, she opened her eyes.

"Just one quick read through."

It didn't take long to go through her work. It was easy to form an opinion too – an opinion that covered the whole batch. She hadn't written any good sketches.

Now what?

She had spent good money on train tickets, come all the way to London and disrupted an old friend's routine. And for what? Just to give Ian Crawford-Troy a good laugh? God, she hated him. She also wondered if he'd help her. He certainly owed her. Or did she simply have too much pride to place herself in his wandering hands?

6. DELIVERY

Erin opened her eyes and checked the clock. It was four a.m. Something lingered – part-dream, part-idea. It was Prime Minister John Major dealing with the Devil and it felt funny. Something lingered in the room, too – the stink of stale cigarette smoke from the pub. She got up and sniffed the power suit hanging from a hook on the back of the door.

Ugh...

Pulling on some casual clothes, she crept out to the kitchen. It was quiet in Kilburn Park at night.

"Right then..."

She placed a sheet of paper in the typewriter and began typing.

Yikes. The little hammers sounded like the Forge of Vulcan.

She tried typing very quietly – only then the stupid hammers made no impression on the paper.

She took the typewriter back to her room, and under the duvet, to type up her brilliant idea. Only...

For some reason, the idea of John Major doing a deal with the Devil no longer seemed funny. Still, she had to try. What if John Major *was* the Devil? That would be an unexpected twist. An ineffectual Satan with a rebellious team. Was that funny? She couldn't be sure. It was a shame she couldn't call on a second opinion.

Her gaze wandered to the ceiling and the room above.

No.

No?

You cannot wake Trish at 4:05 a.m. and ask her if John Major would make a funny Satan.

Erin threw off the duvet. The room felt cold.

Cold…

What if John Major sold ice-cream? What if John bloody Major, the Prime Minister, had an ice-cream van? Was that funny? *Was it?*

She closed her eyes.

John Major. Prime Minister. Living at 10, Downing Street.

By day.

Yes.

And, *by night*, he sold…

A knock!

On… the door?

Where…?

"Sorry to wake you, Erin," came a voice from the hall, "but I'm going out. Are we still on for lunch?"

"Oh… er… morning, Trish." Erin checked the clock and then her watch. Either way, it was ten-past eight. "Yes, lunch. Yes, I'll see you at… lunchtime."

"You've got the address?"

"Yes, I… yes, I'll see you there at twelve-fifteen as arranged."

"Good luck then. Hope it goes well."

"Thanks Trish."

Erin heard the front door close. She got up and stretched. It was time to do something amazing.

She donned the power suit and visited the bathroom. She hated doing it that way round, but had no idea if she was alone in the house.

Later, fortified by coffee and toast, she sat at the kitchen table, kept her conversation with Wayne and Frances to a minimum and went over her sketches. In the light of day, they weren't so bad. Not great, but not awful. She made a couple of amendments with a biro and then got to typing them up afresh.

On the platform at Kilburn Park Station, waiting for a Bakerloo Line train, Erin studied the full London Underground map.

Out East you could visit Barking. She imagined a canine village. And wasn't there a place called Catford? She couldn't see it among the stations listed.

She shifted her gaze to the western side of the map.

Hammersmith.

It made her feel funny. Up until the age of six, she'd been a Hammersmith girl, and she had good feelings about a half-remembered early childhood there.

When the train pulled in, she took a seat and attempted a Zen-like state with eyes closed. Only, she quickly opened them again for fear of dozing off and ending up miles away from Broadcasting House.

Yes, Broadcasting House – she was heading for one of the oldest and most trusted broadcasters in the world.

Calm yourself, girl.

She lowered her gaze and found herself staring at Hugh Grant's brother. At least, he might have been.

It was an old adage that the best comedy was based on great characters. If you didn't understand character as a concept, you might struggle. Luckily, Erin felt she was good at 'character', although a little practice never hurt.

So...

His jacket was a lovely shade of midnight blue. A good quality worsted. The sky blue shirt looked Italian. The tie, crimson silk. It seemed odd to match that lot with denim jeans and a brand new pair of black suede shoes, but Erin guessed Hugh Grant's brother would look good inside most outfits.

Right – what's he up to?

He looked up from his magazine. Eye contact.

Erin switched to studying her nails.

Got it! He's going to a job interview at one of those funky, happening London companies. Advertising, perhaps. He didn't want to wear a suit for fear of coming across as a dinosaur. On the other hand, he couldn't go with the rugby shirt look in case they were all wearing Savile Row suits. This was a clever compromise. She liked men who could negotiate a tricky wardrobe decision. She wondered what he thought of her power suit.

Eye contact.

Damn. Twice is bad. Twice means he knows.

She checked her nails again and, for the briefest, briefest, briefest possible moment, he was on top of her, naked, thrusting – but it was so brief it didn't count. What magazine was he reading? If they were to be the only two survivors of a shipwreck, cast away on a scorching desert island for six months while they waited for rescue...

It looked suspiciously like a football mag.

Did she really want to spend the next six months on a paradise island with a guy who droned on about football? No. If she'd wanted that, she could have married Rancid Phil and gone to Ibiza for a fortnight, which would have felt like six months.

The train screeched to a halt at Regents Park Station.

She got up and smiled at the would-be advertising guy.

"Good luck with the interview," she said, not knowing why.

How long his bemused reaction lasted was lost to her. She was away, sweeping through the train doors and onto the platform.

That's when it occurred to her that she might have just left Mr Right. What if he wasn't a football nut? What if he'd boarded the train and the magazine was a discard on the seat opposite? What if, trying to be cool about his massive interview, he'd simply picked up the mag to flick through?

A middle-aged man barged past her. *Bloody cheek*. He was obviously in a hurry. She followed him to the exit. Yes, he was late for something. You could always tell. It was the determined stride and... was his mouth slightly open to let in more air? She'd written a character like that in her play, *The Angry Stonemason*; he was going 'somewhere important' – to murder his tool supplier.

Erin put on a burst to draw level with Hurrying Man. Yes, the eyes, the jaw... he flashed a look of annoyance, so she slowed. Some people just couldn't act normally under pressure.

She arrived at Broadcasting House around half-eleven. While she waited for the receptionist to finish with a woman who seemed to have no idea what she wanted, Foot Injury Man came in, smiled at her, signed himself in and mock-hobbled to the escalator. No Clash t-shirt this time though. Had he gone off them? Or was it a case of having other t-shirts?

Feeling a bit of an amateur, Erin signed her name on the list beneath that of... Paul Fielding. For a moment, she wondered if to follow him up the Escalator of Possibilities, but opted for the stairs to the Corridor of Opportunity because she required the Loo of Convenience before arriving at LE.

Five minutes later, she breezed in to the LE reception area to find Paul Fielding sipping coffee from a large branded cardboard cup. Where did he get that? Was it an Escalator of Possibilities thing?

"What did you cover?" he asked.

"Oh, this and that."

"You too? Damn. Who would have thought?"

Erin smiled. Paul Fielding, she decided, was nice.

Passing through to the inner sanctum, she found script editor Gavin Gould chatting with Sarah Bryce the broadcast assistant. It felt like progress to know people and their roles.

"Hi guys," she said, proffering sketches.

"Those for me?" said Gavin, as if she bore gold, frankincense and myrrh.

"There are three," said Erin, "so you might want to space them out in the show. That's a joke, by the way."

"Or it could be the truth," said Sarah. "You never know."

"I shall read them straight after lunch," said Gavin.

Erin smiled. She was glad having Gavin read them. She knew he'd be a tough critic but he was sympathetic – the sort of person who could make the rejection of your sketches seem like a superior outcome to them being on the show.

"Will we see you next week?" asked Sarah.

"I hope so."

"Great," said Gavin.

Erin got in touch with her brain and mouth.

Why did we say that? We're not coming back.

Leaving the inner sanctum, she found Paul Fielding seated in the LE reception area, sipping his coffee and skimming a newspaper.

"Could I give you an official souvenir before you go?" he said.

He put the coffee and paper down and indicated that she follow him into an office. Erin did so. There were two female staff busy inside.

"Hi guys," said Paul, "this is......?"

"Erin Goodleigh," said Erin.

"Yes, remember that name," said Paul. "Erin, this is Carol and Joanne, the admin team. Very important people."

"Hi," said Erin, exchanging smiles.

Paul threw his empty biro into a bin and took a couple of new black pens from a box on a shelf. He handed one to Erin.

"Your official BBC souvenir pen."

"It says BIC."

"Nit-picker."

"Has that bloody fax come through yet?" blasted a male voice that materialized into a middle-aged man coming into the office. Without ceremony, he grabbed the papers off the fax machine, skimmed through them, dumped them aside and stormed out again.

Erin looked down at the discarded faxes. Some looked like sketches.

"Okay, so the souvenir's rubbish," said Paul. "I can give you two handy tips though. Interested?"

"Go on."

He indicated she should follow him out again.

"Okay, so tip one: always read the notice board." He inclined his head to a board with various notes and newspaper cuttings fixed to it. "And tip two: make as many friends as you can. Networking is half the battle."

"Thanks for sharing."

"You're welcome." He smiled, grabbed his coffee from the table, and headed to the inner sanctum. Only he stopped by the open doors. "You *are* coming back?"

"I might. I mean I definitely want to do something with my life."

"Well, you have to, don't you? Old Father Time won't stop and wait. He's not the type."

Paul smiled and headed off to the writers' room. Was that the last time she'd ever see him? She was surprised at how she felt about that.

"Goodleigh, are you stalking me?" It was Ian coming in from the main corridor with a script.

"It's the only reason I came to London, Ian."

"How did it go?"

"Not sure. Gavin's got my stuff."

"Best of luck then. Will you try again next week?"

"Possibly."

"You should? How about lunch?"

"No, I'm going back to Taunton soon."

"Oh right. Listen, if you see my mum, tell her you've seen me with your very own eyes and I'm fine. She's convinced I haven't eaten, slept or done any laundry since I've been here."

Erin smiled. "Mums, eh?"

"Good luck, Erin. Hope you get something on and we see you again."

She watched him disappear in the direction of the writers' room.

She hadn't intended coming back to London and yet Ian, Paul, Gavin and Sarah all seemed to think she wouldn't be a one-week wonder. Well, she wouldn't. The idea, surely, had to be sending the sketches in.

Sarah emerged from the inner sanctum.

Yes, Sarah.

"Sarah, if I can't make it next week. It's just that I'm based in Taunton and…"

"You were wondering if I could help."

"Yes, it's just that I need someone to fax my sketches to. I could phone first, so you'd know."

"I'd love to say yes, but I'm doing a couple of days a week at TV Centre. You can always fax them marked for Gavin's attention."

Erin had a flashback to a grumpy man dumping faxes aside.

"Okay, I'll send them to Gavin then. Could you ask him to keep an extra-special eye out."

"The only thing I'd say is we get a lot of one-time writers. Not yourself, of course, but they have one go at getting something on the show, fail, call the show a pile of poo and never come back."

"I'm seriously not like that, Sarah."

"Absolutely. Send them to Gavin. I'll tell him to keep an eye out. And maybe you could come up occasionally, so you get to know the producers."

"Thanks Sarah. I'll try."

Making her way out of the building, Erin let out a sigh. It was like finishing an exam. Now she could enjoy lunch with Trish before boarding a train back to Taunton. As for *It's News To Us,* it was in the lap of the gods now. And as for any decision about her future involvement – that would have to wait until she'd listened to the show on Friday night.

7. TAUNTON

A hundred and fifty miles southwest of London, Erin arrived home to the intermittent triple-beep of the answerphone. Dumping her bags and kicking off her shoes, she hit the 'play' button.

Beep. "Hi, this is Jane at Fraser and Carbury Estate Agents. I have a Mr James who would like to view the property on Saturday morning, preferably around eleven a.m. Could you get back to me and let me know if that's convenient? Many thanks. Bye."

But Erin didn't want to sell the flat. With Phil gone, it was the only place she wanted to live. And she certainly didn't share his annoyance at the seasonal sluggishness of the housing market: four months, five viewings, one derisory offer. It was just a shame she couldn't afford to take it on solo.

Beep. "I had the estate agent on to me. I thought we agreed certain conditions for you to stay there until the sale – like dealing with viewings. Sort it out, please."

Bog off, Phil. But he was right, of course. They had an agreement and he was keen to get his half of any money due to them. As soon as the sale went through, she would have to sort out a smaller, cheaper place. There was no way she could move back in with her parents.

Beep. "Hey, let's meet for drinks and a bite to eat. You

can tell me all about London, then… well… I'll be in the Red Lion at five."

Jane, Phil and Charles. All wanting something.

Erin put her shoes back on and headed out.

The Red Lion wouldn't be properly busy until after eight but it already had a Thursday after-work feel to it – not quite the weekend but what the hell. Charles was at the bar, a half full pint glass in his hand, having a laugh with the barmaid. When he spotted Erin, he immediately ordered a large chardonnay.

"How was London?"

"Tiring."

"See anyone famous?"

"Not really. Would it be alright if we had an early night?"

"You sex-crazed woman."

Erin pasted on a smile. Had this relationship run its course? Was it time for the untangling process to begin? Or was she simply tired from her travels?

The barmaid served up Erin's wine. She took a sip.

"Mmm. Just what the doctor ordered." *Followed by a hot mug of Horlicks and eight hours' sleep.*

"Drink up," said Charles. "I want you to see my mate's flat."

"What?"

"It's brilliant."

"Do we have to?"

"It's tradition. You have to toast the flat. It's a luck thing. Anyhow, there'll be champagne, so it can't be all bad."

Erin took another sip of her wine.

"Come on, you can knock that back in one. Come on, come on…"

Unable to disengage with his rugby club cajoling, she

drank until the wine was gone.

"There," said Charles, "what did I say?"

Erin gasped. Three units of alcohol in less than a minute.

As they walked to the flat, her brain was fizzing. She wanted to go back to London. Not just to be with Trish again, although that would always be a massive plus, but also because it offered something. Besides, what did she owe Taunton? It wasn't even the cradle of her dreams, her love of stories, her desire to become a writer. Hammersmith was. That's where the lovely old lady next door, Elsie, had looked after her and her brother when Mum and Dad were out. That's where the stories and songs had come from.

She wondered – how was Elsie? Was she even still alive?

"Not too shabby, is it," said Charles.

From the outside, the small 1960s-style block didn't look too bad. Inside, the hall and stairs were mercifully clean.

"Let's not stay too long, Charles. I'm looking forward to an early night."

"Princess, you shall have an early night. I promise."

At a plain blue door marked with a brass number 4, Charles produced a key. Erin was surprised.

"Shouldn't we ring the doorbell?"

"No need – it's my flat."

"Yours?"

"I've been keeping it a secret. I only signed the papers this morning."

They entered what Erin could only describe as a drab apartment. Knowing Charles, he'd soon have it knocked into shape, but for now… well, it was barely okay-ish.

"Right," said Charles, clapping his hands together.

In the small kitchen, he opened a fridge crammed to the max with cans of beer. No, not completely crammed – from between the cans, he extracted a bottle of chilled champagne.

"There should be some glasses in that cupboard."

Erin obliged and found some hideous catering goblets. Charles popped the cork and poured them a glass each.

"To home ownership," he said.

"To a happy home," said Erin, meaning it. She wanted Charles to be happy.

They clinked glasses and took a slurp. The fizz went straight up Erin's nose.

"Nice bubbly," she said.

"It's on offer at Sainsbury's. Only nine quid."

"Nothing wrong with that. You'll need all your pennies for redecorating."

"One day we'll share it," he said. "When the time is right."

That felt a bit odd. She wasn't exactly desperate to move in with him, but even so. Then she got it. His mates would be up here watching sport on TV and consuming vast quantities of booze. Then she *really* got it. If she moved in at a later date, it would be a matter of *her* contributing to the cost of running *his* flat. Typical lawyer. Unless he meant something more solid, more permanent. Marriage, for example.

Charles put his glass down.

"There are actually two traditions when it comes to breaking in a new flat. One is champers, the other is… any guesses?"

His lips were on hers. His hands were in action. And Erin felt too exhausted to fight tradition.

Once they were in the bedroom, he clapped his hands together again.

"Right, let's get you out of that uncomfy suit."

It wasn't an uncomfy suit. It was a power suit. And this habit of clapping his hands together? She'd barely noticed it before but it was now getting on her nerves. All the same, she was soon undressing.

"Are you going somewhere?" she asked, annoyed that he was still fully dressed.

"Don't be daft." He dropped his trousers and boxers. "There we are. Ready for action."

"Can't you get properly undressed?"

"No, it's… no."

He kissed her. What was going on? Was it a fantasy? He never shared stuff like that.

"This fantasy of yours," she said, having pulled free.

"No, it's not like that."

"Are you pretending to be at work then?"

"Don't speak."

Time to buy a book on male psychology. Find out what goes on in those Neanderthal heads of theirs.

He pushed her onto the bed. It was lumpy. Any hope of some much-needed foreplay was crushed by him lowering himself onto her, entering without ceremony and thrusting like a Victorian steam engine.

Who did he fancy at work? Was he about to utter "Oh Charlotte?" Assuming he worked with a Charlotte. Did he?

She hoped he wouldn't take too long.

He didn't. Rolling off, he flopped onto his back, his tie only slightly askew.

Erin stifled a sigh. It was fine. It wasn't Charles' fault. And anyway, it didn't always have to be romantic. It could be lusty and furious on occasions. She'd learned that with Phil.

"Stay?" he asked.

"I won't, Charles. I'm worn out. It's been so busy,

what with going to London." She didn't mention that his flat felt like a one-star B&B. "I'll see you on Saturday for lunch, if that's okay?"

Around eight o'clock on Friday morning, sunlight was pouring through the crack in the curtains in Erin's bedroom.

"Mmmm…"

She rolled onto her side enjoying the feel of being in her own bed. But it wasn't a day to waste.

She got up and donned her dressing gown. Today was going to be a big day. Well, a big night. The theme tune to *It's News To Us* would blare from half a million radios at eleven p.m. By half-past, she would know her fate.

Scary.

In the hall, a couple of bills and a white envelope awaited her on the mat. Putting the kettle on, she pondered her best strategy regarding the white envelope. Judging by the neat handwritten name and address, it had to be from Mears and Bibber, agents specializing in representing novelists and playwrights. Established in 1908, if she remembered correctly.

What if it's a rejection?

She couldn't bear the thought.

What if it isn't?

Was that likely? Was a whole new future about to open up? Had it in fact already opened up and all she needed to do was open the envelope and learn the details?

Of course, she would retain hope for longer by not opening it. That way she could ponder having to choose between writing for the BBC and writing for the Royal Court Theatre.

Or could she do both?

She imagined it: the whirl of writing and the endless taxi rides between Portland Place and Sloane Square. Maybe she'd open the envelope during *It's News To Us*. That way she'd learn of her fate on two fronts at the same time.

Exciting…

After a hard day's cleaning the flat for potential buyers, Erin left at half-six bound for the pub. She had fallen into an end of the week routine with Cat and Rose from Goodleigh Packaging Ltd and was grateful for it. Rose was a twenty-six-year old mum of one whose own mum had her little boy on Fridays. She was currently on a bit of a high due to an incident called 'meeting Alan'. Cat was a twenty-eight-year-old divorcee who liked drinking a sizeable chunk of her wages in chardonnay. She was also TADS' leading lady for younger roles.

Entering the pub, Erin spotted them at the bar with large glasses of white wine and cigarettes on the go. They looked set for a good night.

"Here she is – the next head of television," said Cat.

"Can we have more *Friends*?" said Rose.

"I can only get you more wine."

"Yay!"

"So how did it go?" asked Rose. "Did they offer you a contract?"

"No, there are loads of people trying to climb aboard. I'll be lucky to make an impression. If I could just get a sketch on though…"

She caught the barman's eye and ordered the drinks.

"See anyone famous?" asked Cat.

"No, it's more of a behind-the-scenes place. You know, people making shows."

"I've always wanted to go to London," said Cat. "Get an agent, try for theatre and TV work – and radio, of course."

"Why haven't you?" asked Rose.

"It's such a big step. Imagine sorting out a place to live and not getting any work."

"It's the same for writers," said Erin.

"Maybe one day," said Cat. "If I ever work up the courage."

Talking about London soon morphed into Rose's shopping plans for Saturday. Talk of buying shoes then led to Rose's love affair with Alan from the baker's, which opened out into a more general discussion on boyfriends, which led to Charles.

"Decided if he's marriage material yet?" asked Cat.

"It's still early days. Who knows, we might not be right for each other – long term."

Cat shrugged. "My cousin Kate's looking forward to her nuptials. Can't bloody wait to get that ring on."

Erin had never felt like that about Charles. She hadn't really felt like it with Phil either although she would have worked her socks off to make their marriage a good one.

"I saw Phil out and about yesterday," said Rose.

Erin didn't wish to hear it.

"Do tell," said Cat.

"He was in a car."

"Ooh... going somewhere, eh?"

Erin enjoyed gossip as much as the next person, but seriously, "Phil Seen In Car" was hardly front page news.

"I suppose that's the thing with selling the flat," said Cat, "you still hear from him."

"Every time I hit the play button on the answer machine," said Erin.

"You're well shot of him, Erin. Charles is so much

more of a catch."

"You make him sound like a haddock."

"He's big," said Cat. "I like big."

"How are you getting on with David?" said Erin, changing the subject. "Still a work in progress?"

"Yes, I'm still training him." But then Cat nudged her. Two young, nervous-looking men were smiling at them. Erin's inner alarm bells started ringing.

"They look like schoolboys," she said. "There are laws against that kind of thing."

"They are not schoolboys. Twenty-two? Twenty-three?"

"Can't we just get drunk and dance till we fall over?" said Erin.

"No, I want a man," said Cat.

"They are not men."

"I want a boy-man then. The one on the left, in fact."

Erin smiled. As far as boozy nights out went, she didn't have her heart in this one. And that wasn't fair at all. Cat and Rose just wanted a good time. You couldn't stand there being constantly distracted by the fact *It's News To Us* would be on the radio at eleven and that she planned to be home in time to listen to it. Of course, she felt like sharing her deepest hopes and fears about the future, but not with Cat and Rose. It was different with Trish. You could tell Trish anything. Share any thought, any feeling, any emotion. She sighed. Why did Trish have to live in London?

Erin was sitting on the edge of her bed quite sober. The clock clicked over to 22:59. The radio was burbling at a low volume. She had enjoyed her night with the girls, although they were disappointed to lose her early. She hoped they were enjoying their Chinese meal and, in some ways, wished she was there with them, eating and drinking and talking and laughing without a care in the world. Perched on the bed with a huge knot in her chest – this was no way to spend a Friday night.

She increased the volume.

"And now on Radio 4, it's time for some late night mirth with *It's News To Us.*"

The theme tune rasped, Erin's bowels rumbled, and the show's leading man, Brian Grainger snapped: "The Prime Minister said *what?* It's news to us!"

The first sketch featured beleaguered Prime Minister John Major having a dream. Erin's throat tightened. Her head pounded. She hoped she'd breathed enough in the preceding minute otherwise she would pass out due to insufficient oxygen.

But… *oh, you crappy little…* John Major wasn't Satan; just John Major waking up next to Mrs Major with a new vision for Britain. What, another one, said Mrs Major. I don't think Britain can take any more visions.

The adrenalin remained high, although it lessened as the half-hour passed as a form of psychological torture.

Then…

"It's News To Us was performed by Brian Grainger, Hannah Dobson, Anne Garston-Green and Ben Tidy. It was written by Gavin Gould, Martin Dobbs, Josh Steinman, Phil Holston and Nick Ferris, Shaun Donoghue, Dave Singer, Simon Driver, Paul Fielding, Oliver Goldman and Joe Harrington, Kirsty Gray, Simon Yeovil, Stephen Green, and Dave Boynton. The producer was Caroline Felby."

Erin switched the radio off. Silence filled the room. She wasn't really disappointed. Just drained. She wouldn't bother again. It was too much trouble. It wasn't as if she could build up a head of steam from Taunton. Besides, there were only a few more shows before the three-month summer break. She was glad that Paul Fielding had got something on though. Hearing his name had given her a tingle, and that surprised her. Hearing people's names didn't usually result in a tingle.

The phone rang. It was Erin's mum, Jenny.

"Any luck?"

Erin was acutely aware that her mum would have listened to the show. Maybe she thought they didn't read out the names of new writers.

"No, Mum."

"Oh well, at least you tried. There aren't many people who can say that."

"I know. Thanks."

"The song was fun."

"Yes." One of the sketches had been a musical ditty, not that it mattered.

"Now, onto other matters," said Jenny, "we landed that new contract with the video distributer."

"That's great, Mum. That should keep the firm busy."

"Keep *our* firm busy, Erin. Fifteen years from now, Dad and I will have retired, which means you'll be... any guesses?"

"Forty-five-years-old?"

"Experienced enough to take over."

Fat chance. They'd never retire. Not properly. Grandad retired years ago but he still came in every day trying to call the shots.

"Okay, Mum. Look, I'm going to turn in. I'll see you over the weekend."

"Okay, love. Night-night. And remember, there's a big future in front of you."

"Night-night, Mum."

Erin put the phone down and went into the kitchen. It was still there. The white envelope. She tore it open and scanned the contents. There was a fair bit of blah-blah-blah but bits leapt out: 'some interesting ideas', 'not quite what we're looking for' and 'we wish you better luck in the future'. Erin let the letter fall to the table. Was that it? Had the Fates decided she would never be a professional writer?

8. BIRTHDAY GIRL

On a warm, pleasant Saturday evening in June, Erin was stationed at a picnic table in her parents' garden with Cat and Rose, drinking bubbly and smiling occasionally at friends and family dotted around like human shrubs. While she felt overdressed in a black cocktail dress and heels, Rose and Cat had both opted for off-white summer dresses and smart sandals. The look showed off Cat's salon-tanned body perfectly while accentuating Rose's sunburn.

Erin was currently suffering the consequences of having revealed she might try writing a novel.

"Write a bonk-buster," said Cat. "Sex and yachts sell well."

"You could put a serial killer in it," said Rose.

"Make it historical."

"Yes, and romantic."

"And funny."

Erin weighed it up. "So, a hysterical historical rom-com psycho thriller."

"With boats," said Cat.

While Cat went on to flesh out the two main characters – Roger and Fanny – Erin's mum, Jenny, tied a shiny metallic helium-filled balloon to the back of a plastic chair.

Happy 30th Birthday!

That was its message. Its sole purpose in a vast universe was to remind everyone that Erin Goodleigh was thirty. Still, there was plenty to be positive about. Indeed, Tony Blair's landslide victory in the recent general election was still fresh in the mind and his theme song, "Things Can Only Get Better", continued to resonate.

"Is Charles coming?" asked a passing aunt.

"Yes, he'll be here soon," said Erin.

Everyone liked Charles. It was weird to think she had almost ditched him. Now she could put that temporary insanity down to her brief flirtation with fame. As someone, somewhere had pointed out, Charles was a catch – a well-paid lawyer who dressed well and took her to nice restaurants.

Cat poured the last of a bottle of champers into their glasses.

"Dead soldier," she declared, placing the empty bottle under the bench.

"I'll get us a fresh one," said Erin.

"Three cheers for Erin," said Cat. "Hic-hic – hooray! Hic-hic…"

On the way into the house, Erin caught her reflection in the glass patio doors. Charles was right. She did look good in a short black dress and the push-up bra did wonders with what she had. The high heels weren't too bad either. You got used to them. She had always been a flat-shoe girl but Charles reckoned high heels made a woman's posture dead sexy.

Inside, Erin's dad Ralph was putting the latest Bee Gees album on. Well, he was a leading Rotarian and member of the Chamber of Commerce, so it wasn't likely to be the latest Radiohead offering. Could she imagine him singing along to 'Paranoid Android'? No.

Before she could grab a fresh bottle of bubbly from the fridge, there was a fuss by the front door. Gran and Grandad had arrived and Jenny was trying to take Gran's cardigan – more than enough provocation for Gran.

Erin went over for a hug and a hello.

"Ah, my little Erin," said Grandad.

"Our little jewel," said Gran.

While Grandad scooted off to grab a beer, Gran handed her a large open bag stuffed with what looked like dark green bedding.

"A little something for the bottom drawer," she explained.

"Thanks Gran, but we haven't made any plans to live together yet."

"It's a duvet set," said Gran.

"Thanks," said Erin, warmly – despite the fact that she didn't like green, which was ironic for someone whose name literally meant Ireland. No, her future shared bedroom would be off-white with a hint of rose. Charles wouldn't mind.

"Where's Jonathan?" asked Gran.

"He couldn't make it," said Jenny. "Work."

"That's a shame. We hardly ever see him these days. You did say he's in Bristol, not Brazil?"

"Now, now, mother-in-law," said Jenny. "Jonathan's perfectly entitled to flee the nest. He *is* thirty-two."

"Yes, and now Erin's thirty."

"Erin's not going anywhere," said Jenny, possibly mindful that Gran held her personally responsible for failing to stop Jonathan leaving the family business to work for a shipping firm.

"Is that right, Erin? You're not going anywhere?"

"Erin's my special project," said Jenny. "I'm guiding

her to take over."

Yes, come back in twenty years when she starts letting me make actual decisions.

"Mum, hello…" It was Ralph appearing with a glass of champagne, which he deftly placed in his mother's hand.

"Ooh bubbles. You clever boy, Ralph."

"Let me show you my new mobile phone, Mum," he said, prior to steering her to the garden. "Jen didn't think I needed one, but it's amazing…"

Erin paid a quick visit to the loo and then returned to the kitchen for the bottle she had come for. On her way back to Cat and Rose she got as far as the patio.

"Erin, there you are," said Gran. "We were just talking about when your father came back to Taunton."

"How time flies," said Ralph, holding the mobile phone they obviously *weren't* talking about.

"Just think," said Gran, "had Ralph come straight back after National Service, you would have been born in Taunton, not Hammersmith."

"Had I come straight back," said Ralph, "I wouldn't have met Jenny."

"Had you returned from London sooner then."

Erin didn't like the way this was going. Her brother's departure to Bristol had been like a rock dropped into a pond. A year on, small waves were still rippling over certain parts of the family.

"The past is the past, Gran. It doesn't matter where I was born."

"Jenny made a great sacrifice, as you well know," Ralph reminded his mother. "She was a brilliant young actress with genuine star quality."

Erin sighed. She had heard the story of When Ralph Met Jenny countless times. After his stint of National Service, Ralph took a job in London, met an aspiring actress, they married, had two kids and had to leave London as Ralph's best prospects were in Taunton working in the growing family packaging business.

Erin headed for her friends. Minor conflicts aside, her parents had put together a good party. There was plenty of bubbly, the jasmine smelled divine and, thanks to Dad's considered placement of the barbecue, they weren't overwhelmed by the smell of burning sausages.

"About time!" complained Cat. "We thought you'd been abducted by aliens."

Cat and Rose did the *X-Files* theme.

"We were just about to call Fox Mulder," said Rose.

"I wouldn't mind him doing a spot of investigating," said Cat.

Erin popped the cork and topped up their glasses. Okay, so it wasn't like her twenty-ninth birthday, which had involved the three of them plus Sue from work and Erin's mate Amy. What a massive booze-up that had been. It was a shame Sue didn't hang out with them anymore. Amy too, although getting married and moving to Plymouth had been a factor. Of course, celebrating the Big Three-0 was always going to be a big affair and Phil would have had a fit if she'd tried to squeeze everyone into the flat while it was on the market.

"Just think," said Cat, "if you'd had a bit of success you might have left us for London."

"Boo hiss to London," said Rose.

Yes, boo hiss to London.

Erin wondered – why had she written a sketch the other night? *It's News To Us* had almost come to the end of its current run and even if it hadn't Erin wouldn't have sent it in. It was just that after a few glasses of wine on the Wednesday she found herself at her computer with an idea about Tony Blair's pledge to spend National Lottery cash on hospitals and education. And Blair's bumbling deputy, John Prescott, was comedy gold, wasn't he…?

PRESCOTT:
Er… twenty-six… twelve… thirty-two… oh, hello, Tone.

BLAIR:
Prescott! What on earth are you doing filling in a lottery slip? We've got a government to run!

PRESCOTT:
But Tone, you promised we'd spend lots of lottery cash on hospitals and education.

BLAIR:
And?

PRESCOTT:
Well, I'm buying a fiver's worth of tickets. I mean if we win, we'll be able to do a lot of good.

BLAIR:
Prescott! You absolute…

PRESCOTT:
..Genius, I know. Now come on, dig deep. Another couple of quid's worth and we'll increase our chances of winning the jackpot… er… Where are you going, Tone? Rushing off to buy a couple of scratch cards?

"Erin." It was Charles.
Cat and Rose cooed like a couple of lovesick teenagers

as he kissed her.

"Good to see you, Charles. I was beginning to think you might have ditched me for a younger woman."

"Younger? You're the perfect age, Erin."

Erin noticed a couple of strangers hanging back. The guy looked smart in a suit and shirt *sans* tie, while the woman looked stunning in a black cocktail dress.

"I brought a couple of friends from work," said Charles. "I thought it was time you met Tony and Tiffany."

Tiffany? Wasn't that the name of his boss?

They exchanged greetings.

"I turned thirty a couple of years ago," said Tiffany. "The pain soon fades."

"I'm not too bothered," said Erin. "Life has to take its course."

But something was bugging her. It was Tiffany. They shared similar cheekbones, eyes, nose... although Erin's hair having highlights like Tiffany's had been at Charles' suggestion. They were also the same height. Although that was down to Erin's three-inch heels and Tiffany's flats off-setting their natural height difference. God, they even had similar clutch bags.

Erin had a weird feeling.

"You're lucky to have Charles," said Tiffany.

"Yes..."

Erin wondered about that. They were supposedly getting closer as a couple and yet he'd never once said he loved her. Applauding when she downed half a pint of cider seemed to be his way of saying 'you are my world'. On the other hand, he made Cat and Rose drool, so wasn't that a plus?

The conversation continued, but Erin stood on the edge of it.

What are you up to, Trish?

And what about those non-comm writers? What about Paul? In the pub, most likely. Or did he prefer to stay at home? What if he had a dog he walked during the evening? Or what if he was writing a screenplay? Didn't real writers get on with that kind of thing, rather than keep putting it off? After all, who stole the first half of 1997? One minute it's New Year and you're starting out with Charles, the next it's June and you're...

A couple of Charles's rugby club mates arrived, leaving a gap for Erin to politely withdraw to rejoin Cat and Rose.

"Charles is looking hot tonight," said Cat, handing Erin a glass of champagne.

"He's probably standing too near the barbecue," said Erin.

"Guard him jealously," said Cat. "There's more than one girl who'd be in there like a shot."

Erin looked over to Charles, who was laughing and pushing one of his mates in some kind of show of strength.

"I'm sorry," said Erin. "I'm being a party bore."

"No, you're not," said Rose. "You're trying to be a dignified thirty-year-old. A few more glasses of bubbly and you'll forget all that nonsense."

Ralph called from the dining room.

"Phone, Erin!"

"Excuse me, ladies."

Erin went inside. The phone was on the hall table, the receiver off the hook. She picked it up.

"Hello, Erin speaking."

"Hello, party girl."

"Trish! It's so good to hear you. I've really missed you."

"Me too. How's it going? I thought I'd better get in now before the carnage gets under way."

"No, it's pretty quiet. Cat and Rose are here. And Charles."

"Well, I won't keep you. I just wanted to wish you all the best for your twenty-tenth."

"Ha, thanks Trish. No such word as thirty, eh?"

"Get drunk. Make a fool of yourself. It's not like your parents can send you to your room, is it."

Erin had a flash of Charles in her room, wanting to get on top of her, to huff and puff...

"So what are you up to, Trish? Going out?"

"I'm meeting a few friends in Covent Garden."

"Ooh, I'm jealous. That's sounds great."

"Well... I'll see you when I see you, eh?"

"I'll call you in a couple of weeks – on your twenty-tenth, okay?"

"Great. Look forward to it. The call, I mean, not the occasion."

"Don't worry, I'll be over my post-traumatic stress by then and be able to talk you through it."

"It's a deal. Take care, Erin. Lots of love."

"And you, youngster. Bye."

Erin put the phone back on the hook and sighed. She missed her best friend. Yes... her best friend. That's what Trish was. You didn't have to see someone every day for that.

What a shame returning to London wasn't an option. The likelihood of earning a living through sketch-writing was... well, if not zero then close by.

She could get a job, though – a flexible job that allowed her Wednesdays and Thursdays off to write sketches that probably wouldn't be used by the BBC. Could it be done?

Ian Crawford-Troy...

Yes, Ian must have had a plan when he first went up there. How did he survive?

The champagne in Erin's system insisted she open her mum's phone book at 'C' and scan down the handwritten entries until she came to the latest addition: Liz Crawford-Troy.

She was soon tapping in the number.

"Hello, Liz, it's Erin Goodleigh. It's about Ian. We got on brilliantly in London back in April, but we forgot to swap phone numbers. I just need to ask him something. If you have his number in London...?"

"You can speak to him here, Erin. He's staying with us for a few days."

Erin heard Liz call out to another part of the house. "Ian, it's Erin Goodleigh for you." And then, as Ian obviously neared, "She says she had such a lovely time with you in London, she wants to see you again."

See him again?

A familiar voice came on the line.

"Erin? Is this a belated invite to your birthday bash?"

"Um... yes. Come over. I need to talk to you."

Erin put the phone down. How did Ian know about her party? The am-dram group, obviously. The TADS mafia.

She returned to the garden, wondering how Ian's views might weigh on her future. If he described the process as a grim endless escapade, the toils of Sisyphus, simply down to endless endurance but based on pure luck, would she try again? Probably not.

Half an hour later, Ian arrived with a bottle of cabernet-sauvignon and a cartoony birthday card. Erin, by now beginning to wonder if that sixth or possibly seventh glass of champagne hadn't slid down a little too rapidly, greeted him with a hug and a thank you. Once Ian had finished being interrogated by Jenny, Erin grabbed him away.

"You must meet Charles," she said.

You're the one who can make him see it's possible.

Charles was lecturing Tony and Tiffany. "Trust me, no-one's going to trade with Hong Kong once we hand it back. People trust Britain with their money. China's a different ballgame."

"Well, it's happening next week," said Tony, "so pull your money out, people."

Erin gave a little ahem and barged in.

"This is Ian, an old school friend who lives in London." She eyed Charles. "He writes for the BBC."

"Ooh, how exciting," said Tiffany.

Charles raised an eyebrow.

"So you've known Erin a long time."

"Yes, good ol' Gullible Goodleigh."

"Er… that was a *very* long time ago, Ian." *And not what I got you here for!*

"Do tell," said Charles, as if enjoying her discomfort.

"She used to like this boy called Henderson," said Ian.

"I was eight or nine," said Erin.

"Fourteen," said Ian.

"Yes, happy days. So, about London…"

"So we told her Henderson's dick could whistle."

"Oh no," said Charles, laughing along with Tony and Tiffany.

Erin's eyes fired death lasers at Ian.

"I never believed you," she said.

"One day, we saw her coming through the park, so we got Henderson to sit on a bench in front of some bushes and we hid behind them. Then, when Erin came along…

I whis… hahaha …and Erin looked… haha at his groin… hahahaha…"

Charles was cracking up too.

Erin sighed. "Boys…"

"So you'll be trying again?" said Ian, suddenly more serious. "It all kicks off again in September."

"No," said Charles.

This annoyed Erin. She was perfectly capable of saying no herself.

"It would have been tough," said Ian. "The real problem is no-one has instant success. I'm sure if you asked the current batch of commissioned writers, they'd tell you it took them a fair while to get going. No problem if you live in London and have a flexible job to support you. Not so easy from Taunton. I didn't get anything on for two months."

"Two months?" gasped Tony, somewhat unhelpfully.

"That's when I started working under a like-minded producer and got an amazing four-week run. It took me a year to get a commission."

"A year…" Erin mulled it over.

"Some people spend longer and still don't make it," said Ian.

"But there's always hope," said Erin.

"Of course," said Ian, "but a commission only guarantees you a small fee whether you get stuff on the show or not – that's all."

"Yes, although it must get you access to shows that aren't open to non-commissioned writers," said Erin.

"Yes, but then you have to do the whole thing again, only on a new level."

Erin was regretting having invited him over.

"You've managed well enough, Ian. You've made a success of it."

"Yes, but there's always more to aim for. For example, each year, one or two get awarded a one-year full-time BBC contract putting them on a number of shows. That's one of my current targets."

"But," said Charles, "from what you're saying, some of those who get commissioned still struggle to make money."

"Yes, they carry on writing for *It's News To Us* and go no further. It's a long road. Not everyone's going to make it like I have."

"Erin's too smart to take that kind of risk," said Charles.

"I need more champagne," said Erin, heading off to find a bottle.

The end of the night was a bit hazy. Although that wasn't a bad thing. You needed lots of champagne when you had too much to think about.

She spied Charles with Tiffany and found herself humming her current chosen song, Sarah Brightman and Andrea Bocelli's 'Time to Say Goodbye'. Were Sarah and Andrea trying to tell her something?

Men… Ian was a Grade One twit. Charles was a grown man who spent his Saturdays playing Super Mario on his Nintendo 64. Paul was…

Charles came over and kissed her on the cheek.

"How's the birthday girl?"

"You're a good man, Charles. Maybe you should find yourself a good woman."

"I already have."

"I'm a failed writer who wants to go to London but can't see any point in doing so."

"You're not a failed anything. You're just trying to find

your way. I understand. I really do. I've been there myself."

"You have?"

"I started in accountancy, remember. It took me two years to work out that numbers weren't for me."

"So you came up with a plan."

"Yes, I thought about the alternatives. It's called thinking outside the box."

"It's hard to think outside the box when you work inside the box factory."

"There's nothing wrong with packaging, Erin."

Erin sighed. She was too drunk for this.

"Charles, I know there is nothing wrong with packaging. It's a great job in a great business with prospects and thingies. Writing's not better. It's just more... me. It's what I want for little old me. I'm thirty, you know."

"I know."

"Thir-bloody-tee."

"I'll get you some coffee. Then we can go back to my place. I'll soon take your mind of your age."

While Charles headed for the kitchen, Erin sat down in a bush. She liked her job at Goodleigh Packaging, but it didn't put out the fire that burned inside. She wanted to write – and *not* as a hobby.

Old Father Time won't stop and wait. He's not the type.

From deep down, a sensation began to rise. Despite all the obvious impossibilities, it had to be worth one great big final push. All or nothing. One last go before she placed all her dreams into an endless succession of small, medium and large cardboard boxes.

She needed to decide. The show would return at the beginning of September. Could she spend a few months in London? God, living with Trish and the others would be fun – although that might not be possible. She might have to sit watching *Friends* and *Frasier* in another house-share. Still, she could meet Trish down the pub. And she would spend her days writing. What would she lose? Apart from her salary at GPL? Okay, so she would have no money beyond the money from the sale of the flat. After she paid off her part of the mortgage it would be about ten grand. Wasn't it a huge risk though? What would a sensible person do?

Charles returned, put the coffee down on a table and helped her out of the bush.

"Thank you, Charles."

"Right, this is what we're going to do. You'll move in with me. We can split the bills fifty-fifty. Deal?"

Deal?

"Ah, the modern version of the prince going down on bended knee. Well…"

"It's not marriage, Erin. It's us being more jointly responsible."

Erin huffed. *More jointly responsible for paying your mortgage on your flat.*

"I'll get everyone together," he said. "Let them know we're taking the next step."

"Charles…"

He started calling. "Gather round, everyone. I've got an announcement to make."

Erin steadied herself as best she could and stepped in front of him.

"No, Charles, I'm the one with the announcement."

9. THE RETURN

A bird. High in a clear September afternoon sky. Swooping. A hawk of some kind? Ornithology wasn't Erin's strongest point, although when she was young, Dad often had her help fill up the bird feeders in the garden. God, that hadn't only been in Taunton. They'd had bird feeders when she was a little girl in Hammersmith.

She lowered her gaze. The number of buildings was increasing now – their density as good as an announcement that she was approaching a city. Whether it would be a long stay depended on certain factors. Success, for one. There was no way she could justify months of failure. Besides, her parents had only agreed to keep her job open for a limited period. They wanted to see results. But success was all in the future. For now, it was enough to know that Anthea had moved out of the grotto and her room was Erin's for as long as she needed.

Mum's last words came back to her. "Are you really sure about this?" Jenny had been a bit tetchy ever since Erin's announcement. She seemed to think her daughter should have settled down with Charles.

Dad's last words came back to her. "Be careful." The words he'd spoken away from Jenny also came back to her. "I'm glad Charles gave you an ultimatum. I was worried you'd end up with him when you deserve someone who doesn't stifle the life out of you."

Cat's last words came back to her. "See you next week." Cat had of course followed it with a big smile and a hug – and a reassurance that she was joking.

And Rose's last words came back to her. "You're brilliant, Erin. Go get 'em."

Well, she was ready. No power suit and neat hairdo this time, just a comfy jacket, T-shirt, jeans and ponytail – the look of a writer too busy to worry what she looked like.

The train was slowing now... and coming to a halt. But not in the station. A moment later, a customer service announcement stated they were being held outside Paddington Station to allow for 'a freight movement'.

It sounded like one of Auntie Gertie's trips to the smallest room and Erin could only pray it didn't last as long.

Across the tracks, a small open-air station platform displayed a sign: Royal Oak. Behind it, dozens of London taxis sat idle by what looked like a cafeteria. What a strange place for an eatery, tucked away by the sidings, hidden from anyone on the streets above – although not from anyone stuck on a train. Erin imagined dozens of people waiting at the Paddington Station taxi rank wondering where the hell all the cabs were – and here they were, parked out of sight, with their drivers consuming fry-ups and cups of tea.

She checked her watch and sighed. She wasn't the only one. Others were sighing too, while the man behind her began humming the chorus of "Don't Look Back In Anger".

A thought occurred to her.

What am I doing?

It was a recurring doubt.

Getting off at Paddington, weighed down by her bags, Erin found the atmosphere unusually quiet. As the few dozen Tuesday afternoon passengers made their way along the platform to the gates, she wondered if it was down to Princess Diana's funeral, still raw in the public mind from the weekend. Of course, London wasn't so big and powerful that it couldn't be subdued by something so shocking. For Erin, it seemed unreal that the most famous woman on earth was no longer with them.

Passing through the gate, she headed for the taxi rank… which hosted around thirty people and no cabs. Erin hoped the cabbies choked on their bacon rolls.

Ten minutes later, aboard a northwest-bound Bakerloo Line train, she willed herself into a positive frame of mind. She would write great sketches and avoid men to become a commissioned radio writer. It was the ninth of September. By the ninth of October, she would see genuine progress towards that goal.

She would also squeeze in other types of writing – such as the TV comedy-drama script she had begun in August. It was quite a good one, so far. She had only written the opening scenes but now wondered if creating an outline of the whole story first might have served her better. Or was it more exciting to write without one? What it definitely needed, apart from a middle and an end, was a better hero. Not a goody-two-shoes, but a plausible champion. A nobleman's aide living a double life, perhaps. By day, a dutiful servant of the aristocracy; by night, a crime-fighting genius – a bit like Jeeves crossed with Sherlock Holmes.

Did Ian Crawford-Troy write brilliant TV drama scripts? No, of course he didn't.

Around half-five, emerging from Kilburn Park station, she found Trish waiting.

"Great to see you," she called over the sound of Duck Voice Man performing "Wonderwall".

"Long time," said Trish, giving her a big hug. "Sorry to hear about you and Charles."

"It was for the best."

"So… you're definitely here for the long haul then?"

"Yep. I am absolutely bloody determined to make it as a writer."

"Good for you."

"And what about you? How's the course?" Erin asked, referring to Trish's one-year Post-Graduate teaching-training commitment.

"We don't start until Monday, so I'm having a week of doing nothing."

"Lucky you!"

"I know. But what about your job in Taunton? Will you lose it?"

"Mum's brought in a temporary replacement. A nice girl called Sharon. To be honest, I'm not sure how this is going to pan out."

At the grotto, they got comfortable on the sofa with cups of tea and a lemon drizzle cake that Trish had bought.

"I'm only a tiny bit worried," Erin admitted. "Nothing massive. Just a teensy bit of doubt."

"Erin, you're going to have to keep it ramped up, girl. I need to see wide-eyed enthusiasm day in, day out."

"I know. Maybe I just need a couple of glasses of vino down the Kings Head."

"King's Arms."

"Yes, we could pop in there too."

"You're not here for a pub crawl, my girl. Are you?"

"I'm thirty, Trish, I've split up with Charles and I'm worried I might be a rubbish writer."

"Cancel my previous statement. You *do* need a pub crawl. I'll arrange it." Trish clicked her fingers. "There, it's arranged."

The King's Arms was smoky and quite noisy for a Tuesday evening. *Be Here Now* was blaring out from the CD player, but that was okay as Erin didn't mind a bit of Oasis.

"So, Charles is just a memory," said Trish as they took their seats armed with large glasses of chardonnay.

"Yes, he's all yours."

"What, after he chucked you? I think not!"

"Yes, well, let's not use the word chucked."

"Absolutely right. What was I thinking? The way I see it, he was an amoeba in a suit and you let him slither away."

"Him saying 'enjoy your slide into the sewer' wasn't the nicest thing I've ever heard."

"You're well shot of him. No amount of robust bed exercise is going to keep a girl in his grasp. Well, not all girls. Actually, tell me more about the robust bed exercise."

"Trish, will you put Charles' dangly bits away. We're just two single girls who don't need men spoiling things."

"Right again. Down with men."

An hour later, they were in another pub. Erin didn't notice the name on the sign outside but it had a bar and served drinks, so it was just fine. They clinked glasses, drained glasses and left to find another pub.

They found it. It was the King's Arms again.

"Hooray, we're home," said Erin.

They lined up more drinks and got into some serious talk about men, jobs, London, Liam Gallagher and whatever happened to the Stone Roses. At which point, two men eyed them up.

Erin was adamant. "No more men!"

"She's going to be a writer," Trish explained.

"Get some traffic cones around me, Trish. Set up an exclusion zone."

"It's the artistic temperament," Trish further explained.

The two men turned their attention to a fruit machine.

Later, at the grotto with a coffee and *Newsnight* on TV, Erin was sniffing her post-pub clothes. Even if you didn't smoke, it was impossible to avoid reeking of stale tobacco ash.

"So, definitely no men?" said Trish.

"Defi-maybe. No, that's a big fat no. Defi-no-be. Writing not writhing."

"Next stop Broadcasting House then."

"Yes, tomorrow I'll bowl in there like I own the place. I just hope I don't make a complete pig's breakfast of it."

"You won't."

"I wish I had your belief in me."

"It's like falling off a bike. You just have to get back on and ride."

"I'm nervous. I didn't get a single thing on last time."

"It'll be different this time. You know what to expect."

Erin took a sip of her coffee and tried to concentrate on the news. Trish was right. Tomorrow was another day. She'd be fine.

10. HERE I GO AGAIN

As Erin paused at the art deco entrance to Broadcasting House, a woman hurried out talking on a mobile phone. Then two men rushed in discussing something called pro-tools. Somehow there seemed to be more anxiety in the air than back in April.

"Here we go then…"

On entering the light, airy reception area, the noise of Portland Place faded away. The man behind the desk looked up but Erin just smiled, said "It's News To Us" and signed in. Then, rejecting the Lift of Plummeting Doom and the stairs to the Corridor of Opportunity, she opted for the Escalator of Possibilities.

It felt odd riding up an escalator inside the BBC. It made the building feel more like a shopping mall. There was a nice sense of travel though, as if she were going somewhere in life. Maybe there was a series in that? *The Escalator*. Our hero rides up the moving staircase, unaware of what this week's episode would bring – a bit like *Quantum Leap*.

At the top, she was pleased to discover a small counter selling proper coffee and tasty-looking Danish pastries. Of course, she wasn't in the building for that. Then again, she was only human.

Descending down some stairs to the first floor with a

coffee in one hand and the unchomped half of a Danish pastry in the other, Erin found herself by the entrance to Light Entertainment. It made her stomach flip.

Entering, she was greeted by half a dozen new faces. At least, they weren't faces she recognized. Maybe they had done years on the show barring her single week in April.

One of them – a rare female – smiled.

"My first time," she said. "I heard about it from a friend."

"Good for you," said Erin. "The main thing is to stick with it and not give up if you don't click straight away."

"I've heard there's a high turnover."

"Ignore that. You heard about the show, you came up and you'll come back next week regardless."

"Is that how you started?"

"Yes." *Kind of.*

Paul Fielding came in, coffee in hand. He looked just as she remembered, although with a little stubble. No Danish pastry though, which made her feel weak-willed.

"Paul. Hi."

"Hi. Um…?"

Um? Hadn't he spent the entire summer dreaming about her?

"It's Erin."

"Erin, of course. The heavy tackle from behind. It's been a while. Did you have a good summer?"

"Brilliant. You?"

"Yeah, I managed to scrape a week in Newquay."

"Nice."

He smiled and then continued through into Light Entertainment's inner sanctum. Erin followed.

"I didn't come back after my first week," she explained. "I didn't quite click with the show, then there was stuff at work and…"

They stopped alongside a dozen people outside the writers' room. The door was closed for the commissioned writers' meeting, although someone inside was playing the piano and singing.

"If you're starting again," said Paul, "try to remember the old proverb: a journey of a thousand miles begins with…"

"A single step?"

"No, a stupid amount of optimism."

Erin smiled. She liked that.

"Kirsty, Ollie and Joe got commissioned."

Erin didn't know Kirsty, Ollie or Joe but smiled all the same.

"What about you, Paul? Is a commission on the horizon?"

"I hope so. We've got a good run at December now so it's every man for himself. And woman, of course."

Erin frowned. "December?"

"The next commissions. You know how it works, don't you?"

"You smile at the producer?"

"*Producers*, plural. But no, they just add up the number of minutes we non-comms get on the show. Come December, they look at the league table and pick the top two, three or four, depending on how many they want to commission."

"I see – and it was three last time?"

"Two," said another writer. "Ollie and Joe are a team."

"The bottom line," said Paul, "is we're relying on this lot of commissioned writers to get aboard other shows to make room for us."

Erin wondered – how would she accumulate enough minutes to get into the top two or three? It sounded like a case of getting off to a really good start and not letting up for the next few months. But that seemed a tall order.

The door opened and ten or so people emerged. Around twenty-five non-commissioned writers eventually shuffled inside to replace them.

"Everyone have a good summer?" asked Gavin Gould. There were murmurs. "Okay, most of you know I'm an alien overlord posing as Gavin Gould the *It's News To Us* script editor. For new people, that was the producer and commissioned writers you saw running away. It's nothing personal. The producer has gone through the news stories and they'll now try to resist the lure of alcohol in order to write lots of lovely sketches. My job is to go over the stories with you so you can beat their efforts with brilliant sketches of your own. Any questions?"

A hand went up. Male, mid-twenties.

"Should we cover different topics to those covered by the commissioned writers?"

"Just write brilliant sketches. Second guessing what others will or won't write will drive you to crack-cocaine – although I can supply you at reasonable prices."

Most people laughed, including Erin. Gavin was so nice to these one-time-only attendees. And to regulars like herself, of course.

"Who's the musical genius?" she asked.

"Modesty prevents me naming that genius," said Gavin. "Oh, alright, yes, it's me and I do a musical sketch each show."

Gavin soon got going through the week's stories, with a big proviso to steer clear of any Princess Diana ideas. Sticking to politics seemed to be the best bet and the producer had given a few hints on what she was after. Erin felt reasonably positive – a couple of ideas were already brewing.

After the meeting, as the crowd of non-comms disappeared in the direction of the LE reception, Erin poked her head into Sarah Bryce's office.

"Hello," said Sarah, sitting with a pile of what looked like scripts on her lap. "Can I help?"

"Hi, I'm Erin Goodleigh. I was here in April."

"Er…?"

"Sorry, Sarah, I'm being dim. I came up in April but I'm trying again."

Sarah smiled. "Yes, I remember you now. Most writers give up far too easily. You won't get a better opportunity than this."

Erin smiled. "Thanks Sarah. How many times have you dished out that piece of advice?"

"Oh, once or twice."

"I can imagine."

In the LE reception, Erin found Paul checking the noticeboard.

"I see *Newslines* is up for an award," he said.

"What's *Newslines*?"

"Our show's evil twin."

Erin didn't get it, so Paul elaborated.

"*It's News To Us* is made in a small studio without an audience for Radio 4, check?"

"Check."

"*Newslines* is made in a theatre with a live audience for Radio 2. LE makes both of them."

"I see. Well, I'm sticking with *It's News To Us*. At least for now. One show is more than enough."

"Good call. Some of the more experienced writers work on both, but it's not easy."

"I've written for a live audience before," she said, defensively. "At Edinburgh."

"Sure, but *Newslines* is a tough gig for writers. It's a lot harder to get stuff on."

"Is that a warning?"

"No, of course not. Are you sticking around for lunch?"

"No, I'd best be getting away. Lots to do."

"See you tomorrow then."

"Yeah."

Erin left by the Corridor of Opportunity, where two men in overalls had the middle double doors off. The majesty of Broadcasting House had to be an ethereal thing. In reality, it was a complete dump.

Outside, in bright sunshine, she wondered briefly if she had just turned down a date with Paul Fielding. No, of course not. He obviously just wondered if she would be sticking around to eat some food.

She strode up Portland Place with great purpose, ignoring the 'Freedom for Tibet' demo outside the Chinese Embassy on the other side of the street. This was no time to be filmed and labelled an enemy of the People's Republic. She was a writer on a journey to deliver satire to half a million listeners. What a thought. Half a million people chuckling away at her jokes. Or more likely, frowning at the radio. *You call that funny?*

Reaching Marylebone Road, she crossed into Regents Park. In need of a clearer mind, she walked deep into the park, perhaps for half a mile, before she found herself a nice quiet bench. It wasn't like being in Central London. You could hear the birds and monkeys.

Monkeys?

Ah, the zoo. It had to be nearby. Either that or an ape was about to leap out of the bushes and eat her notepad.

Now what? She had no idea what to write. Still, in a few hours, she would be seated at Trish's recently-bought second-hand Amstrad word processor, finishing off her third or fourth sketch. It wouldn't seem so bad then.

11. WRITE ON

Around twelve the following day, suppressing a yawn, Erin walked into the LE reception area with a cappuccino and an apricot pastry. She had been up since half-six, re-writing and polishing her work before printing it out on the daisy-wheel printer that almost shook the house apart.

She found Gavin in the doorway to the admin office and handed him her sketches.

"Wonderful! Thank you so much."

From there, she wandered into the writers' room where a few people were polishing their work. A couple of them were discussing the England win over Moldova on Sky Sports and the Princess Di tribute, with the crowd singing along to "Candle in the Wind".

Paul appeared at the door.

"Erin, hi. Do many sketches?"

"Three. Well, I started with four but even I could see one of them was a dud."

"Three's good. I did three."

"We have an equal chance then."

"Yes, although as a deadly rival for a commission I hope you fail miserably."

Erin smiled. "And may your sketches curl up at the edges and spontaneously combust before the producer sets eyes on them."

"Good – we understand each other. Are you coming back for feedback?"

"Er…?"

"Nobody tells newbies, but come back at four and Gavin might have a tweak or two for you. It's always worth it."

"Is that what you're doing now – just waiting around?"

"Not exactly. I'm waiting for Toby Lock to show up. Do you know him?"

"No, can't say I do."

Paul indicated she should follow him. They ended up in Toby's small office around the corner from the writers' room.

"I've got some ideas for a sitcom I want to run by him. Nobody will tell a newbie, but it's the sort of thing you should think about."

"What, chat with producers about possible sitcoms?"

"Why not? I mean you've made the effort to come up from…?"

"Taunton. Can't you tell by the accent?"

"Only in a general West Country-ish kind of way."

"I'm told it's not particularly strong. Perhaps it's because I was born in London. Are you a Londoner?"

"No, I'm from Huntingdon. I came down to London for work."

She wondered – how old was he? He looked a little older than most of the writers who inhabited LE. Thirty-five? She liked a man who was old enough to have lived a little. What had Paul done with his life?

"I thought of you in the summer," he said.

"Really?" Erin's heart began beating faster.

"I was in Cornwall and there was a woman who looked just like you."

"You remembered what I looked like but not my

name?"

"Confession time. I did remember your name. It's the name of the most important woman in my life."

Erin tensed up. "Your wife?"

"No…" Paul laughed. "My despatcher."

"Your despatcher?"

"I'm a motorcycle courier. If I'm nice to our Erin, she gives me better jobs."

"I don't think I'd like riding a bike around London. It looks pretty busy out there."

"Yeah, it can get a bit lively."

"So this woman in Cornwall…?"

"She was selling t-shirts on the beach. I have to say things got quite intense between us. Passionate, even. Especially when I offered a fiver for a ten quid shirt and she told me to eff off."

Erin smiled, glad that Paul could joke with her, and glad that his liaison with a t-shirt seller hadn't developed.

"So," he said, "any sitcom ideas bubbling up?"

"No, but I'm thinking of writing a comedy-drama."

"Fair enough. But this opportunity is miles more special than some people realize. You don't play football on a tennis court, Erin."

"Erin!" Ian Crawford-Troy was standing in the doorway.

"You know ICT?" said Paul. "Ah, the West Country connection."

"We were at school together," said Erin.

"So how's your mum?" asked Ian. "Still worrying you'll be carried away by some grisly Londoner? We should catch up. Loads to talk about."

"I'd better go see if I can find Toby," said Paul, departing.

Erin smiled but wished the ceiling would collapse on

Ian. Of course, Paul had raised a teensy, tiny, minuscule micro-question. What did you do if you fancied a fellow writer but had taken a vow to steer clear of men?

The afternoon went slowly. Having taken a stroll down to Oxford Circus and Regent Street, and having popped into Hamley's toy shop where she bought a rainbow pack of pens, she returned for feedback at four. An hour later, she was still waiting for Gavin to show up.

Where was he?

Around five, she was wondering if to give up, but several others were still waiting.

At half-five, Gavin finally returned, full of apologies and feedback news – only there was none for Erin. Gavin suggested she was free to hit the pub while these less fortunate oiks had to stay behind and toil. She couldn't decide if that was good or bad.

Later, after fish and chips, Erin and Trish popped into the King's Arms. Liam the barman was playing *OK Computer* – quietly, so as to not scare away the older regulars. Erin wondered about him.

"Do you think you'll be serving drinks until you retire, Liam?"

"Me? No, I'm off travelling once I get the money together."

"Oh, good for you. Where might you go?"

"Thailand, Australia… a long way from Kilburn Park, that's for sure."

As soon as Liam went to serve another customer, Trish nudged Erin.

"So what about you? What will you be getting up to

tomorrow? A nice lie-in till lunchtime?"

"No, I need to write. Seriously, I really do need to use the time I'm at the grotto to get some kind of career launched."

"Any ideas what you'll write?"

"Not yet. Something funny, I think. Well, hopefully it'll be funny. I've got a comedy-drama idea, but…"

Paul's comment came back to her. Shouldn't she be writing a sitcom? But what was wrong with writing a comedy-drama? What was the difference?

Friday morning saw Trish reading heavy-duty materials linked to the course she'd be starting on the Monday. That meant Erin had no excuse for any kind of procrastination.

So what would she write? She wasn't sure how to set out a sitcom. Or what kind of characters to put in it. Or what sort of mishaps they might get up to. Or how to make any of it funny. Perhaps she could continue with the comedy-drama and delay the sitcom until she could get a bit of guidance, possibly from Paul.

"Trish, what's the difference between a comedy-drama and a sitcom?"

"One's got a bit of drama in it?"

Maybe she shouldn't bother with comedy-drama. Maybe she should just adopt a straightforward, no-nonsense *two-fold* attack on becoming the kind a professional writer she'd like to be – a writer of sitcoms and novels.

Great thinking.

So what kind of novel?

A thriller?

She went to the kitchen and filled the kettle. What had

Paul said about staying focused? *You don't play football on a tennis court.* Was he right? Or was he failing to take into account those who could multi-task? She didn't strictly need to incorporate comedy into *all* her writing, did she? Why couldn't she make it as a writer of hilarious sitcoms *and* serious novels?

While the kettle boiled, she considered what that might entail. Obviously a prolonged massive effort on the comedy front and, yes, a prolonged massive effort on the novel front…

Two massive efforts.

Paul was right. When faced with an opportunity to impress producers who made comedy, why not come up with ideas for comedy?

She thought for a few minutes.

Two people…

She opened a fresh document and began typing.

LIFE BEGINS AT THIRTY
A TV Sitcom by Erin Goodleigh

Episode 1: "Home Comforts"

EXT. ESTATE AGENTS – DAY

Elizabeth and Piers are looking in the window at the photos of houses for sale.

ELIZABETH:
They're so expensive, Piers.

PIERS:
Don't worry. We'll find something we can afford. What about that one?

ELIZABETH:
(SQUINTS) What's that little box behind the
satellite dish?

PIERS:
That's the house.

That wasn't too bad, was it? She could build on that.
What was the point of it though? Was it to show how
tough life could be for two middle-class people who
could only afford a small house? What about the majority
of people who couldn't afford any kind of house? And it
was a TV sitcom. Did that matter?

She needed to talk to someone. Paul or Ian? No, not
Ian. Toby Lock though – he was a producer. Paul was
right. There were opportunities staring her in the face.
Learning directly from people who actually worked in the
business wasn't something available to most amateur
writers. She really couldn't afford to throw that away. She
shut the computer down. She would talk to Toby before
taking another step. No more wrong turns or dead ends.
She grabbed a magazine and began reading.

It wasn't a great Friday evening session in the King's
Arms. Trish was up for it, but Erin couldn't get her mind
off a certain radio show that would be going out at
eleven. Still, it was great to hear all about Trish's hopes
for the course and her future.

They left the pub at ten to eleven. Erin went to her
room, set the radio-cassette player to 'record' and turned
the volume down. She knew she should be absorbing and
learning how the show worked but she couldn't take the

pressure. Sipping coffee on the sofa in front of the TV with Trish, she skimmed through a newspaper. All the while, she kept glancing at the clock and wondering – what if one of her sketches was being broadcast to an entire nation right at this moment?

When the clock reached 11:27, Erin went to her room and turned up the volume. There was a sketch about Bill Clinton.

Then…

"*It's News To Us* was performed by Brian Grainger, Hannah Dobson, Anne Garston-Green and Ben Tidy. It was written by Gavin Gould, Martin Dobbs, Shaun Donoghue, Josh Steinman, Simon Driver, Paul Fielding, Dave Singer, Oliver Goldman and Joe Harrington, Jamie Strand, Stephen Green, and Dave Boynton. The producer was Caroline Felby."

Erin's blood turned to ice.

Nothing on.

12. A WRITER?

It was a rotten weekend full of self-doubt and questions. Erin wasn't a negative person, but failure to get anything on *It's News To Us* was an open wound that made her feel like avoiding people. Fellow failures at LE might joke about it, but surely, like her, they felt sick inside?

Trish was great, naturally. She had lots of ways to keep Erin distracted, including a canal-side café lunch at nearby Little Venice, home to a myriad of beautifully-painted narrow boats. It's what best friends did. The wine they had in the pub helped too.

Monday had a slightly different feel to it. With Trish going off excitedly to her first day at teacher-training college, Erin's sense of disappointment was replaced by a growing sense of opportunity. By the time Trish returned at five, full of enthusiasm. Erin couldn't help but be full of enthusiasm too.

Tuesday was a good day. Erin made a list of sitcom ideas and decided she would talk to Sarah at LE to get her ideas on who would be best to approach. There was no sense in assuming that *any* producer would be a good fit.

Wednesday saw Erin's stomach butterflies return. Entering Broadcasting House, she felt weighed down by the prospect of facing everyone as a failure.

In the Light Entertainment writers' room, she

recognized a few of the twenty or so non-comms. There were plenty of new faces though and she could only assume that quite a few people had dropped out – hardly a good omen.

"Okay," said a cheery Gavin, "most of you know I'm a member of the Royal Family posing as Gavin Gould the script editor. For new people, that was the producer and commissioned writers you saw fleeing the building. No, there's not a fire. The producer will have gone through the news stories with them and they'll soon be writing lots of lovely sketches. My job is to go over the stories with you so that you can knock their efforts into a cocked hat. Okay, any questions?"

A hand went up. Male, mid-twenties.

"Is it worth avoiding what the commissioned writers will be covering?"

"Don't worry about them. I'll take you through the stories the producer is interested in and you'll have your targets."

Paul arrived.

Tsk, late.

Gavin got things under way and Erin took notes. Thankfully, at least two good ideas came to her before the meeting ended.

Disappointingly, Paul had to get away for some reason and they had no chance to speak beyond a quick hello. Sarah wasn't around either, so Erin gave up on finding a producer to talk with about a potential sitcom.

She spent the afternoon and evening writing sketches. It was easy enough to tell Trish she would try harder this week, but she had tried bloody hard last week and it was difficult to see what she could do differently. Besides, Trish had enough on her plate with homework from her course.

Sleep didn't come easy that night. Failure seeped into her dreams. Staying in London as an unsuccessful non-commissioned writer wasn't an option.

Thursday lunchtime came around fast and Erin was back at Broadcasting House handing in her sketches. That done, she headed out for a sandwich and a long walk in the late summer sunshine. Later, she returned for feedback.

Intriguingly, there were a couple of notes from the producer, which gave Erin hope. She bagged an electric typewriter in the writers' room and did the re-writes as requested. Once she was done, she sought out Sarah for any tips on producers. Sarah thought Jane Clearwater would be perfect, but she was away on holiday and wouldn't be back until the following week. Erin wasn't sure whether to wait another week, so she went round to Toby Lock's office.

There was no sign of him. Was he ever there? No, in fairness, he was probably busy working on a show. She was about to leave when she noticed a sitcom script on the desk. "Buck House" by Paul Fielding. Did she dare read it? She didn't know Paul that well and he'd been kind to her. He might not like her nosing through his stuff.

Even so…

She turned the page. There was a statement in capitals.

THE WHOLE OLIVER CROMWELL
THING NEVER HAPPENED. BRITAIN IS
STILL RULED BY THE REIGNING
MONARCH.

INT. A WEATHER STUDIO. DAY.
Map of Britain. The Queen facing camera.

THE QUEEN:
Good evening. It's turned out nice again, what?
A bit nippy though in one's kingdom of
Scotland... which played havoc with Philip's
knee yesterday. Ahem. Now, the cold front will
be with us until the Duchess of York returns
to her own place on Friday.

Erin put the script back. Firstly, it wasn't a radio
sitcom. It was a TV sitcom. So she was right about that –
you could write for TV even if you were currently without
a commission in radio.

Or had Paul got special permission?

The rest of her day began to take shape: go back to the
grotto, think up sitcom ideas for TV and radio, get eight
hours sleep.

Friday morning, eating toast while catching up with the
news on Ceefax, Erin mulled over her sitcom ideas. Just
as well, too, as the weather had taken a nosedive.
Checking her list, one of the sitcom ideas, set in an
insurance company's regional office, showed some
promise. It was staffed by a Charles-a-like, his rugby
mates and Tiffany, who would be called Bethany. Or was
that just a rubbish idea masking a need to put the boot in?

In the end, it was a stop-start kind of day as she
couldn't really find the point of anything she wrote. It was
as if she was trying to cobble together various sketches
with the same characters in the hope that they might
merge into a sitcom.

Friday evening was spent in the pub with Trish and
Frances, although Frances ducked out at nine as she was
going to a club in Soho with a couple of mates. Trish, of

course, couldn't stop talking about her new course, and Erin was happy to hear it. Inside, the anxiety of waiting for *It's News To Us* at eleven was a bit like toothache.

Around half-nine, a couple of thirty-something men appeared at their table.

"Hello ladies, I'm Craig," said a confident tanned blonde guy.

"And I'm Tim," said his confident tanned dark-haired mate.

Erin's disinterest was trumped by Trish's smile.

"I'm Trish and this is Erin."

"I work in a packaging factory," said Erin, hoping they would go away.

"She's management," said Trish.

"Meet the boss, eh?" said Craig.

"Very junior management," said Erin. "It's my parents' firm, which means I don't get to make any decisions, apart from whether to have tea or coffee – and that's only if my parents aren't there."

"Erin's also a writer," said Trish, unhelpfully. "She's written for the BBC."

"No way," said Craig. "What have you written?"

"Trish is being a tease," said Erin. "I've done a bit of radio but I haven't managed to get anywhere."

"My sister works in books," said Tim. "At an agency."

Erin was suddenly intrigued. "What kind of agency?"

"Not sure. They have a famous author according to Denise, but I can't remember the name."

"So it's an authors' agency? Representing authors?"

"Yeah, Denise does the admin."

"Whereabouts in London?"

"Soho somewhere."

An agent. Oh, to have one.

"Erin's thinking of writing a novel, aren't you," said

Trish. "Maybe we could sort out an introduction to this agency."

"Possibly," said Tim.

"What sort of novel is it?" said Craig. "Dirty?"

The boys laughed, which annoyed Erin.

"Actually, if you wouldn't mind leaving us to get on with our evening…?"

The boys shrugged and left.

"Sorry Trish, but I'm not stumbling out of here drunk and singing "Bitter Sweet Symphony" with their hands all over us.

"You don't know that would happen," said Trish.

"Alcohol-fired pheromones, Trish, seeping into our brains and gradually turning Laurel and Hardy over there into Hugh Grant and Bruce Willis."

"I think the seeping's already under way."

"Okay, keep your eyes on me, Trish, and tell me all about teacher training again."

Back at the grotto, at 10:59 p.m., Erin set the radio-cassette player to begin recording then went to watch TV. At 11:27, she returned to her room and turned the radio up. There was a sketch about the Queen followed by a lot of names, but not her own.

Argghhh!

This was a slow, slow death.

The weekend and the first couple of days of the following week were a blur of writing up ideas accompanied by the constant dull pain of failure. The only welcome positive was Trish's boundless enthusiasm for teacher training. For Erin, a slow-motion form of panic was setting in. She wasn't freaked out, nor had she lost her head, but it was like those old movies where the bit-part actor was up to his knees in quicksand. It didn't look too bad but you knew where it was heading.

Still, on the Wednesday, she managed to absorb, via Gavin, what the producer wanted for *It's New To Us* and, on the Thursday, handed in three appropriate sketches. All the while, she kept her distance from Paul and he made no move to close the gap. She was also aware that producer Jane Clearwater was in the building but decided it would be too embarrassing to talk to her about sitcoms before she had got at least one sketch on the show.

That evening, after feedback, she popped into the Crown & Sceptre, a pub just around the back of Broadcasting House. She had heard that Paul and a few others might go. He didn't, although the others – some of the more regular non-comms – did.

While at the bar, waiting to be served, she found herself alongside three guys discussing topical comedy sketches and sounding very much like writers.

"Do you write for *It's News To Us?*" she asked.

She was greeted with three men scoffing.

"*Newslines*," one of them said.

"Oh right. I'm new – to *It's News To Us,* I mean."

"Good luck," one of them said.

"That's where I started," said another. "Good show to learn the craft."

"So your show's recorded in front of an audience? It must be fun to hear the laughs."

"Yes, and terrifying to hear the silences."

"Ah the silences," said the third writer, reverentially.

"I was being unkind," said the first. "It's just that *INTU* writers get an easy ride. You know, writing chin-strokers for the discerning Radio 4 audience in the Home

Counties. You getting much on?"

"Not yet. But I live in hope."

"Good for you. It's not your fault it's a terrible show."

"It's not that bad," said Erin.

"It has no house style," said the first writer.

"I hear some people write for both," said Erin.

"Very few. Almost none, to be more accurate."

"You wouldn't recommend I try both then?"

"Get commissioned on one first. Don't dilute what you have to offer. Your show's actually both better and worse to write for. Better because you get a different producer every few weeks and—"

"—worse because we get a different producer every few weeks?" interrupted Erin.

"Exact-o-mundo."

"So *Newslines* has one producer?"

"Yes, just the one, covered in dust and cobwebs, never allowed to leave the building."

Erin knew they were right about sticking with one show. There wasn't much point in failing at two.

Two hours later, in a different part of the part, with a different group of writers, all thoughts of failure had been washed away by Foster's lager.

"You know Ian Crawford-Troy then," said a long-haired writer called Miles.

Erin didn't want to talk at length about Ian, but didn't like to be rude.

"Yes, we were at school together."

"Ahhh… very handy."

"How do you mean?"

"Well, it's who you know, right?"

"Who I know?" This was preposterous. Ian was about as useful to know as a dead budgie.

"Yes, who you know. Do you want a pint or

something?"

"Er... Foster's please."

She followed him to the bar.

"It's a drain on the pocket," he said.

"It's certainly that. I've never been so broke."

"You know Marylebone Road?" he said.

"Yes...?"

"You know the offices by the station?"

"Er... yes?"

"They need cleaners."

"That's not funny."

"It's not meant to be funny. It's a job opportunity. One of the non-comms over there – Steve someone – he's doing a bit for rent and beer money. I mean who knows how long it'll take to make it, eh?"

Erin reflected on it. Was it okay to be a writer-cleaner? What would Mum say? An image of a volcano exploding came to mind.

She found the Steve in question at a table with a few people. When she expressed a slight interest in the cleaning option, he jotted the agency number on a beer mat.

A couple of hours later, sitting on the edge of her bed feeling drunk and uncertain of the future, she pondered the idea of getting a part-time job. She only needed enough to cover expenses. The money she earned from writing sketches would be a bonus. The downside? She wouldn't be a writer who did a bit of cleaning. She'd be a cleaner who did a bit of writing.

Twenty-four hours after Steve had given her the agency number, Erin was somewhere near Marylebone Road pushing a vacuum cleaner down an office corridor. She was officially a cleaner who did a bit of writing. Still, it was only from six until nine p.m. and it meant sixty quid a week, cash in hand. Of course, if she was successful with a radio sketch that exceeded a minute in length, she'd be able to flip her status back to a writer who did a bit of cleaning.

It was while emptying a waste paper bin into a black rubbish sack that a figure popped into her head. *Mrs Reed.* The elderly woman who did exactly this at Goodleigh Packaging, where, until recently, Erin had been part of the management team. What would Mrs Reed make of all this? She'd probably think Erin had lost her mind.

She grabbed an office phone and called home.

"Hi Mum, how are you?"

"Erin, darling. How lovely to hear from you. You're not wasting money in the pub, are you?"

"No, Mum, I'm working."

"At the BBC?"

"No, I've got this handy little job to help with the rent."

"Not in a burger bar?"

"No, Mum, it's in an office."

"Oh Erin, you have an office job here. What are you playing at?"

"It's just for a while. You know, until I get some sketches on…"

"Is that where you're calling from now?"

"Yes."

"At eight o'clock on a Friday night? Get the hell out of there, Erin. They're exploiting you."

"It's fine, Mum. Honest." Erin didn't like misleading people, but there was no way she could let on about her current duties.

"Erin, I'm disappointed. You went to London to

become a writer."

"I *am* a writer." She averted her gaze from the vacuum cleaner. "A good one."

An hour later, she finished her shift and stopped at McDonald's before making her way home. It was a relief to find the house empty when she got back. She put the television on but didn't watch anything. Making a cup of coffee used up a bit of time too.

At eleven, she pressed 'record' and turned the radio-cassette player's volume down.

It was funny how one person's decision could affect your life. Justin Moore, this week's producer, had the power to raise Erin to the level of the gods, or plunge her down into the pit of hell. She hoped producers understood this power and wielded it judiciously, and not randomly or lazily. Justin had read her sketches, hadn't he? Or had he? What if he'd just skipped over them?

She took a breath. Maybe the coffee was making her agitated. Why didn't they have de-caf at the grotto? She made a note: "buy de-caf."

The minutes dragged.

Did Cat listen to the show? Or Rose? What would they make of it? It wasn't the greatest show in the world. Far from it. Some of the sketches were okay though. The cast certainly gave it everything.

Patchy. That's what someone in the pub had said about it. Someone else had pointed out that it was a training ground for tomorrow's big names. Was she going to be a big name tomorrow? She didn't feel like a potential big name, although Erin Genevieve Goodleigh wasn't exactly a small name.

Finally, she turned the radio up. It was sketch about Tony Blair arguing with his cabinet about something or other. Then… a lot of names, but none of them hers.

Erin felt a cold sweat.
I'm not a writer, I'm a cleaner.

13. PROGRESS?

Erin spent the morning of the first day of October in Regent's Park. The weather was glorious and it filled her with hope that, writing-wise, she might crack it this time – before it cracked her and she went completely mad.

Around half-eleven, she headed to Portland Place for the *INTU* non-comms meeting. Annoyingly, Ian Crawford-Troy was hanging around in the LE reception area.

"Erin, hi. You come to see me?"

"No."

"Just kidding. I was going to say there's no queue."

Normally, Erin liked a self-deprecating man, but Ian just couldn't lose the smarm. It also occurred to her that he might be a stalker. After all, he was only too aware that she would be in the building for the meeting.

"What are you up to?" she asked.

"Oh, I've got a nice little gig on a new sketch show. It's a six-week run starting next week. The commission's only three minutes a show, but I can build on that."

Only three minutes? Erin wished she had that guaranteed every week.

She pushed on into the LE inner sanctum where the short corridor leading to the writers' room was full of non-comms. A few minutes later, the commissioned writers emerged along with a new producer. Gavin Gould followed them out and addressed the waiting non-comms.

"That's your producer," he said. "All wave to Jane Clearwater – a very funny psychopathic vegetable grower."

Once they were gathered inside, Gavin closed the door.

"Okay, most of you know I'm Lord Lucan posing as Gavin Gould the script editor…"

The door opened again and Paul came in muttering his apologies. Erin was relieved to see him. Paul giving up would be a big dent to her own determination to carry on.

Paul… he looked scruffier this week. Messy hair, an old sports shirt, jeans and trainers. Thinking about him meant she missed the funny thing Gavin said.

After the meeting, she waylaid Paul.

"Getting a bit slapdash, aren't we?"

"Oh, busy at work. Lunch?"

"What, me and you?"

"It's not a date. We regulars often have lunch in the canteen."

"Okay."

"Wait there. I just need to photocopy a few things."

Paul went off, leaving Erin to recall comedians like Eric and Ernie making gags about the BBC canteen.

"Waiting for Paul?" asked a writer – a man in his mid-twenties. Erin knew him as a regular non-comm face.

"Yes, we're going to the canteen."

"You might as well come with us," said a second writer – a female non-comm regular, also in her mid-twenties. "If we hurry, we might nab a table."

Erin checked her watch. It was five-to-one.

"Okay."

"I'm Colleen, by the way. This is Simon."

"Erin."

"So, how's it going for you?" Colleen asked as they made their way to the lifts.

"Not so good. As in nothing on the show."

"Anything in the script?" asked Simon.

Erin didn't understand. Her frown must have shown it.

"The show is twenty-seven minutes long," said Simon. "The script is much longer."

"You mean they record more than they need. Of course they do. Why wouldn't they?"

"There's usually about forty-five minutes in the script," said Colleen. "They cut that during the read-through with the performers."

"They record around thirty-five minutes," said Simon, "then trim it to twenty-seven in the edit."

It hadn't occurred to Erin that she might have had stuff read by the performers… or even recordings of her sketches cut during the edit.

"How do we find out?" she asked.

"Grab a script," said Colleen. "Do you know Sarah?"

"I do."

"Ask Sarah."

"I will," said Erin, feeling a tiny bit excited.

The canteen was at the top of the building. Far from looking like something from a cautionary tale, it was clean and shiny. The food looked good too. Opting for fishcake and chips, Erin followed Colleen and Simon to a table in the far corner.

"Good view," she said, peering through the window over part of central London.

"We'll go outside later," said Colleen. "You can see more."

Paul joined them with a plate of fishcake and chips.

Snap.

"So you've met Ms Nicholls and Mr Driver."

"Simon Driver... I've heard that name a few times in the credits."

"Simon's top of the non-comms at the moment," said Colleen.

"Only until they work out I'm crap," said Simon.

"So who are the commissioned writers?" asked Erin.

Colleen squinted slightly, possibly visualizing them. "Gavin the script editor, Martin Dobbs, Shaun Donoghue, Kirsty Gray, Dave Singer, Ollie Goldman and Joe Harrington... Simon Yeovil, Stephen Green... Dave Boynton..."

"We've got eleven or twelve at the moment," said Simon, although a couple of them are working on other things."

Erin understood. "So, the leading non-comms just have to wait for some of the commissioned writers to leave the show."

"Yes," said Paul. "Colleen, Simon, Jamie, Josh, me... we're all waiting to pounce."

After their meal, they adjourned to the roof terrace; a large open space with a few seats dotted around. Here, Erin learned that Simon was a former London School of Economics student from Ipswich who lived in Willesden Green, and that Colleen was a Neasden-based Liverpuddlian who had attended Cambridge University and knew a few members of the famous Footlights.

Later, when Simon and Colleen broke away to scrounge cigarettes off people they knew, Erin was left with Paul.

"Great views," she said.

"Er... average views. We're not quite high enough, are

we."

"That's the Telecom Tower, isn't it?"

"Yes, hard to miss."

Erin eyed his sports shirt.

"I saw you in a Clash t-shirt once. Are you a fan? Or is it because they're cool again?"

"Cheek. I'm actually old enough to have been a fan when they first got started. I saw them a few times in the late-seventies."

"In Huntingdon?"

Paul laughed. "No, in London. Nothing happens in Huntingdon. We're even lumbered with John Major as our MP."

"Did you come to London after university?"

"No, I didn't go to university."

"Oh. So what sort of work have you done?"

"All kinds. For three years, I put up marquees. That's your cue to make a joke about erections."

Erin felt warm. "Erections are no laughing matter, Paul."

"No? I could name a dozen sitcoms that think they are."

"Tell me – how did you get into this?"

"By mistake. I was meeting a mate in a pub – the Crown & Sceptre round the corner – and some guy thought I was part of their crowd."

"He thought you were a non-comm writer?"

"Yeah, he's long gone now. Did about three shows. Anyway, I think we agreed that I should give it a go."

"How long ago was that?"

"Oh… a year? Must have been late September. See? I might be old but the memory's still working."

"Why, how old are you? Oh God, no, sorry, that's incredibly rude. Thirty-five-ish?"

Paul laughed. "Thirty-seven. And no, I don't need an afternoon nap."

"No, you've got stamina. You've stuck it out when most don't."

"It's patience you need. It was six weeks before I got anything on. I almost gave up."

"I'm having the same problem."

"Don't give up. Most of the commissioned writers say they clicked with a certain producer and that was it."

"Who have you clicked with?"

"James Laine, but he left in June."

"Ah well."

After lunch, Erin popped down to find Sarah. It wasn't long before she had a copy of the previous week's script. It was a strange creature; lots of photocopied sketches in different fonts, with different line spacing and layouts. A cover sheet and a big staple in the top left-hand corner bound them into a single entity: an *It's News To Us* script. Erin flicked through. Her Bill Clinton sketch was near the end with a diagonal line across it in biro.

Progress?

The following day, she was back at Broadcasting House with her sketches.

"Oh no, a rival writer," said Paul. "I was hoping your computer monitor had fallen on you and pinned you to the floor."

Erin was worried that she was becoming obsessed with Paul because him saying 'pinned you to the floor' had an effect on her.

"Funny you should say that, Paul, because I was hoping you'd had trouble with your hard drive."

Stop it!

Once the sketches were handed in, they went to lunch in the canteen and chatted about trying to make a living from writing.

"I'd love to buy a computer," said Erin. "I'm using my friend Trish's Amstrad at the moment but it's very limited. What do you use?"

"I share a Windows 3.1 with my girlfriend."

Girlfriend???

"You mean you… have a… 3.1?"

"I'd love to get a Windows 95 but they reckon it'll be replaced next year. Still, the 3.1's okay. It's got Word on it so you get all the fancy fonts. Mind you, some of the writers swear by the Apple Mac."

"Yes, well, I suppose it doesn't matter what you've got. It's what you do with it that counts."

When they returned for feedback, they ended up making their changes on manual typewriters as two of the electric models had been claimed, while the third was dead. Once Erin had made her small changes, she went off to get a cheeseburger before heading up to Marylebone Road for her evening shift cleaning offices.

Friday arrived with its usual offering of writing time for Erin. She couldn't work out what to do with the three sitcom ideas she had though, so she tried to think up some ideas for a sketch show she could pitch to a producer – once she'd got a sketch on *It's New To Us*, of course.

The main problem seemed to be how to package the sketches to give the potential show an identity. What was needed was some kind of wrap-around idea. A fake news channel? Aliens spying on the Earth?

Yes, a fake news channel.

She started writing a scene to introduce the characters. But this began to take on the feel of a sitcom, so she went with that. A new sitcom, *The News Room* by Erin Goodleigh. Two hours later, it dawned on her that a sitcom called *Drop The Dead Donkey* was set in a newsroom and had won many BAFTA's.

Crap.

Why had she never watched it?

At lunchtime, fancying a break from work, she went to see *The Full Monty* at a local cinema. While she felt their pain at being unemployed, watching Robert Carlyle and co. strip off for an audience made her extremely grateful to be making a few quid via cleaning.

Later, pushing a vacuum cleaner around offices in Marylebone, she made time to phone her mum – again, avoiding the exact nature of her office job. Then, after work, she caught the Tube back to Kilburn Park and popped her head in the King's Arms. Trish was there with Frances and Wayne. Flush with a week's wages, Erin joined them.

Apparently, there had been a bit of excitement at the school where Trish had been placed as part of her course. The police had to be called due to threats from a disgruntled post-divorce dad with a bad temper and child access issues. That aside, Trish was excited about her first placement. Although she had spent three years in a classroom as a teaching assistant, the training course placement meant being in charge of the class as a teacher – which felt completely brilliant, even though it was under supervision. She was absolutely certain that this was her new life taking shape. Erin was thrilled for her. It all made so much sense because it engaged Trish's personality and skills. Talking about an unsuccessful writing career felt very second-rate.

"Oh, I meant to say," said Trish, "fancy a different job?"

"What different job?"

"Liam's leaving."

"Liam the barman? Is he off to Australia and Thailand?"

"Not quite – he's got a new job at a restaurant."

"Oh. And you reckon I should step in?"

"It's four nights a week instead of five – although it's Thursday to Sunday."

"Thursday to Sunday…" Erin fancied it. The pub was just around the corner from the grotto and she'd have three evenings off instead of two. "When did you find out?"

"When I came in."

Erin went straight after Dale the owner and it was all quickly agreed that she would start the following Thursday, doing seven till eleven at twenty quid a night.

When she returned to their table, it was apparent that a guy was trying to get into Trish. Erin was annoyed that Wayne and Frances didn't seem to think anything of it.

"This is Matt," said Trish. "He's a friend of Wayne's."

Okay, he was Wayne's friend. *Even so…*

But Erin relented. Trish was entitled to team up with whoever she wanted. She worked hard all week and if having a guy paying you attention was her way of unwinding, then fine. Erin couldn't deny missing that kind of thing herself.

Later that night, in her room, she tuned in to Radio 4 and listened to *It's New To Us* from beginning to end. It wasn't the greatest half-hour she'd ever spent.

14. THE FUTURE?

Three weeks later, life was chugging along. Erin was working in the pub and had got sketches in the script three times, Trish was happy with her course and showed it by constantly humming "Barbie Girl' and "Spice Up Your Life', and Erin's dad had unexpectedly taken up gardening – which puzzled Erin until she caught sight of new TV gardening show, *Ground Force,* and water-feature expert Charlie Dimmock's ample bosom wobbling about under her open shirt.

On the Wednesday, Erin said hello to Paul at the non-comm writers meeting and worked hard to please producer Caroline Felby. The following day, she was up at six a.m. rewriting and polishing her work.

A few hours later, approaching the main entrance at Broadcasting House, she found a uniformed concierge standing guard.

"Do you have a pass?" he asked.

"A pass?" She'd never been asked that before. "No."

"I'm sorry – no entry without a staff pass. There's a security alert."

"I won't be long. I just need to hand my sketches in."

"Sorry."

"I write for *It's News To Us.*" She pulled her sketches from her bag and waved them at him. "If they don't get these, there'll be no show."

"As I say, no pass, no entry. Sorry."

He smiled at a woman flashing her staff ID card and stepped aside to let her in.

Erin hadn't budged.

"Could you phone producer Caroline Felby in Light Entertainment? She'll vouch for me."

"It's staff pass-holders only."

"Do I look like a security threat?"

"I'm sorry, until further notice there's no access for anyone without a pass."

Erin felt ill. She couldn't miss the show. She looked around. What would the other non-comms do? Maybe she could wait for a commissioned writer and get them to take her stuff in. But she didn't know any of the commissioned writers. Not personally. She knew them by sight and name only. Still, they wouldn't mind taking in a rival writer's work, would they? Sketches that might knock their sketches off the show? Or maybe Ian would come along any minute now. Ian, her old friend.

"I can't believe this is happening," she said.

"Look," said the concierge, "the best I can do for you is put them in the internal mail."

The way he enunciated "internal mail" made it sound like the seventh circle of hell.

Then… coming along the street… a commissioned writer.

Shaun someone…?

"Hi, Shaun…?"

"Hi."

Shaun Someone flashed his ID card at the concierge and received a smile.

"There's a security thingy," said Erin. "I haven't got a pass and they're worried I might destroy the building.

Could you take my sketches in for me, please?"

"Sure, no problem."

She barely knew him, and technically they were rivals, but she handed over her work.

He held them to his ear. "Can't hear any ticking…"

"Could you give them to Gavin?" said Erin, feeling this was no time for comedy.

"No problem at all."

He took the sketches and entered the building as if it were nothing – but would his first stop be LE or the nearest rubbish bin? Erin felt sick not knowing which.

Friday morning, she woke up with a knot in her stomach. The anxiety over her sketches hadn't gone away at all. Feeling that it would be impossible to write, she chose to spend the day mooching around London.

She took the Bakerloo Line to Piccadilly Circus, where she had a look at the statue of Eros and the old shops in Jermyn Street. Then she overheard some tourists discussing the whereabouts of Trafalgar Square and followed them. From there, she went along Whitehall, past Downing Street and along to the Houses of Parliament and Westminster Abbey.

She then made for Westminster underground station, where a Tube map revealed that Hammersmith wasn't far. She had been in London a while but hadn't engaged much with her past.

Why not now?

Did she have time? It would hardly impact on her day.

Exiting the Tube at Hammersmith, Erin looked for any recognizable signs. It didn't help that the traffic was ridiculously busy and everyone seemed to be hurrying somewhere. Even so, this was it. The place she started out. The place that helped shape her. The place where her love of stories took hold. A place so important and yet so vague and fuzzy in her mind.

Were the houses still there? The little park? She recalled a bench where she loved to swing her legs. Where had six-year-old Erin Goodleigh existed? She wondered about her old neighbor, Mrs Haddon, but she would be ancient by now. If still living, she'd likely be in an old people's home.

The school though…

"Excuse me," she asked a passing woman. "Do you know Queen Victoria Primary School?"

"Sorry, I don't live round here."

She tried a young man with a briefcase.

"I only work here. Sorry."

She tried an older man.

"Yes, isn't that the one called Greenbank?"

"Er, no idea. I lived here a long time ago."

"Well, I think that's the one." He pointed the way. "Up there about a quarter of a mile. If you can't find it, just ask again. You'll certainly be a lot nearer."

"Thanks," said Erin.

She did get a lot nearer, because when she asked again, she was directed to a side street.

The past and its ghosts… she felt intoxicated. Standing on the corner, looking down the street, it all came back to her. Small children running up to the bigger road while their mums called after them to wait at the corner. In the summer, there would be the ice-cream van outside. She'd ask Mum for a "99" but get a raspberry ice-pole.

She ventured down to the school gates. And there it

was – the playground. It looked smaller somehow. They used to run around it laughing and squealing. The boys would play football, the girls hopscotch or, if they had a rope, skipping. What was that skipping song?

I am the Lady of the Lake
These are the actions I must take
Salute to the General
Bow to the King
Kiss my true love
Wear his ring.

So much happiness. A child cocooned in a safe world. It didn't feel so much a long time ago as a completely different life. Where had the years gone?

She turned back up the street feeling a little happier, and a little sadder.

A few hours later, at work behind the bar of the King's Arms, Erin was pulling pints and pouring wine for the Thank God It's Friday crowd. They were in such a good mood that she was offered enough drinks to float a boat. Of course, she accepted some of them. While getting drunk behind the bar was a complete no-no, there were no rules to say you couldn't pass these free drinks on to Trish, Matt, Wayne and Frances.

One of the Friday crowd, a young man, maybe in his late-twenties, paid her particular attention, commenting on such details as her friendly manner and nice smile.

"All part of the service," she told him, hoping he'd take a hint and a hike.

"What time do you get off?"

"Oh, late, late, late. Then it's straight to bed as I have to be up very early for something."

What a liar.

"Busy tonight," said Dale the guvnor in his faux-world weary manner. As usual, his smiling eyes gave away the fact that he loved having his pub packed to the rafters.

Still, Erin didn't mind being busy. It made the time fly and kept her from dwelling on *It's News To Us* and whether she'd get anything on this week.

At around ten-to-eleven, with customers waving money at the bar staff, she prepared to make her move. It was a good job Dale's wife, Janey helped out when things got extra busy, otherwise Erin might never have got away.

"Just popping to the ladies," she told Dale.

Dale didn't look too impressed.

She ran out of the packed pub, down the street, into the grotto, into her room, pressed 'record', closed the door, ran out of the house, back up the street, into the pub and back behind the bar. She was breathing like a marathon runner.

"Christ, what were you doing in there?" asked Dale.

Erin threw herself into serving the last orders rush and helped with the tidying up. Although her hours were to seven to eleven, she never got away until midnight on a Friday. Still, the boss always stuck an extra tenner in her hand.

As she prepared to leave, Wayne and Frances decided to go to an Indian restaurant. Trish and Matt weren't sure if to go with them. Erin couldn't eat. She had to know what had happened on the show.

Back at the grotto, the tape had ended. She took a breath and rewound it a bit, watching the little wheels spinning furiously.

She clicked "play' and heard something to do with Whitehall officials and some unspecified crisis. She wound forward a bit. Now it was a Royal Family musical skit. A little more… The end credits theme tune came up.

Her heart was thumping.

This is insanity. I'm actually going insane.

"It's News To Us was performed by Brian Grainger, Hannah Dobson, Anne Garston-Green and Ben Tidy. It was written by Gavin Gould, Martin Dobbs, Shaun Donoghue, Oliver Goldman and Joe Harrington, Colleen Nicholls, Simon Yeovil, Paul Fielding, Jason Edwards, Kirsty Gray, Simon Driver, and Erin Goodleigh. The producer was Caroline Felby."

Erin couldn't breathe.

Fame and I'm going to die from heart failure!

Maybe she'd misheard. Was there an Aaron Goodleigh? Or maybe they had recorded her sketch and then deleted it during the edit but forgot to cut her name from the credits. God, that would take an age to explain.

She rewound the tape a bit and hit 'play'... nope... and rewound it a little more... nope... and a little more...

'...sorry Tone, I was trying to park me Formula One racing car and the chuffin' new tobacco ad flipped up in me—'

Erin hit 'stop'.

"Mine," she gasped. "Good grief, half a million people heard my sketch."

Her throat felt tight. Her eyes became misty. She rubbed them and rewound the tape a little. Then she grabbed her copy of the sketch.

"This is crazy..."

She pressed 'play' and followed it on the page.

TOBACCO SPONSORSHIP

BLAIR:
Right, Cabinet, I want to... hang on, what's that noise?

F/X: RACING CAR... CRASH.

PRESCOTT:
Chuffin' heck! *(coughs)* ...sorry Tone, I was trying to park me Formula One racing car and the chuffin' new tobacco ad flipped up in me face. I think the glue's still wet.

BLAIR:
Yes, if we could just get on with the meeting. Right, New Labour... as I see it, we're currently going from strength to strength...

HARMAN:
But we're thinking of going back on our pledge to ban cigarette advertising, which means we'll have darts back on the telly.

PRESCOTT:
Fast cars *and* darts – great!

BLAIR:
Yes, thank you, Harriet, thank you, John, but I don't actually think that comes under the heading of good publicity.

Erin pressed 'stop'. She didn't need to hear the rest of the sketch. She knew it by heart. Besides, a little phrase was bubbling up from the depths and breaking the surface.

"I have seen the future!" she gasped.

She fast-forwarded to the credits again. Yes, she was still there. She rewound to the start of the show to listen to it whole. Halfway through, she heard Trish and Matt come in. She went to hit the stop button, but they rumbled straight up the stairs. Erin continued listening. It was important to get a real grasp of the show's structure. As it was, her sketch sat very nicely about twenty minutes in. *Good work, Caroline Felby.*

The future opened up to her. Lots of lovely sketches on the show. A successful sitcom on the radio. It gets picked up by TV. She wins a BAFTA. She writes a screenplay. Hollywood beckons…

Back in the here and now she pondered something more prosaic. How much would she be paid? She rewound the tape to her sketch and began to time it. As soon as it went over a minute she stopped. She'd get paid for two minutes. Two times £36.

£72.

"Ha-ha!" Okay, so it wasn't Hollywood rates but it meant more than that – it meant the world.

She couldn't keep it to herself any longer. News of this magnitude had to be shared. She went into the hall. The lounge and kitchen were empty so she climbed the stairs. Up on the first floor, a shaft of light was coming from under Trish's door. Had the insipid Matt gone home?

Unlikely.

She leaned close to the door. The rhythmic punishment the bed was receiving left her in no doubt.

Why, Trish? He's no good for you.

She returned to her room and sat on the bed. A wonderful moment felt a little less wonderful when you had no one to share it with.

It was okay though. She was doing fine. And the warm glow soon returned. She'd be able to phone Mum in the morning. And what's more, they repeated the show Saturday lunchtimes. God, the heat that would generate.

Jenny Goodleigh's daughter Erin had something on BBC Radio 4. She'd have to phone early. Jenny would need at least four hours to call everyone she knew to make sure they tuned in for the biggest event since she was appointed a Justice of the Peace at the local magistrate's court.

Erin settled down in bed. She couldn't sleep, but now she could dream. And why not dream about Hollywood? The weather would be lovely at the party on the back porch at Eddie Murphy's place overlooking the beach. And... god, Bruce Willis... in his swimming trunks... he was smiling at her... and wondering if there might be somewhere quiet they could go... except Paul Fielding was sitting alone at a table beneath a huge yellow sun umbrella reading a book. And Erin knew then that she wanted him. And, as it was her dream...

15. JOY

The following Wednesday, Erin was in the LE reception area half an hour early, struggling to contain her joy. If only Paul were there to share the news. She'd checked the writers' room and all the LE offices but there was no sign of him.

A familiar face came in. Her knight in shining shirt and jeans.

"Thanks ever so much for taking my sketches," she said.

"I nearly left them in the loo," he said. "Then I put them on a window ledge while I tied my shoelace and they almost blew away. And then an eagle swooped down and tried to grab them."

Erin smiled. "You mean it wasn't just my imagination?"

Paul came in and swapped hellos.

"So, friends with Shaun Donoghue now, are we?"

"He's brilliant."

"I'm blushing," said Shaun, before heading into the inner sanctum.

"Clever," said Paul. "The quickest way to the top is working with people already at the top."

"You think Shaun would work with me?"

"Honest answer – no. So which sketch was yours?"

"Blair, Prescott, Formula One tobacco advertising."

"Funny sketch. It sounded nice and long, too. Well done. I only got a Prince Charles one on. Forty seconds."

"Ah well, you stick with me and I'll teach you how it's done."

"Bit of a nightmare getting the sketches in, though," said Paul. "I had to phone Gavin and get him to meet me at the side entrance. What we need is… what she's got."

He was indicating the female writer who had just come in from the main corridor. Erin knew it was Kirsty Gray, although they had never spoken.

"Kirsty," said Paul. "Show us your pass."

"You and your chat-up lines," said Kirsty, in a warm, soft Scottish lilt.

The sight of the BBC ID card got Erin excited. Under Kirsty's name, it stated her job title as Freelance Staff.

"Thanks Kirsty," said Paul. "You'll always be my undying love."

As Kirsty disappeared into the inner sanctum, Erin wondered if she was the only one noting her attractive flame hair and great figure.

Don't forget you're in a relationship, Paul Fielding.

Erin's thoughts then returned to the more pressing matter.

"I want an ID card," she said.

"You could try Carol," said Paul. "That's where they're issued."

He was indicating the admin office just off the LE reception area.

"I can't afford to be locked out again," said Erin.

She went in and found Carol doing some filing.

"Hi Carol, you probably don't know me very well – Erin Goodleigh. I'm a new writer on *It's News To Us* and I had a sketch on last week's show."

"Well done you. Great stuff. You'll need to fill in a form so you can get paid. Just take one off the desk there."

"Thanks," said Erin, taking a form. "Only, it nearly didn't happen. There was a security alert."

"Yes, a nuisance, aren't they. It has to be safety first though."

"Absolutely. Only, I noticed that writers with staff ID cards were allowed in."

"Yes, the commissioned writers get one."

"Yes, I understand that. I was just wondering if any of the non-comms get one?"

"Some do – if a producer backs them."

"Right, well, I'm not quite at that stage yet." *Obviously.* "Thanks anyway."

Leaving, she almost bumped into Ian.

"Hey, I heard your name in the credits. Well done."

She looked for Paul. He'd gone.

"Thanks Ian. It's a start."

"You bet. Onward and upward, eh?"

"Hopefully."

"What you need now is some genuine inside info."

He was right, of course, but she had come a long way since seeing him as the only source.

"What I need, Ian, is more success on the show."

"The show's only a part of it. You need to build your engagement with the department. You need to target producers with other work. You need to get a staff ID card and come up with a plan for getting TV work."

"Yes, well, obviously I do intend to make a move into all those areas."

"I mean now. Today. Come out with me for a proper chat and I'll explain all. Seriously, Erin, don't do what the others do and just have fun hanging around the building.

There's only one time to get started properly and that's right now. Anyone who tells you otherwise is either an idiot or they're bitterly jealous and want to see you fail. Believe me, they're out there."

"I don't get that vibe from the other writers. It always feels…"

She was going to say supportive, but Ian had a point. They were all rivals for a very limited number of commissions. Even so, Ian made it sound like a horrible dog fight, which it wasn't. And anyway, if anyone was going to help her, it would be Paul. Although, Paul didn't have Ian's experience.

"Okay, Ian. We'll talk."

"Great. How about tonight?"

"I'm writing sketches."

"Tomorrow night?"

"I'm working in the pub. Right through till Sunday."

"Monday night then."

"Okay, Monday night."

"Great. Here's my number. Keep in touch."

He gave her a business card with his details. Handy, she supposed. After all, you never knew who you might bump into. Certainly Steven Spielberg would be unlikely to hang around while you searched for a scrap of paper and a pen.

She found a scrap of paper, dug out a pen from her bag, wrote the grotto's communal phone number on it and handed it over.

"See you soon then," he said.

As Ian disappeared into the inner sanctum, Paul passed him on the way out.

"Erin, after the meeting – lunch?"

"Ooh, do I want to have lunch with Paul Fielding, now that I'm a hugely successful writer? Um… ooh…

hmmm…"

"I've already been in touch with the canteen. The champagne has been arranged and there'll be six trumpeters for the fanfare."

"Only six?"

Over lunch, she wondered – would Paul reveal more about his girlfriend? Erin didn't want to cause problems. It was just… well, she had to know the situation. Of course, there was the other difficulty – her vow to avoid men. But who was she kidding? She tried to shift the conversation onto the importance of working for a good relationship.

"Too right," said Paul. "Sasha and me are getting on well now but we had a big wobble a while back. How about you?"

"Me? Oh, I was with the wrong man… *men*. Phil and Charles. At different times, obviously. I'm not seeing anyone now. As free as a bird. Just waiting for lightning to strike. Not that birds like being hit by electrical bursts." Paul didn't seem too interested. "No, just kidding. I'm here to work. I think I told you that before. Work, work, work. Work is good, lust is bad. Bad lust."

Shut up, Erin. Shut up!

"You're right to focus on your career. It's not easy making headway. Did I tell you I've got something in with the PDG?"

"PDG?"

"Programme Development Group a.k.a. a bunch of producers and the senior script exec. I've got something called *Buck House* in. It was a TV idea but Toby Lock persuaded me to re-write it for radio, so I spent last week doing just that. If they like it, they'll offer it to Radio 4."

"That's great."

"Or they might just throw it out."

"Not so great."

"Or I might get a seedcorn."

Erin's brow furrowed. "You'll have to explain."

"They sometimes pay two hundred and fifty quid for a sitcom. It's not a commission, it's more a payment that says your sitcom has failed but we don't think you're complete and utter rubbish – here's some cash, be encouraged and feel free to try again."

"That doesn't sound too bad."

"No, but I'd swap it for a commission any day."

"Yes, particularly any day they decide to turn away non-comms."

"It might have happened again this week. Just as well the big day is Friday."

"What big day?"

"The Queen's coming."

"What, here?" said Erin, a little surprised.

"She's opening the new Visitor Experience."

"Really? Well, I sincerely hope she's got an ID card."

The following day, Erin arrived at lunchtime with four sketches. She saw Paul in the LE reception area but he was busy talking to a producer and didn't break off. After her sketches were safely lodged with Gavin, Erin found Paul at the photocopier.

"Lunch?" she said.

"Not today. I'm a bit busy."

"Oh. Righto."

For some silly reason, it spoiled the rest of her day.

*

Erin came up to Broadcasting House on the Friday. Seeing the Queen in the flesh seemed odd, as if she wasn't a real person who you could touch. Not that you could touch – too many security types about. Although it was cold standing in the crowd outside the building, there was a lot of warmth towards Her Majesty – much more than Erin would have imagined.

At tea-time, she phoned her mum to let her know she'd rubbed shoulders with royalty. Jenny also had big news – Phil had left a message for Erin to say he'd accepted an offer on the flat. After the mortgage and fees were paid off, they'd receive around seven thousand each. Not as much as she'd hoped, but still…

Later, Erin did her stint in the pub and listened to the tape of the show. She didn't get anything on. Neither did Paul. She went to sleep feeling like her insides had been scooped out. She was a shell. Hollow, with no meaningful substance.

16. IAN

Erin went up to Brent Cross on the Monday to amble around the shops. She was meant to be writing something that would further her career, but her impending evening meeting with Ian Crawford-Troy was playing on her mind. Firstly, she didn't want to meet him, and secondly... well, secondly, she didn't want to meet him in any kind of social setting that might be misconstrued on his part – particularly *that* part – as a date.

No, that was unfair. Ian was just awkward around women. If one evening with him could save her months of wrong turns then it had to be worth it. He'd called the grotto on Sunday morning to confirm. Even then he irritated her with his "I thought we'd go Italian and I know just the place..." She'd considered feigning pasta intolerance, but no. She had to do this.

That evening, they met in a pub in Covent Garden. The hellos and small talk were quickly exhausted and Ian seemed keen to move straight on to the nitty-gritty.

"Do you know *Them & Them*?" he asked.

"The Channel 4 show?"

"They accept non-commissioned gags."

"Do they?"

"Erin, please don't take this the wrong way, but you don't seem to know very much about the world you're trying to break into."

"That's a bit harsh, Ian. I'm only just getting started."

"You need shortcuts. You might earn yourself some money."

"I'm okay for money."

"I heard you were cleaning."

"I was – now I'm working part-time in a pub."

"One gag on *Them & Them* pays a hundred quid."

"Does it?"

"All that time you spend serving pints and cleaning up? I probably earn more spending two minutes writing a gag about a two-faced politician."

Erin tried to find a fault in where this was leading – but it did seem that she needed Ian in her life.

"So how do I go about contacting them?"

"All in good time, Erin. Now answer me this – which LE producer is reading your latest sitcom?"

"Er… well… I've got some ideas for a sitcom or possibly a comedy-drama."

"Do you actually know the difference?"

"Er… remind me."

"Erin, really – I should phone your mum and tell her what a lazy girl you are. Seriously, you are a mile behind the curve. Now – how about another drink before the restaurant."

"Er…" She hadn't finished her first one.

"It's on me. I got two gags on *Them & Them*."

Erin watched him go to the bar. He wasn't all bad, she supposed. In fairness, most of her thoughts about him were at least a decade out of date. Ian had clearly been working his socks off and was now prepared to share his writing secrets with her. That was friendship, wasn't it? Or would he be expecting something in return, like the Ian of old?

Oh, give the guy a chance.

Ian returned with their drinks and smiled.

"So the room in Kilburn Park?" he ventured. "Is that long-term?"

Erin puffed out her cheeks. "I wish I knew. I normally have a plan. I *am* the girl with the plan. But…"

"We all have to start somewhere. We just need someone in our corner. I had that in sixth form. Remember?"

"You mean us writing the school play?"

"I mean *you* writing the school play and letting me take some of the credit."

Honesty from Ian? Wow.

"That's a long time ago, Ian."

"I was mad about you back then."

"I guessed as much. But you've since found Ms Right?"

"Possibly."

She wasn't entirely sure what he meant.

"So where do you live?" she asked, changing the subject.

"I'm renting a two-bed place in West Hampstead with a flatmate who works in the City."

"It sounds ideal."

"It is. But tell me about you and Taunton. What's happening where you work? I mean it's a family firm, so…"

"It's fine. Mum and Dad are okay, if not overly enthusiastic."

"And you'd love to get out of packaging. It makes you feel boxed in."

"Very funny, Ian." *Not.* "It's a brilliant firm with great staff. I'm really happy there. *Was* really happy there. I can be happy there again if I go back. But I have to know I've given this everything. I can't be like my mum, forever irritated about the acting career she gave up."

"Tomorrow night," said Ian.

"Tomorrow night what?"

"I'm taking you to a comedy club. It's vital you get to know the comedy scene. You can't trade on ten-year-old Edinburgh memories and a spot of small-town panto writing. Deal?"

"Er, yes. Deal."

The following evening, Erin stood shivering outside a south London station. She'd been waiting for ten minutes when Ian popped out, all smiles and bonhomie.

"It's not far," he said, setting off.

"So it's new acts night," said Erin, recounting what Ian had told her. "They're brave."

"It's a great way to see performers who could be the next big thing."

The action took place in a room above a pub just around the corner from the station. There were about twenty people in the audience.

"Stand-up comedy is a rising movement," said Ian as he got them a drink at the bar. "There are comedians popping up everywhere and the number of venues has shot through the roof."

Erin tried to work out what you did if you spotted the next Ben Elton. Did you climb aboard their wagon while there was room? Was that Ian's ongoing mission? If so, where did she, as a writer, fit in? Did he see her as a rising star? Or did he have something else in mind?

Erin enjoyed compare Joe Reece's introduction, particularly his observations about British pubs and camping holidays.

"He's good, isn't he," said Erin.

"He's not who we've come to see."

But Erin liked him. He had warmth.

"Anyone go to the British Folk Festival last summer?" asked compare Joe. "I went, of course. Well, I tried to go. I wasn't sure where the venue was so I just followed the crowd… and ended up at the Ikea sale."

Joe soon introduced the act Ian thought was brilliant. Erin felt less enthused. The guy swore at least twice a sentence and Erin felt no warmth at all. She didn't mind the swearing but wondered why he would squander such a valuable tool in the comedian's arsenal. He got plenty of laughs though, which left Erin less sure of her judgement.

After the show, Ian dragged her to an Indian restaurant for a biryani and a beer. She wasn't in the mood but played along. After all, he was helping her get her career launched. The only thing that bugged her was the thought that she might be dating him without agreeing to it.

"Are you interested in co-writing a sitcom," he asked over the poppadums.

"With you?"

"I've got a producer interested in a radio sitcom but I'm struggling with the female part."

"And you think I can help?"

"You'd get the female stuff right. Think about it, Erin. It could be a big hit on Radio 4 – and that means a fair chance of a crossover to television."

It was true that numerous Radio 4 shows had transferred to television, and this seemed to offer her a crack at it right from the off.

"Maybe," she said.

"We should discuss it. Why don't you come back to my place and take a look at the script?"

Alarm bells!

"Let me think about it, Ian. I've got some ideas of my own."

"I've got a producer practically gagging."

"Sorry, Ian. I can't make a decision tonight."

"No problem. I've got another female writer in mind. I just thought I'd ask you first."

God, do I trust Ian Crawford-Troy or not?

The following day, just before the non-comms meeting, Erin found Paul in the LE reception area chatting with Simon Driver. She attempted to join in but Paul seemed distant somehow.

Oh well. Maybe he's affected by only getting a short sketch on.

"I think I'm getting to understand Caroline Felby," said Erin. "Another big effort should pay off, I reckon."

"It's Toby Lock this week," said Simon. "Difficult to know what he wants. Mood swings."

Damn.

That evening, to the sound of fireworks in a nearby garden, Erin wrote sketches in three different styles: a silly one, a satirical one and one based on TV sitcom *Dad's Army*.

The following day, she handed them in but couldn't find Paul. Was he avoiding her?

On the Friday, she worked on her revised sitcom idea relating to an insurance company and the twits who might inhabit one. In a way, it was a pity she'd never worked in such a place. She felt she might have found more to make fun of.

After her stint working in the pub, she sat on the bed listening to the end of the tape. She failed to get a mention in the credits.

Crap…

Keeping Ian at arm's length was beginning to seem really stupid.

17. ELSIE

The following Wednesday, despite the weather turning cold, Erin was being positive. It was just a case of finding the right formula. She had long passed the newbie phase of questioning the ability of producers to pick out a good sketch. There were non-comms being successful week after week and it was simply a matter of trying to match them.

Up at Broadcasting House, Paul seemed a bit happier. Well, he'd got a long sketch on, so why not. That said, he still seemed to be putting distance between himself and Erin. She knew he had a girlfriend and she respected that. They could still be friends though, couldn't they? Or didn't he trust himself to behave?

After the meeting, Paul went off with his friends. Erin didn't receive an invite so went back to the grotto to write. It was probably for the best, but she felt down at being left out. Maybe it was time she forged her own little gang.

On the Thursday, having handed in her sketches and responded to feedback, she returned to Kilburn Park and reported early for work at the King's Arms.

On the Friday, the mood to explore Hammersmith took

Erin's fancy. She emerged from the Tube with a notebook and the hope that the area would throw up some sitcom settings. She had also come armed with a *London A to Z* map book.

It felt odd to have the street where she grew up sitting there on the page. Not for the first time, she wondered if the houses were still there. She wandered along Brook Green, looking for anything familiar.

A few minutes later, she turned a corner and…

It was Mrs Haddon's house. Wasn't it?

She rang the bell.

It took a while, but eventually the door edged open to reveal a round-faced, white-haired elderly woman in a emerald housecoat and fluffy pink slippers.

"Yes?"

"Elsie?"

"Yes?"

"Hello, I'm Erin Goodleigh. I used to live next door."

"Erin? Little Erin?" The door opened wide. "Is that you?"

"Yes, I've grown a bit since 1973."

Five minutes later, sipping tea in the lounge, and having gone through a speedy catch-up, Erin cast her gaze around a room that looked familiar and yet unfamiliar. Although something was coming back to her. The stand-up gas fire in front of the fire place…

"I remember a coal fire filling the room with a really warm glow. Or am I imagining that?"

"No, you're not imagining it – it's just that Norman wanted gas."

"Norman, of course. How is he?"

"No longer with us, unfortunately. Heart."

"Oh… I'm sorry to hear that, Elsie."

"Long time ago now. You get used to being on your

own, sort of. Anyway, tell me more about you working in radio. What show are you writing for?"

"You won't have heard of it – it's called It's News To Us."

"On Radio Four?"

"You've heard of it? Haven't you got better things to do on a Friday night?"

"Yes, I have. That's why I listen Saturday lunchtimes."

"A fan of the show. You're the first I've met."

"Well, I wouldn't go that far. I tend to put Radio Four on when I come down for breakfast, and it stays on. Keeps me company."

"Nothing wrong with that, Elsie."

"So where do you work? Don't tell me it's Broadcasting House?"

"Yes, Broadcasting House. Until they knock it down."

"Oh, Broadcasting House... that brings back a few memories. I used to sing there."

"Really? That's amazing. When was this?"

"1938 to 1940. Then the bombs stopped it. We did broadcasts from around the country after that. Then I left to join ENSA. That was a War unit. We travelled to entertain the troops fighting abroad. Happy days."

"Fancy that. Lucky Broadcasting House didn't get bombed."

"Oh, but it did. Twice. The news teams had to move out. They went to Oxford Street, as I recall."

"Thank God it's safer now. We only have the IRA to worry about. Was anyone hurt, Elsie?"

"Yes... sadly. The first bomb crashed through into the music library on the fifth floor. I think seven BBC staff died in that."

Erin shivered. The place she worked, writing funny sketches, and people were killed there.

"That is sad…"

"Typical BBC though. They had old Bruce Belfrage reading the news in the basement when it went off, so most of Britain heard the bang. Bruce paused for a second or two, brushed the dust and plaster off his head, and carried on reading the news."

"Amazing."

"There was a second bomb a few months later. Landed in the street outside it did. Killed a policeman and caused a fire."

"Incredible. So you were there in those days."

"Yes, we were singers. Me and the others."

"What others, Elsie?"

"The Wednesday Club. That's what we called ourselves. We used to meet up socially on Wednesdays, see. We sang backing to some of the top singers of the day. It was fun, I can tell you. We still reminisce about it when we meet up."

"You're still in touch with the other singers?"

"Yes, and we can still hold a tune, you know."

"I'm sure you can."

A little idea fizzed in Erin's brain but died away again.

"More tea?" Elsie asked.

"Yes please."

18. BACK AND FORTH

Come Friday night, Erin didn't get anything on the show. Rather than be down though, she decided to be extra positive. After all, some people had worked at Broadcasting House in far more trying times.

On the Saturday, she popped out to a local shop that sold second-hand computer equipment. She'd had her eye on a piece of kit for some time and decided to take the plunge. It was a beauty, too. A three-year-old burgundy Windows 3.1 laptop with a matching mini-printer. *Talk about style!* The £300 price tag price was a bit steep, but she simply had to have it. That afternoon, she worked out how to use Word, installed an internet service provider's software and set up a Freeserve e-mail account. *Miss Modern or what!* She was soon finding her way around Lycos and Ask Jeeves. She had never been more determined to succeed.

The following Wednesday, she was standing outside Broadcasting House, looking up at the side of the building facing onto Portland Place and imagining wartime…

Up in LE, prior to the non-comms meeting, there were at least three new faces. Erin tried to get a smile to each of them. One, a female, smiled back with a question written into her expression.

"First time?" asked Erin, knowing it to be exactly that.

"Yes."

"Just take a few notes during the meeting. Try to feel what resonates for you and don't worry about what anyone else might write."

"Thanks."

"The main thing is to stick with it. Come back next week and the week after."

"I will."

After the meeting, she caught up with Paul.

"The latest thinking is they'll commission two or three," he told her.

"Where are you on the list?"

"Third."

"That's promising."

"Not if they commission two."

"True. How exactly do you shift immovable commissioned writers?"

"A stick of dynamite?"

But Erin didn't want to talk about the show. "How are things with you?"

"Oh... busy."

"We haven't managed to catch up for a bit, have we."

"No. No... maybe tomorrow. I have to scoot right now."

"Okay. Tomorrow."

Back at the grotto, Erin worked on her ideas for *INTU*. She felt a bit like a hamster on a wheel. Even so, she wrote four sketches.

Around nine, she phoned home. After the initial greetings were over, Mum mentioned the upcoming TADS Christmas show.

"We're going with *Jack and the Beanstalk*. The one you wrote four years ago."

"Good idea."

"It's just that everyone's asking if you're coming home to update the jokes and generally run us through it."

"I can't."

"It's just a few days and the local charities really benefit."

A few days spread over two weeks.

"Can't you do it, Mum? You know exactly what's needed."

"Of course I can. I just thought you'd want to do it. You always have such fun. And TADS is as much yours as it is mine."

That didn't ring true. Jenny Goodleigh ran TADS in much the same way she ran Goodleigh Packaging Limited – Erin never got to make any actual decisions.

"I can't, Mum. Sorry."

The following day, Erin took her sketches to Broadcasting House, handed them to Gavin and then waited for Paul. When he arrived, he seemed in a pensive mood.

Up in the canteen, they had a quick catch-up. Erin thought Paul was doing brilliantly and had to keep going.

"I know," said Paul. "Sasha says exactly the same thing, only not as nicely."

"Sasha's your girlfriend, right?"

"Yeah, we get on really well. There's just one problem. Last April, she got really excited. I think I led her to believe I'd get a commission."

"You went pretty close."

"She's fed up, Erin. Absolutely bloody fed up. She

thinks I can do a lot better in life. And do you know what? She's right. I know enough about the courier game to start my own little firm. She can't believe I'm piddling about up here with a bunch of ex-students who are happy to earn a bit of beer money getting the occasional sketch on the radio."

"Have you pointed out that it's a stepping stone?"

"I'm two-and-a-half years off forty. This is a game for youngsters like you."

"I'm thirty, Paul."

"Exactly. A youngster. I'm the only old non-comm around here. Everyone else my age is either an established writer or a senior producer. If I don't get a commission soon, I'll have to give up. Forty's a big thing. By then, I need to be a full-time writer or running my own courier business. I can't be stuck between the two. We're getting to decision time sooner rather than later."

"Is this you or Sasha talking?"

"Me. Sasha thinks I should have started the courier firm in the summer."

"Don't give up hope, Paul."

"I'm not. At least not yet."

"Give it everything. You'll get a commission next month. I'm sure of it."

"Thanks, but if I don't... um... are you coming up tomorrow?"

"What for?"

"There's a TV writing opportunity they're opening up. Commissioned writers only."

"That's a cheek. What about the non-comms?"

"They're doing that after Christmas but I'd prefer to be ahead of the opposition."

"Will they let us in?"

"No. Fancy trying though?"

*

The following morning at a quarter to eleven, Erin emerged from the Tube into thunder, lightning and hail – hardly the gods smiling down on her. She waited ten minutes for the skies to return to a drab grey and then ran all the way to Broadcasting House.

Paul was waiting for her in the main reception area. On seeing her, he nodded and they approached the desk.

"We're due at a meeting in Light Entertainment," he said.

"Do you have passes?" asked the new security man at the desk.

"No, but we're seeing Jane Clearwater and Gavin Gould."

"I'll just phone. Let them know you're here."

"Don't bother. We're a bit early. We'll pop back a bit later."

They trudged outside. The skies looked threatening.

"That went well," said Erin.

"They know which days non-comms can walk in off the street, and it's never Friday."

"So what do we do?"

"Come on."

"Where to?"

"The side entrance."

"They have different rules there, do they?"

"I have no idea. I just know some people go in that way."

They entered through the side entrance, where a young security guard was sitting behind a small desk reading a newspaper. He looked up and smiled.

Paul held up some papers. "We're going to the *It's News To Us* feedback meeting."

"Isn't that Wednesdays and Thursdays?"

"No, this is the feedback meeting for soon-to-be commissioned writers. Paul Fielding and Erin Goodleigh. We're meeting with Jane Clearwater and Gavin Gould."

"And broadcast assistant Sarah Bryce," Erin added.

"Okay, whatever."

They signed in and slipped into a lift. Erin waited for the doors to close.

"We did it! Let's hope he's a regular."

LE was busy with commissioned writers and others milling around. Ian was among them.

"Erin, hi. What did you do – dig a tunnel?"

"They let us in as they see Paul and me as the future of the department."

"Well, if you ask me, this is a complete waste of time. Coffee?"

"No thanks."

Ian left and Paul leaned in close "Shall I translate for you?"

"No need. I speak fluent Ian. By complete waste of time, he means go away and leave this to me."

"That's no way to talk about your boyfriend."

"My what?"

"I thought you were going out with him."

"What? Of course I'm not."

"He said he took you to a pub, a restaurant, a comedy club. Full of it, he was."

"He did but that was just a catch up."

"So you're not *seeing* him then?"

"No, I'm not *seeing* him."

Bloody Ian. What the eff had he been saying? She'd tie his balls in a knot.

They were soon called to the writers' room where a producer called Callum Court from BBC Television welcomed them to the inaugural *Comedy UK* meeting. Ian was there, of course, taking copious notes.

"Spend your prep time wisely," said Callum, dishing out a business card to each of them. "This is your ideas period, so don't waste it. Once we're through the Christmas holidays, I'll clock in again and we can review your material, give approval and you'll be able to book in to get acting pool talent attached for your shoot."

"So we're looking at January," said a disappointed Erin, tucking the business card into her pocket. She had no plans to be in London after Christmas.

"Think more February," said Callum. "Think the last week of January for submitting your firmed-up ideas to me."

Erin felt the rest of the air leak out of her balloon. It wasn't like this was a paid gig. If approved, they would get to film a couple of sketches and submit them to *Comedy UK*. It didn't mean they would make it onto the show.

Later, after her shift at the King's Arms, she listened to the tape recording of the show. She had a short sketch on.

Yes.

But it was only a small 'yes'. She was studying Callum's business card. It bore the BBC logo and his details: Callum Court, Development Producer, plus a phone and fax number.

Was a £36 radio sketch in late November really enough to change her plans for January and February 1998?

The following Wednesday, Erin was back at Broadcasting House for the non-comms meeting. It was funny how a short sketch could make her feel good about chatting with other writers. There was nothing like a bit of success to oil the social wheels.

After the meeting, she told Paul she really needed to get away to write her sketches.

"Lunch first?" he asked.

"Oh, go on then."

"Did you fancy going to the pub?"

A date?

"Is that a good idea, Paul?"

"Colleen and Simon seem to think so. It was their idea."

So, not a date. Just as well...

Standing at the bar of a nearby establishment with her three writing colleagues, waiting to order ploughman's lunches, Erin took in the INXS soundtrack that many of pubs were going for in the wake of Michael Hutchence's tragic demise.

"Hey, it's Leanne Fuller," said Colleen, indicating an area by the side door.

"We should be getting in there," said Simon. He turned to Paul and Erin. "We pitched something a while back."

"There's nothing like getting them off-duty," said Paul. "Go on."

Erin watched them home in on their prey. Then she turned to Paul.

"Just me and you then."

"Don't blame them," said Paul. "This is all about taking your opportunities."

Grabbing a small table, they sat down with their drinks and waited for their food.

"So how's it going with Sasha?"

"Oh, you know. We've been together three years on

and off. I don't think we're brave enough to split up."

"You'll resolve it, Paul. You sound like a good couple."

The rest of the week went by in a blur. The conveyancing solicitor confirmed that contracts had been exchanged on the flat and that the sale would go through on completion in three weeks. So that was it – bye-bye little flat in Taunton. On the writing front, she had submitted five sketches to *INTU* but couldn't get away from her duties at the King's Arms in time to record the show. Sitting on her bed after midnight, she wondered – as she always wondered – *what am I doing?*

Saturday was quiet. Everyone was off to other places. Erin bought a copy of *The Times* and enjoyed a good read aided by tea, toast and an apricot Danish.

At lunchtime, she sat on the edge of her bed and stared at the radio-cassette player. Would she even bother to listen?

She switched it on all the same. But she couldn't go through a half-hour of torture. She hit 'record' and went into the garden for some air.

It wasn't a bad garden; it just didn't look at its best in late November. That said, it hadn't looked much better in September. Maybe a house-share would never result in a beautiful garden. Why should it? Not many people put in the same effort as Dad since he'd become a Charlie Dimmock fan.

At 1.27 p.m., Erin came in and turned the volume up.

It was a Tony Blair sketch. Then the end credits theme tune came up.

Although she should have been used to it by now, her heart thumped.

Come on, girl, you can do it.

"It's News To Us was performed by Brian Grainger, Hannah Dobson, Anne Garston-Green and Ben Tidy. It was written by Gavin Gould, Shaun Donoghue, Paul Fielding, Martin Dobbs, Oliver Goldman and Joe Harrington, Colleen Nicholls, Josh Steinman, Simon Driver, Erin Goodleigh, Dave Singer, and Michael Holbrook. The producer was Ruby Edwards."

Yes! Thank you, Ruby Edwards, thank you!

She grabbed her sketch copies, rewound the tape a few minutes… and hit 'play'… nope… and rewound a bit further… nope… and…

"Erotica as far as the eye can see…"

She hit the 'stop' button.

Crikey, it was her sketch about a cabinet minister visiting Britain's first-ever erotica exhibition. She pressed 'play'.

"What's that on the top shelf? An inflatable Margaret Thatcher?"

"The label says Ginger Spice. It must need blowing up a bit more."

Erin hit 'stop'.

What a way to live.

She rewound the tape. She would listen to the entire show to get a sense of what the producer liked. It was therefore a surprise when she also recognized the show's second sketch as one of hers. Despite trying to stay calm, Erin's heart went into overdrive.

Two sketches! Oh… my… God!

19. THE END OF THE RUN

The first couple of weeks of December raced by. Erin failed on one show then succeeded on the next. Paul was still third in the writers' league table. Erin was sixth. On the money front, Erin and Phil's solicitor completed the sale of the flat and Erin received just under seven thousand. While she was grateful to have some cash, it would never be the deposit for a new flat unless she started earning real money and qualified for a mortgage. That was probably why she needed to return to Taunton.

On the romance front, Trish split up with the insipid Matt. To help her get over him, Erin took her to see *Seven Years In Tibet* at the cinema. Having rapidly fallen in love with Brad Pitt, they came out to a little flurry of snow. Hardly Tibet, but surely an omen that one of them would meet Brad. Of course they argued over which of them it might be before settling for a drink and the hope that he might have a twin brother.

Erin also went to see Phil Collins at Earls Court. She hadn't planned to but Sarah at Broadcasting House was let down by a friend and, as it was a Tuesday gig, Erin could make it. Of course, it was always difficult to listen to Phil Collins. Not that she didn't like his music – it was just that when you'd nearly married a Phil Collins…

The following lunchtime, she was at Broadcasting

House for the final show of the year. It meant making firm plans, which was proving difficult.

After the non-comms meeting, she got chatting with Colleen Nicholls.

"I'm shaking apart," said Colleen. "Come on, I need a ciggie."

The BBC had ban on in-house smoking, apart from in the disgusting 'smoking room', in which people didn't only exhale smoke but also part of their soul. That meant accompanying Colleen to the sixth-floor rear balcony.

On the way up, Colleen babbled on about the minutes she had racked up and whether it was enough... and whether sketches she'd written could have been longer... and the occasions she had failed to follow the feedback advice...

"The last show will sort it out," said Erin as they stood on the balcony looking down at the street below.

"The last show? No, they'll be talking to people this afternoon."

"Oh?"

No-one had told Erin. Then again, they probably didn't trouble those who had no chance. Colleen, who until recently had been just ahead of Paul, continued wittering on, but Erin wasn't listening now. Below, a parked van's radio was blaring out 'Perfect Day'. You reap what you sow.

"Lunch?" said Colleen, stubbing out her ciggie.

"Yes, lunch," said Erin.

They met Paul and Simon Driver in the canteen. The talk, unsurprisingly, was all about who would get a commission. It didn't help that someone had hidden away last week's scripts. Erin could see Paul trying to play it cool. She guessed that inside he was burning up with anxiety. The way he picked at his food backed up her diagnosis.

After lunch, they went down to the writers' room where the other leading non-comms were hanging around. It wasn't long before Jane Clearwater and Sarah came along.

"Okay," said Jane, "you know the drill, so I won't mess you around. Colleen, Simon and Josh, congratulations. You'll be commissioned for one minute per show from the January re-start. Paul and Jamie, commiserations. You were both close but we just don't have the space. Keep trying though. I'm sure next time…"

After Jane and Sarah left, there were five minutes of animated chatter. Then it was just Paul and Erin left in the room.

"I'm really sorry, Paul. You must have been so close."

"How about trying to get into the party?" he said, as if she hadn't just spoken.

"What party?"

"The LE party. There's one every Christmas. I thought I might try to get in."

"What, you're not invited?"

"Some non-comms get an invite, but only those who have a working relationship with a producer."

"Oh Paul, you don't deserve to be a non-comm."

"It's done, Erin. Are you up for getting into the party or not?"

"Yes, of course. I don't see why the comms should have all the fun."

"You've got that right. They'll be waving their tickets in our faces soon enough, burbling on about whether they'll go or not. Pay no attention to that crap. Those tickets are gold dust. You get TV producers there, TV writers, actors, all sorts. And, what's more, there's free beer."

Erin feigned a swoon. "Did you say… free beer? Is it okay to trample over TV producers to get to the beer?"

"It's the thought of all those undeserving comms guzzling free booze and moaning about too many non-comms getting sketches on the show. It's us and them, Erin. Us and Them. Until we become them, of course."

"So how do we get in?"

"It won't be easy. Getting into Broadcasting House might be straightforward but getting into the party is another matter entirely. Have you been to the Radio Theatre?"

"No."

"No? Oh, you must. To see a show, I mean. Not ours, of course – that's done in a studio. *Newslines* is done in the Radio Theatre. Lunchtimes. Today, in fact. Come on, we can catch the end."

As he led her down to a part of the building she had yet to visit, Paul explained that, among other things, the Radio Theatre was where the party took place each year.

A minute later, pushing through a doorway, she found herself at the back of a surprising space. It was a genuine theatre, over half full with people watching a show. It was quite plush, too, if a little faded. They were standing by the control booth. Inside, three people appeared to be in charge of recording.

A big laugh erupted from the audience. Erin laughed too.

"Sounds like a good show," she said.

"It is, but it takes a while for the producer to trust your comedy – if at all."

"So I've heard."

"Spread yourself thinly across two shows and you'll get halfway to nowhere twice."

"So this is where they have the party, is it? Seems easy enough to get in."

"No, they'll be checking tickets."

"Right, so we definitely need a ticket."

"No chance. What we need is a plan."

Erin tried to take it all in. A BBC party would be a brilliant send-off. One last hurrah before she returned to a box factory in Taunton with her parents running the show. It was fitting that it was pretty much a year since Liz Crawford-Troy walked into a Taunton church hall and turned her life upside-down. And here she was, nearing the end of that journey. She could dream though… her own comedy show on Radio 2… it transfers to BBC TV…

"Jamie was saying he got a seedcorn," said Paul. "Two hundred and fifty quid – not a bad Christmas present."

"A seedcorn…" Erin's insurance company sitcom bubbled up.

"It's been done," said Paul.

"What has?"

"Whatever's in your mind."

Erin gave up. It didn't matter. She wouldn't be coming back after Christmas.

"Do you have a white blouse and black trousers?" he asked.

20. THE BBC CHRISTMAS PARTY

Erin wrote her sketches and took them in the following day. It seemed pointless, but a credit wouldn't do her any harm. Paul meanwhile fleshed out the plan. It just meant a trip to Marks and Spencer's for a blouse and she'd be set. He'd also strongly advised her to take the Friday evening off work. Thankfully, Dale the pub boss was already aware of her intention to return to Taunton and had someone lined up.

Friday came around and Erin felt a mixture of excitement and anxiety. The BBC party would be brilliant. But what if they couldn't get in? As suggested by Paul, under her raincoat she was wearing a jumper over a white blouse and black trousers. They met by the side entrance and gained access to the building on the basis of a spurious involvement in an *INTU* edit.

Once inside, they dumped their coats in an empty LE office and went down to the Radio Theatre. Outside, trolleys laden with bottles of beer and wine had appeared. There were snacks too. Erin noticed how the sole BBC caterer in view was a man wearing a white shirt and black trousers. They just had to wait a few minutes for him to be busy.

"Right," said Paul.

Erin took a deep breath. The plan was a simple one.

She whipped off her jumper and handed it to Paul. He stuffed it with his in a Sainsbury's carrier bag. They then grabbed a trolley each and pushed on straight past the man at the door checking tickets. Working on the basis that no-one ever paid attention to catering staff, once inside they left the trolleys by the front of the stage and moved a safe distance away with the carrier bag. Paul handed Erin her jumper and headed for the toilets. Erin left it a moment then did likewise. The plan was to stay in a cubicle for fifteen minutes. By then, no-one would recall how they or the trolleys had made it into the theatre.

Playing it safe, Erin left it twenty minutes before she emerged into a much fuller space and took a free bottle of lager. With plenty of people standing around chatting and drinking, Erin, in her blue woolly jumper, blended in nicely.

She wondered briefly if Elsie and the Wednesday Club had attended BBC Christmas parties in this very location. Then she spotted Paul with commissioned writer Dave Singer. Approaching them, Erin was distracted momentarily by a well-known actor. She couldn't recall his name but she had seen him in countless television dramas.

"Erin, hi," said Paul.

"How many new non-comms have come through the door since September," said Dave, "only to disappear again?"

Erin shrugged while enjoying Dave's ignorance of the Great Escape In Reverse plan that had just been enacted.

"Sixty, seventy?" she said.

"Sounds about right," said Dave.

"I reckon it's Gavin's aftershave," said Paul.

"How long have you been submitting, Erin?" asked

Dave.

It was odd to think they had been submitting sketches for the same show without really knowing anything about each other.

"Since September, although I was here briefly in April."

"Did you hear they're thinking of testing e-mail submissions? Just for commissioned writers initially. Can't afford to clog up the system with non-comms. No offence."

"It's not the non-comms, it's the computers," said Erin. "They take an aeon to download anything."

"Broadband," said Dave, seemingly at home with technological talk. "One of the studio managers was talking about it. Apparently, it's a lot faster than dial-up."

Erin shrugged. "Not heard of that."

"You can't get it for your home yet, but it's coming to the BBC," said Dave. "Once they've updated those knackered old computers."

"It's not just about the technology though," said Paul. "There's no point in e-mailing if you're a newbie – you need to meet producers face-to-face."

"Yes, well, there's a lot of talk about changes to the security arrangements," said Dave. "It's mainly speculation, but there are supposedly long-term plans. I've personally overheard a few things in the canteen."

"Like what?" asked Erin.

"Okay, so feel free to ignore this, but they might – at some point – stop writers walking in off the street."

"Never," said Paul. "Not in a million years."

"It's the IRA thing. From what I've heard, the talk is they'll close Broadcasting House for major renovations…"

"That wouldn't surprise me," said Erin. "It's falling

apart."

"… and when it reopens, they'll have proper security screens. No more scruffy oiks stumbling in, eh? By then, the computers will be state-of-the-art and non-comm submissions will be via e-mail."

"It'll never happen," said Paul.

Erin agreed. You had to come in for feedback. The producer wasn't going to waste time typing notes for non-comms when she was trying to put a show together for a recording in less than twenty-four hours.

"Hey, Kirsty," said Dave.

Kirsty Gray joined them. "Hello writers. How are we today?"

"As happy as a writer with a free beer," said Dave.

"Disgruntled," said Paul. "If you want the gruntled, Driver and Nicholls are over there somewhere."

"Yes, I heard. And Josh too. He's good, isn't he."

"So what about you, Kirsty?" said Paul. "What are you up to? We haven't seen much of you at *INTU*."

"Ah well, I managed to knock out a few sketches, but… exciting news, I've been head-hunted by Priority Productions. We're making a new show for Channel 4 in the New Year. Brilliant or what?"

"A proper TV writer," said Paul, patting her on the arm. "Fantastic."

"Coo-ee!" It was someone calling Kirsty away.

She bade them farewell and scooted off to share her good fortune.

"I must leave you, too," said Dave. "I need a long talk with Jane Clearwater. Until later…"

They watched Dave trundle off then both took a swig of beer.

"So," said Paul, "are you coming back in January?"

"No."

"No?"

Erin took another swig of beer. She felt awful.

"Let's meet up a bit later," said Paul. "Right now, I need to do a Dave. Not with Jane, with Toby Lock."

"Right, good."

She watched him go off.

Bloody hell! This isn't a free booze-up; it's a free opportunity!

It was clear – if she could make a good impression, she might be able to make a meaningful contact. Yes, she'd be in Taunton, but it wouldn't hurt to know a producer in London. She could send in ideas. Maybe come up on the train occasionally.

She looked around.

Who do I know?

She spotted Caroline Felby, who introduced her to an actress called Kay before moving on. Erin ended up talking with Kay for an age, fascinated how this talented woman could want to know so much about her. It was probably twenty minutes later that Paul nudged her and whispered.

"Don't forget to mingle with producers. Networking with actors won't get you any work."

Erin felt naïve. It hadn't occurred to her that Kay was also networking and had assumed Erin to be a successful writer – and why wouldn't she? Only good writers got into this party.

"It's been great, Kay, but I must talk to Simon Driver."

Grabbing a third, or was it a fourth beer, she joined Simon and three others. He introduced them as Octopus people. That didn't mean anything to Erin and it took her a while to work out that Octopus was a production company. By then, the Octopuses were swimming away. Simon then excused himself to pay a visit to the loo.

Standing alone by the stage, Erin picked up another beer and sidled over to Colleen Nicholls.

"Colleen, how's the networking going?"

"Not bad. I was just talking to Callum Court from TVC."

"You mean he's here and I haven't pumped him for info?"

Erin took off after Callum, joined his small executive-looking group and started talking about comedy ideas.

"Will you be doing anything for *Comedy UK*?" asked Callum.

"Oh… yes… possibly," said Erin.

Or possibly not.

"I did warn you, Callum," said one of the group. "All these busy writers will have your no-budget show at the bottom of their to-do lists."

"Not true," said Erin. "I just might be working in a box factory instead."

They laughed, although Erin couldn't bring herself to tell them it wasn't a joke. She decided to leave them – a trip to the loo, getting another beer and finding a radio producer was a much better plan.

Ease up on the beer though… mustn't get drunk…

Time seemed to race away after that. Erin drank lots of beer and talked to lots of people, although she became less and less sure of who they were or what they were talking about.

At one point, a jolly man she had never seen before responded to her challenge to describe the difference between a sitcom and a comedy-drama.

"Ah well, let's talk television. A sitcom is multi camera, usually with an audience but not always, usually half an hour, usually with a heightened sense of the unreal in characters or setting, whereas a comedy-drama is single camera, no audience, usually forty to sixty minutes, realistic characters and setting but played in a light-hearted way. In radio, LE makes sitcom; the drama department makes comedy-drama."

Erin smiled in a confused way. "You couldn't do that again but slower, could you?"

"Yes, well, it's not written in stone," said the man, moving deftly away. "*Only Fools and Horses* has enjoyed a cross-over of sorts…"

Paul reappeared.

"Pub?"

Erin punched the air. "Great idea!"

"Goodleigh, you're drunk."

"You're right."

The key was to avoid letting him know she liked him otherwise he'd know and then… she lost her train of thought.

"Erin," said Ian, coming to join them, "you are amazing. I never got to go to the ball when I was a non-comm."

"I expect it was different in your day, Ian."

"It was. Back in '95, boys had to wear short trousers until we gained a commission."

"Yes, well, a helluva lotta months have passed since then. We do things differently now."

"I'm just nipping to the gents," said Paul, scooting off.

"You hanging around with that guy?" said Ian. "Isn't he the one who rides a bike for a cruddy little delivery firm?"

"Enough histrionics, Ian. Did I tell you I'm writing a seedcom?"

"A what?"

"A sitcom. Sitcom."

"What's it about?"

"It's about life, Ian. Life. You know, that big thing you ignore while planning things."

"Life – that's a big subject for comedy. Have you thought of narrowing the focus a little?"

"Alright, it's a sitcom about a box factory."

"Hey, that's not bad."

"Yeah, well… really?"

"Yes, really. That's exactly the kind of thing you want to write about. Zero research."

"Yeah?"

Erin wanted to take Ian down a peg or two, but here he was telling her that her sitcom idea was a good one. Could she write a sitcom about a box factory? What would Mum and Dad think? Then she started laughing. She could put them in it. *Ha ha.* Yes, Ian was right.

Mwah!

Ian recoiled. Perhaps she shouldn't have snogged him on the lips.

"Sorry about that, Ian. Box. Box… All the World's a Box…"

She was looking forward to going home now. She was looking forward to Christmas.

Dear family, I bring great news. You're all going to be in a sitcom!

The Crown & Sceptre was packed with dozens of people who could have been writers and/or producers. For Erin, the key was to sober up and mingle. *Yes, mingle and impress those producers. Because producers are the key to success.* She accepted a glass of wine from Paul and turned to a semi-familiar face.

"Hello, I'm Erin Goodleigh."

"Hi, Pam Griggs. I've seen you around the first floor."

"Well, I'm an LE kind of girl. Sketches, sitcoms... you name it, I'm writing one."

Paul leaned in.

"Take it slow."

"Cheers, Paul!" She turned back to Pam. "That's my mate, Paul. He's a good writer. Damned good. Do you have much thing with writers?"

"Yes, I'm the senior script exec. I mainly work with commissioned writers but we're always keen to see new talent emerge. Maybe I could see your latest sitcom. When it's ready."

"Really? Bloody hell, I haven't even... named it yet."

Damn. She wasn't planning on coming back in the New Year. Maybe she would post it.

Paul dragged her away.

"But Paul, I'm now distant from Griggsy."

"It's called leaving a good impression."

"I've certainly done that. When she reads my sitcom she won't know what's hit her."

"Good."

"That two hundred and fifty squiddly-diddlies is as good as mine. Or, even better, a bloody series! What about that, eh?"

"Right."

"What about you, Paul? Are you aware that Ian thinks you work for a cruddy little firm?"

"They're not cruddy. I get plenty of work and they're completely flexible."

"Yes, well... that's alright then. Otherwise, you'd have to start your own little firm. No, hang on, I don't mean that."

"I'm happy with Trident. They pay me more than the BBC so I won't be complaining come January."

"Sasha might. Oops. Personal space. Reverse, reverse,

and drive away."

"Yes, well… that might not be an issue."

"Oh…?"

"She moved out yesterday."

"Oh."

"She said she'd see me in the New Year for a long talk."

"Oh."

"I said I didn't want it spoiling Christmas and that we should have it out."

"Oh."

"So we did."

"Oh."

"Erin, you look like a goldfish."

"Oh."

"Sasha's not coming back."

"Oh."

"Did you see Tim Brooke-Taylor?"

"Er…?"

"He's over there chatting with a couple of the comms."

Erin strained to see. And then gasped.

"I know him. He was in *The Goodies*. On telly."

"Maybe we'll see Graeme Garden or Bill Oddie."

"Yes, maybe."

She wondered – should she kiss Paul?

Yes, good idea.

She prepared to pucker up and move in just as Simon Driver and Colleen Nicholls gate-crashed the party.

"Hey, how's everyone doing?" said Colleen.

Erin decided if she couldn't kiss Paul, she'd sing "Telly Tubbies Say Eh-Oh!"

Paul didn't look too impressed.

While Simon got the drinks in, Erin thought she'd

spotted someone famous making for the exit.

"Famous person alert!" she declared.

"Was that Bill Oddie?" said Colleen.

"Another Goodie?" said Paul. "Can't quite see…"

"Well, it might have been him," said Erin, "and we nearly saw him. What a life, eh?"

For some reason, it now seemed a good idea to sing Robbie Williams' "Angels".

"Are you sure you're okay?" said Paul.

"I nearly married Phil Collins."

"Yes, but not that one."

"No, not that one."

Next Pulp's "Disco 2000" came roaring into her head and out of her mouth, but her little dance caused her to wobble into a cigar-smoker by the bar.

"Are you okay?" he asked.

"We nearly saw Bill Goodie. He was in the Oddies."

"You stay there," said Paul. "I'll get Simon to order you a Coke and ice."

Erin stood next to a man on his mobile phone. He seemed to be arguing with someone. Finally, he huffed and said he'd be right there. Intriguingly, he put his barely touched pint of lager down on the bar and departed.

"Yum, lager," said Erin.

Drinking the free Fosters' she wondered what to do about Paul. Patience was the key. No sense in her turning into a female version of Phil or Charles or one of those Holiday Disco Men. It might put Paul off. Oh what would he be like? Kind, she felt. Considerate. She could see it now – him pulling her top off. If only they weren't in a pub surrounded by millions of writers and producers.

Idea!

She'd lure him back to the grotto. But how? Just ask? *Yes, just ask.* Oddly, after making the decision, she had a vague feeling of sliding downwards… and looking at the ceiling… and not feeling very well.

What a stupid time to be struck down by a mystery illness!

21. PLAN B

Monday, the fifth of January, 1998, was wet and blustery – though, thankfully, not as blustery as Sunday's ninety mile-an-hour gusts, which had seen a substantial number of trees come down. Britain was over the worst now and the early afternoon skies over Taunton seemed to offer a promise of better days to come.

"I must get some shallots," said Jenny, while rooting around in the bottom drawer of the fridge. "I thought I'd make a *boeuf bourguignon* for dinner. Nice to have something solid before we all start back to work tomorrow."

Goodleigh Packaging was closed until the Tuesday due to upgrade work on the production line and new Windows computers being installed in the office.

"Sounds good," said Erin.

"Drat – do I have any bay leaves?"

Erin watched her mum switch from faffing around in the fridge to faffing around in the cupboard where she stored the herbs and spices. As far as Erin was aware, not only would she have a jar of bay leaves, she'd have a back-up refill pack too.

Christmas and New Year had gone fast. Too fast. She missed Paul but...

But what?

Of course, Ralph and Jenny had occasionally raised the topic of Erin's future, particularly on New Year's Eve, just as she was getting ready to leave for a night of serious partying.

"You do see your future in Taunton?" Dad had asked.

"What's your advice?"

"I just want you to be happy. And so does Mum, deep down."

New Year's Eve was fading into memory now, but she smiled at recalling Rose and Cat dressed for action with low heels for dancing and deely-boppers in their hair to symbolize their inner child. Erin had wanted to talk about the future but Rose couldn't stop lamenting her break-up with love-of-her-life Alan, while Cat was too busy partying. Then, during the countdown to midnight, time seemed to slow down. And as the last seconds of 1997 slipped away, Erin Goodleigh wondered what the future held.

Three…

Two…

One…

"Make a wish!" yelled Cat.

Zero.

The crowd roared.

Poppers banged and filled the air with smoke and high-flying streamers.

Yes… a wish…

And now, a few days past all that…

"Are you sure you won't stay for dinner, Erin?"

"No, I have to be going, Mum."

"Right then."

Jenny abandoned her kitchen cupboard search and grabbed her car keys from the worktop. Erin collected her large-ish trolley-case and followed.

Ten minutes later, Jenny was dropping her daughter off at the train station.

"Be careful, Erin."

"I will."

"If you change your mind…"

"I'll call you when I'm there."

"Right."

There was a chalked notice board in the station hall: "Due to yesterday's storms, some services are experiencing delays." Erin checked the electronic departures board. The Paddington-bound service was only running forty minutes late.

"London, here I come – again."

By the time they were passing the London cabbies' secret eating place by Royal Oak station on the approach to Paddington, it was dusk and any weather worries had been replaced by concerns about accommodation. Trish was staying with her parents in Hove for a few more days and, annoyingly, Erin didn't have their phone number. Apparently, Mitch at the grotto did but he was hardly ever there and had failed to return her calls – apart from on one occasion while she was out and Dad failed to take a message beyond writing down "can you call him back?" When she did there was no flipping answer. Well, that was obvious – Wayne and Mitch rarely answered the phone because junior marketing man Wayne was lazy and post-grad psychology student Mitch was scared it might be his interfering parents.

The whole London thing had to work out this time. It really was a final try. No more ifs and buts. Failure to secure a commission by Easter would mean a permanent return to Taunton.

At Paddington Station, she pulled out her Christmas present from Mum and Dad – a Nokia mobile phone. And what a beauty it was too, with the latest analogue technology, voicemail capability, five ring tones, storage space for forty numbers, and a cool on-screen missed call indicator. It was great to be connected to the world, although the call rate of a pound a minute to mobiles and 50p to landlines was ridiculous. Of course, if she waited until seven p.m., it dropped to 10p a minute. Right now though, she needed to sort out a bed for the night.

A pound a minute…?

She went over to a public phone kiosk and called the grotto. There was no answer. *Grrr.*

Half an hour later, Erin and her travel case were on the doorstep in Prince Road ringing the bell. There was no answer. *Now what?*

She was becoming a little scared. The street was dark and it was cold. This was no longer feeling like a home from home. Everything seemed alien. She wasn't expected, neither did she feel wanted. It was tempting to go straight back to Paddington and board a westbound train. She'd be able to sleep comfortably in her own bed.

"Can I help?"

It was a woman of Erin's age coming up the street.

"I'm a friend of Trish's. I've been staying since September, so…"

"Are you the writer?"

Phew.

"Yes, that's right. Erin Goodleigh."

"I'm Lucy. I've got your old room."

Erin didn't like the sound of that, but watched as Lucy produced a key and let them in. Leaving her baggage in the narrow hall, she followed Lucy into the lounge.

"Is it something you arranged with Trish?" asked Erin.

"No, I got it through the landlord. I've stayed in his properties before. Do you know Dean Court?"

"I can't say I recall him."

"No, it's a block of flats in Wembley. From what Trish said, it didn't sound like you were coming back."

"I only decided the other day. Last I heard, my old room was still free. I've tried to get through but there's never any answer."

"Ah well, I'm new and I don't answer communal payphones."

"I was hoping Frances, Wayne or Mitch might be around."

"Not sure where Frances or Wayne are. Mitch stayed at his girlfriend's for Christmas. He's popped back a couple of times, but..."

"Um...?" Erin was looking around the lounge – specifically at the sofa.

"You're welcome to crash in here," said Lucy. "I wouldn't like to say you can use Trish's or Mitch's rooms. I'm new and..."

"No, the sofa's great. No problem. I'll sort something out tomorrow."

It was a difficult evening. Shop-worker Lucy's plumber boyfriend Bob came round and the three of them watched TV in the lounge till gone eleven. Then Frances and Wayne came in from the pub and acted as if nothing was awry – although Wayne said he might be moving out without being specific about a date. Within ten minutes, everyone had gone to bed.

In the silence of the house, Erin settled on the sofa and covered herself with her coat. She was wide-awake when the faint sounds of Bob and Lucy filtered through from the adjoining downstairs bedroom – *her old room*. She felt like going home but refused to give in to it.

*

Tuesday's horrible weather framed perfectly the horrible time Erin endured trying to sort out a place to live. First up, Frances gave her the landlord's number, which led to a possible place to stay in Cricklewood. Dragging her wheeled case up there, she soon found herself viewing what was, even to her untrained eye, a drugs den. One of the young male residents eyed her luggage.

"That, my girl, is one helluva stash."

Another young male resident came in removing things from a leather handbag that looked suspiciously stolen. He tried to sell Erin some items of make-up from it but she was quickly out of the door and away down the street.

She next tried a tatty lettings agent on the High Street but they wanted a ridiculously huge cash deposit. In the end, the agent gave her the number of a contact who did short-term lets for builders. Erin felt ice in her veins. But it was a simple choice. Try this option or book into a hotel.

Or call Paul.

Paul had been brilliant after the BBC Christmas Booze-Up, getting her back to the grotto by taxi and summoning Trish from the King's Arms to assist. Looking back, things were a bit hazy, memory-wise, but she was fairly sure she'd wanted to open up to Paul like the doors of Harrods on the first day of the sales – ready to receive the unstoppable rush. The only unstoppable rush though had been the one she made to the bathroom. *Yuk.*

Yes, she would have called Paul had she known his number. But she'd only just got the mobile phone and so far could only call on the grotto or a few people in Taunton. Popping into the Post Office to check the business directory didn't help either. She knew Paul worked for a courier firm but she couldn't remember the name and there were hundreds of them operating in the capital.

She tried another lettings agent. This one had a list of landlords who let to students. They found her a place in Southgate and accepted a cheque for a month's rent. It gave Erin a flashback to being nineteen and moving out of Exeter University halls of residence into a house-share.

It took an age to get to the Southgate property, but it didn't look too bad. A startled young man who had no idea she was coming greeted her. Still, no matter, she would look at the room and... *and what?* She told the young man that, if she liked it, she would probably take it for three months. That would be enough time to know if she was going to make it as a writer.

"I'm doing stuff for the BBC," she told him. She immediately regretted it. Starting with a boast was no way to behave.

"Yeah, the thing with the room..." the young man was saying, "I mean... well..."

The thing with the room was that it contained two young men who were illegal sub-tenants of the first young man. The bed looked disgusting. If you could get to it across a second bed made up on the floor.

"Great," said Erin. "This just gets better and better."

"You're welcome to crash on the sofa," said the young man. "They've only paid up till the end of the week."

Erin phoned the grotto. There was no answer. So she sat on a sofa in Southgate. It might as well have been Hell.

She kept trying the grotto's number and, around half-seven, she got Mitch.

"Yeah, come down. I've got a few mates coming over.

We're having a bit of party while Trish is away, kind of thing. You know what she's like."

Yes, she'd kick your sorry little arse, you twonk.

"When is she due back?"

"Friday lunchtime."

"Right. Okay. Well, I might come over a bit later. I'll take a chance on Trish not being too angry about me taking her room for a couple of nights."

"Ah, no, see, Jase and Cassie from Manchester are staying in Trish's room for a couple of days. You're still welcome to come over. It'll be a good night."

"A good night? Oh, good night to you!"

Erin ended the call.

What a total bloody nightmare.

Then, as if summoned by a temple bell, four of the Southgate housemates gathered to observe Strange Writer on Sofa. Apparently, news had spread that Erin 'did stuff for the BBC'. Bizarrely, they overlooked the fact that she had nowhere to live and no friends to call on. They were too busy seeing her as amazing.

Erin swiftly left and found the High Street. There she flagged down a passing London black cab.

"The nearest hotel, please. No, the nearest hotel that isn't about to be condemned."

22. STILL HOMELESS

It was Wednesday, just after nine a.m., and Erin was hauling her luggage into Broadcasting House. She was ready to argue that although she was early, it was most definitely an *INTU* day and that non-comm writers should be lovingly accepted into the building without a fuss. As it was, the security guy smiled. It was nice to be recognized. It was also nice not to have him go through her stuff in a security search. Taking the Escalator of Possibilities to the second floor, she bought a coffee and an apricot Danish pastry.

Yum.

"How's the sitcom coming along?"

For a moment, Erin failed to grasp the meaning of the question. Then it came back to her. She had made some kind of promise to this person.

"Not ready yet. Sorry."

"No problem," said Pam Griggs. "What's it about?"

"Oh, er..." *Why didn't I write the stupid thing over Christmas!* "I'll keep it a surprise. I don't want you second-guessing which way I'll go with it."

"Okay, but remember my door's always open, even if you just want to talk through any ideas."

Erin took the lift down to the first floor and headed for the LE reception. There was no-one about so she went to the writers' room where she stuck her stuff beside the piano and took out her burgundy laptop.

So...

She tried to think of something to write, but too much turmoil and caffeine kept her thoughts in a state of agitated disorder. Ten minutes later, she was relieved to hear Sarah's voice just outside.

"Hello Erin. I wasn't expecting you back."

"No, I changed my mind."

"Good for you."

They had a mini catch-up and Erin stressed her desire to work closely with Pam Griggs and producers like Jane Clearwater.

"That's brilliant, Erin. You keep at it."

She felt a warm glow – partly from Sarah's encouragement and partly from the association with the BBC itself. The idea that a complete nobody could get this much personal fuss was beyond all reasonable expectation. She just hoped the stories about the future were untrue and that the crumbling old place would never change.

Apart from a call to her bank to cancel her Southgate cheque, the hours dragged by until it was time for the commissioned writers' meeting. As they arrived, she decamped to the LE reception area and smiled at seeing Simon, Colleen and Josh among their number. It was well-deserved.

Taking a seat, she picked up a newspaper. It was time to get into the right frame of mind for the non-comms meeting in half an hour.

A new face came in. Female. Mid-twenties.

"Hello," said Erin.

"Hello, is this where they have the writers' meeting for *It's News To Us?*"

"Yes, you're in the right place. I'm assuming it's your first time?"

"Yes, I'm a bit nervous."

"You'll be fine. Just listen to what Gavin the script editor says in the meeting and take notes. And don't worry about what the commissioned writers might be covering… actually, Gavin's brilliant. He'll tell you everything you need to know."

"Are you one of them? The commissioned writers?"

"Me, no, I'm Erin Goodleigh, very definitely a non-comm but writing in hope. It's all about remaining focused and being determined. Focused determination. Never give up. Positivity."

Why am I talking gibberish?

"Hello, hello," said Ian, entering LE from the main corridor, "I heard you'd given up – said it was all a waste of time."

"Happy New Year, Ian. You must have misheard."

"Why don't we get together later for a catch-up."

He stared into her eyes. It was very intense – as if his Christmas reading had been *How To Hypnotize Your Victims.*

"Let me get back to you on that, Ian." *When we're the last two people on Earth.*

Ian smiled and disappeared into the admin office.

Paul came in from the main corridor clutching what looked like a script.

"Oh…" he said.

"Oh?" said Erin.

"I didn't expect to see you. Um… I just need to photocopy this."

Erin followed him round to the quiet photocopier corner.

"The Christmas party was fun," she said.

Paul seemed to find it funny. "Yes, Erin, it's amazing how all that booze had absolutely no effect on you."

"So… you and Sasha…?"

"Yes, let's hope things go better with Alice."

"Alice?"

"I met her on New Year's Eve. To be honest, I was drunk and things got out of hand."

Erin's heart sagged. "On your own head be it. I'm focusing on writing and couldn't possibly handle a relationship right now."

"Well, it's nice to see you, Erin. As I say, I didn't think you were coming back."

"No, well, I'm here now."

"Yes…"

Was that a flash of heat… or the photocopier firing up?

"So, who's this Alice who's going to have to put up with your depressing personality and dreary stories?"

"She's a very nice person who works in business recruitment and seems fascinated that I'm in the entertainment and courier businesses. We're going on a third date this weekend."

"Ooh, the cinema, a nice restaurant…?"

"No, Chelsea v. Coventry."

Football? Why hadn't he asked her to a match? Okay, so she wasn't a football fan…

Ian walked by.

"Ian! About that catch-up?"

"Oh right. I just have to…"

He pointed in the direction of someone's office and headed off.

Erin turned to Paul and smiled.

"Happy New Year, Paul."

*

After the meeting, Paul suggested to Erin that they needed to re-double their efforts in targeting producers.

"That's what I was planning to do – with sitcoms and sketch show ideas."

"Yes, but I also mean finding out who they really are, what they really enjoy comedy-wise."

"Good thinking," said Erin, now wondering if she should tell Paul she was homeless.

"It's time to really start using what we know."

"Yes… do you think it's possible for a city to dislike someone?"

"What?"

"It's London. I'm not sure we get on."

Paul sighed. "To settle in London, you have to start seeing it for what it is. People often think of it as this huge entity…"

Tell him you're homeless.

"…but if you look closely, London's actually a collection of villages. It's just they've expanded over the centuries to fill up the spaces between."

"Yes, I see, but…"

"Take Camden. People from Camden are proud to identify with their area. Camden Lock, the market, the pubs… and take Bethnal Green – they barely know Camden exists. They're so busy being in Bethnal Green with the flower market and the great pubs. If you read, say, Samuel Pepys…"

"The thing is…"

"Erin? I've got five minutes if you want to talk," said producer Jane Clearwater, appearing from the direction of the LE reception area. "Sarah said you'd asked about me."

"Oh, right – thanks."

Paul leaned in close and whispered. "Targeting."

"Yes…" She'd grab Paul when she got out.

Jane's office was no bigger than Sarah's, which meant sitting in a space surrounded by piles of scripts, papers and general office junk.

"Sarah says you were talking of giving up."

"Yes, but I changed my mind. I thought I might have a chance this time. Based on what I've learned, I mean."

"*It's News To Us* is a tough assignment. People think anyone can write for it because we let people walk in off the street. You'll have noticed how many of those walk straight back out again and never return."

"I've noticed."

"Caroline Felby and Gavin Gould tell me you should keep at it. You've got something, Erin, so use it. There is nowhere else in the world where a writer with no track record and no script to show off can get direct access to a broadcast producer."

Jane went on to suggest how Erin might draw up a schedule of targets and their delivery. In short, a three-month plan to run alongside submitting sketches to *INTU*. She also encouraged her to reach out to other producers, to see who was a good fit for her style.

"We're not robots," said Jane. "Producers aren't made in a factory to a British standard. We're just people like you doing the best we can. If a producer can't work with you, it doesn't mean you're useless or they're blind. It might just be that you're not meant for each other. It's a relationship, really. That's what you're trying to forge."

"Like finding a boyfriend?"

"Yes," said Jane, "only far more important."

Erin smiled. Jane felt like a good fit. She hoped that turned out to be the case.

By the time she emerged revitalized from Jane's office, Paul had vanished. She tried the canteen where Simon Driver told her that Paul had business to attend to and wouldn't be back until Thursday handing-in time.

Thoughts of homelessness that had drifted away came roaring back with a vengeance.

"You eating?" said Simon.

"No, I'm not hungry."

She returned to LE, where she bumped into Ian. He had a suggestion for a date on the Monday. Erin accepted immediately and got rid of him. She didn't want him knowing her lack-of-bed predicament.

In the empty writers' room, she pulled out her laptop in the most positive way she could manage.

"Sketches then!"

Around mid-afternoon, Erin phoned the grotto. There was no answer. She tried again at five p.m. and 6.15. At seven, she grabbed her shoulder bag, went down to the front reception desk and explained to the security guy that she was just popping out for a burger.

Outside, the streets were dark and cold but it wasn't far to the nearest burger bar. It was quite busy inside and felt like a different world; one with its own concerns. When she left she was almost knocked over by a young man running into her. Fortunately another young man helped her to her feet and even restored to her the paper bag containing her meal.

Back in the writers' room, while she was enjoying her food, Gavin popped his head in.

"Working hard, eh?"

"Hi Gav. I've finished my sketches but thought I'd stay on to work on a sitcom idea." *The Homeless Woman.*

"Unless that's not okay."

"No, no, stay put. I'm here till nine, so feel free. It's lovely and quiet in here too. The sort of place you can really get stuck in."

"Exactly. So what are you up to? Is it *INTU*?"

"No, it's a pilot for a sketch show. It's my own idea but that means loads of unpaid work to get it right. Luckily, Caroline Felby's on board."

"Sounds fun. Best of luck with it."

"Thanks. Can I get you a tea or a coffee?"

"Oh no, it's…"

"Nonsense. We have a kettle and cups. I'm making one for Caroline, so…"

"Okay then. Coffee, milk, no sugar. Thanks Gav. You're a star."

Five minutes later, Gavin returned with her hot drink and a Kit-Kat.

"Gavin Gould, I was right. You really are a star."

Gavin left her to her sitcom idea, which remained thin in terms of substance. Sipping her coffee, Erin tried to work out her best course of action. She could probably leave her baggage by the piano. No-one was likely to disturb it. Then she could find a hotel. There was one opposite Broadcasting House, but it looked horribly expensive. There were plenty near Paddington Station that looked cheaper.

She returned to the idea of a sitcom set in a box factory. In real life, packaging was a varied business. In a sitcom, they would surely just turn out boxes. So, who would be the boss? Did you need a bit of nutcase character like Basil Fawlty? Or someone puffed up with pomposity like Captain Mainwaring in *Dad's Army*.

By the time she'd almost finished writing a two-page treatment of the overall idea, she was quite pleased. This was something she could show to Jane Clearwater.

"Night, Erin," said Gavin. "Remember, the doors into this part are locked after nine." He held up a small black plastic dongle. "If you don't have one of these, wedge a door open if you need the loo, otherwise you won't get back in."

"Thanks Gav."

"Night," said Caroline Felby, coming along from her office.

"Night all," said Erin.

She decided to continue polishing her work for a bit longer. She didn't want to spend too much time in a drab, dreary hotel room.

Boxes, boxes...

Twenty minutes later, she finished work and wondered where to head. On reflection, Paddington seemed a bit far. Wasn't Euston nearer? Surely, they had cheapish hotels by the station. She wondered if she had enough cash for a cab. A London cabbie would alert her if she was about to try a dubious establishment. Only...

Shit!

Her purse wasn't in her bag.

A sinking feeling grabbed hold. The young man outside the burger place. The two of them were working together. One bumps into you, the other rifles through your bag.

Oh God...

How much had they spent on her credit card? A five-year-old could copy her signature. Why hadn't she learned to write like an adult? Finding a pack of A4 paper to wedge open the doors between the inner sanctum and the LE reception area, she tried the admin office.

Empty.

She was the only person in LE.

Finding a phone book, she looked up her credit card contact number and cancelled her card. The guy on the line promised a new one would reach her address within forty-eight hours. Unfortunately, that meant Taunton.

Her next call was an obvious one. She had to get her parents to pre-pay for a room at a hotel. Only, how could she tell Mum? Jenny Goodleigh would be on the next train to London. No, there had to be another way.

She tried the grotto. This time, she got through.

"Hello?"

"Is that you, Wayne?"

"Nah, it's Dan. Wayne's not here."

"Is Mitch there?"

"Not sure. Lucy invited me to stay over. There's been a party, like, and it's still kind of going on."

"Listen carefully. Are there any beds free there?"

"Who is this?"

"Erin Goodleigh. I stayed there from September to Christmas."

"Oh Erin, right. How's it going?"

"It's going great, Dan. Is Frances there?"

"She's out."

"Okay, do you know if there are any bedrooms free there?"

"No, it's crammed full. Me and the girlfriend are stuck with the sofa. I think there might be some space when some dragon called Trish gets back 'cos I've heard she won't tolerate strangers crashing."

Grrr.

"Are you sure Frances isn't there?"

"Is there a Frances here?" he yelled without moving the phone away from his mouth. "Nah, I'm not getting anything. Why don't you come over? There's beer, cider and... well, I won't say over the phone in case you-know-who's listening in."

"So, there's definitely no Mitch? He's not gone to his girlfriend's place, has he? As in, could you go and physically check to see if he's there?"

Dan went off to check. Thirty seconds later, he was back.

"They've gone out. I can leave a message for when they get back."

"No, I'll call again when Trish is back."

Erin ended the call.

Choices, choices...

One of the plusses of London was the many places you could spend the night. Like one of the big train stations. She could hang out at Broadcasting House for as long as possible then walk up to Euston and sit on a bench hoping to avoid the pimps, drug-pushers and muggers. She rifled through her pockets and all parts of her belongings for any spare cash.

Seventy-four pence.

She really didn't fancy Euston Station and she couldn't exactly spend the night at the BBC. On balance, it seemed best to delay any decisions. She could write another sketch. After all, that's why she'd returned to London.

Half an hour later, she popped out to the toilets.

Instead of coming straight back, she sought out the smokers' balcony on the sixth floor for some fresh air. Last time she was there, Colleen had been a bundle of nerves and some van driver's radio was blaring out "Perfect Day". It seemed a lifetime ago.

She sat there for almost an hour. In fact, despite the cold, she was almost dropping off to sleep when the door opened. Erin leapt up. It was a cleaner. Erin wished him good evening and waited for her heart rate to drop a little. It was ten o'clock.

Now what?

Returning to the writers' room, she sat by the piano. Was this a good time to practice her one-finger version of "Chopsticks"? *Probably not.* She took out her note pad and jotted a few lines about a woman who secretly lived at the BBC. Then she left the room and ventured along the inner sanctum's corridor. Further on, there were a couple of small offices in darkness. She slipped inside one and closed the door. She didn't want to cry so did her best to stop it. As she wiped her eyes, she wondered – wasn't there a positive health benefit to sleeping flat on your back on a rock-hard floor?

23. RESCUE

Erin awoke with a start. For a moment, she couldn't understand where she was. Then it all came rushing back. She checked her watch. It was 7.07 a.m. and she was on the floor in Toby Lock's office. Opening the door a crack onto the inner sanctum corridor, she scanned the scene. There was no-one about.

Good.

She was soon sitting at her laptop in the writers' room trying to ponder comedy. Maybe she would write a farce. It certainly seemed appropriate because, for the moment at least, the line between sanity and insanity appeared to be blurred.

No, she would write another sketch for *INTU*.

People began arriving around half-eight but failed to notice her presence. By the time Sarah popped her head in at nine, it seemed slightly more natural to find a writer in the building.

"Someone's keen," said Sarah. "Tea? Coffee?"

"Oh, tea, please."

While polishing her sketches, Erin broke off three times with a view to phoning her parents. But each time, she lost her nerve. Eventually, just before lunchtime, she handed her sketches in then decamped to the LE reception area, where she skimmed through a newspaper while waiting for Paul.

Ian walked in.

Fab.

"Just the person," he said. "Annoyingly, I've got a meeting, but take this and digest it in time for our liaison on Monday." He handed her a large envelope. "That's top secret, by the way. Do not share."

After he'd gone, she peeked. It was his sitcom script.

Paul arrived.

"A lady of leisure, eh? Loafing around without a care in the world."

"If only."

Paul went through to hand his sketches to Gavin. Erin wondered if to mention her homelessness. It was probably worth a quick call to the grotto first though, to see if Trish had returned early.

Not wanting anyone to overhear her business, she pulled out her mobile and went up to the smokers' balcony. The buzz of being able to make mobile calls was a long way from wearing off, although she did wish hers contained a little more joy.

"Hello?"

"Hi, it's Erin. Is that you, Wayne?"

"No, it's Jack."

"Jack? I don't suppose Trish is there?"

"Trish?"

"Yes, she lives there, although she's been at her parents."

"I think she's moved out."

"What? Look, is Wayne there?"

"Who's Wayne?"

"He lives there."

"He's not the other one who moved out, is he? Only I've only just moved in. I might have his old room."

"I don't know if he moved out."

"Right, so shall I leave him a message then?"

"Look, is the sofa free tonight?"

"Sorry, but who exactly are you?"

"I used to live there."

"I'm sorry, you need to phone the landlord. I'm trying to get rid of a guy on the sofa as it is."

"Are you sure Trish has moved out?"

"I'm sorry, I don't know any Trish."

Erin ended the call. Talking to Paul had just become something of a priority. Who knows, maybe she'd sleep on his sofa. Or would Alice be there?

Awkward.

She returned to LE and searched all the likely places she might find Paul. No luck. Just as she was thinking he'd probably gone up to the canteen, she saw Simon Driver.

"Simon, hi."

"Hello Erin. How are you?"

"Fine, thanks. You haven't seen Paul, have you?"

"You just missed him. He's gone up to the smokers' balcony."

"Right, thanks."

Damn. While she was coming down the stairs, he must have gone up in the lift.

Erin went out to get the lift. Why would Paul go to the smokers' balcony? Was he a secret Havana cigar man? No, of course he wasn't. He'd obviously bumped into a smoker and gone for a chat.

Reaching the glass door to the balcony, Erin got a clear view of Paul with a woman. It wasn't a casual chit-chat either. They were laughing and being all super-friendly. The woman was a smoker and Paul had come here to be with her. It all made sense. Paul Fielding was a two-timing bastard rat.

Poor Alice.

Down in LE, she found Sarah's door open and Sarah herself with what looked like a huge box of scripts.

"It's the unsolicited pile. People send them in and they go into my box."

"And a very nice box it is too." *I should know – I'm a former Miss Cardboard.*

"When you're a commissioned writer, you'll be able to read them."

Erin was so in need of sympathetic company that she was happy for Sarah to talk about anything – although this did sound interesting.

"So how does it work?"

"Take a seat…"

Erin made herself comfortable.

"We get lots of sitcom and sketch show scripts," Sarah explained. "Being a public service, we have to respond. To do that, I take a script from my box… thus… and I type the name into my computer here…"

Erin was very happy to watch the process unfold.

"It used to be a list," said Sarah, "but we're now starting to put it all on the computer system."

She copied the writer's name and the title of sitcom, in this case L. Smith and *The Prime Minister's Diary,* and added another name alongside it – Shaun Donoghue.

"So how does Shaun Donoghue figure?"

"I give Shaun twenty scripts and he reads them at four quid a script."

"Sounds intriguing."

"If a script is *really* good, he'll show it to Pam Griggs, our senior script exec. If it's not so good, we'll return it with Shaun's critique attached. At the very least, they get feedback from a commissioned writer."

"And any commissioned *INTU* writers can take part?"

"Subject to approval by Pam. Most don't get involved though. By the time you've read it and worked out a useful critique, it's really just four pounds an hour."

Less than cleaning offices or working behind a bar...

"Shaun does it though," said Erin.

"He'll take the scripts home and go through them at his convenience. For anyone with a brain, like Shaun, it's not just about the money. If he applies for script editing jobs in the future, it'll read really well on his CV."

"BBC script reader. Yes, I can see that."

Seeing the business of being a writer in an ever-expanding way, Erin took another script from the box and read the name and title for Sarah, who typed it into the computer.

"So what experience have you got," asked Sarah, "before coming here, I mean?"

"The short version is the school play, university drama, the Edinburgh Fringe and Christmas panto writing."

"We have time for the longer version."

"You're a soft touch, Sarah."

Erin spent the next twenty minutes ignoring her rumbling empty stomach and the growing need to phone Taunton. Instead, she went through her experiences of writing and putting together comedy extravaganzas for little or no money.

"That's quite a bit of activity," said Sarah, typing in the details of the twentieth script and writer. "Hopefully, you'll get a commission this time around and really take off."

"Hopefully."

"You said you came up from Taunton. Where are you based in London?"

Oh God…

Erin forced back the display of emotion. This wasn't Sarah's problem.

"Are you okay?"

"Fine…" Erin composed herself. "Just having a few problems on the accommodation front. As in, I don't have any accommodation and my purse was stolen yesterday. It had my cash, bank card and cheque book."

"Oh God… where did you stay last night?"

"Don't ask."

"I might be able to get you a room in a house for fifty quid a week. Can you afford that? You wouldn't have to pay until you've sorted out your money."

"That would be brilliant."

"I've got a friend who works for London Transport," said Sarah. "I don't think I can get hold of her now but I can make a call this evening."

"Great…"

"She goes out a lot so I might not be able to get her till late. You can have our sofa for tonight though, if you want. I share a flat with an old university friend who works at the British Library. She's usually at lunch until two. I'll call her then to warn her."

Erin felt the weight lift from her shoulders.

"That would be a godsend, Sarah. If you're sure…?"

Sarah reached for her purse.

"Of course I'm sure. Is a fiver enough to keep you going?"

That evening, a sheepish Erin went east with Sarah. They emerged at Bethnal Green into a dark but bustling street scene.

"I don't know this area at all," said Erin. "How has it

survived so long without me visiting?"

"It's been a struggle without you, Erin, but it has a lot of history. Not all of it good, mind you. Ever heard of the Bethnal Green underground disaster?"

"No."

"During the Second World War, 173 people died trying to get down the stairs we just came up. An air raid siren sounded, a mum with a baby slipped and the bodies just piled up."

"Bloody hell."

"And that park back there behind the station? The library there used to be part of a Victorian lunatic asylum. The sign says Bethnal Green Gardens but the locals call it Barmy Park."

"You can't beat a proper insider's tour."

As they headed up Cambridge Heath Road, Sarah told her of other local points of interest, such the famous Columbia Road Flower Market and the Repton Boxing Club where the notorious Kray twins learned to flatten people. Further on, they reached a structure that reminded Erin of a large Victorian railway station.

"That's the Museum of Childhood. It's part of the Victoria & Albert Museum but most Londoners have no idea it's here."

Something Paul said came back to her, about London really being a collection of adjoining villages. He was right – it made the capital city seem more manageable somehow.

They turned right.

"That's York Hall, one of the most famous amateur boxing venues in Britain, and just a bit further along…" Just along from it was a row of run-down Georgian houses. "…is home sweet home."

"A Georgian flat? Nice."

"Not so long ago, people weren't bothered about Georgian property in Bethnal Green. That's changing fast."

"How long have you lived here?"

"In the flat? Two years – but I was born just around the corner. This is my manor."

Sarah's flat-mate was out, so it was spaghetti Bolognese for two with a glass of white wine while watching TV.

"This is brilliant, Sarah. Thank you so much. And don't worry, I won't tell the other non-comms. We can't have you being overrun."

Later, while Erin enjoyed a second glass of wine, Sarah was on the phone to a friend. It seemed to be good-ish news – a room in suburban Beckenham.

"Unfortunately, it's only for a few weeks," said Sarah, "and it's a bit of a trek, but it's a room. Is that okay?"

"It's brilliant. Thanks."

They spent the rest of the evening talking about their pasts. Erin was staggered to learn that Sarah was only twenty-six. Not that she looked older, but she was so mature. She had heard about the BBC while at the London School of Economics and signed on with them as soon as she left.

Erin went through some of her own experiences in more detail – such as how, at the end of her second year at university, she formed a comedy group that performed at the Edinburgh Festival Fringe three years running.

"Did you refine it each year or was it a completely new show?" said Sarah.

"A whole new show each time, although not by choice. I was one of eight performers and three writers in '87. By '88, that was down to four performers and two writers."

"Ah, onward and downward."

"You're not kidding. In '89 it was a two-woman show, written and directed by me."

Erin explained how, in the following years, she got into writing for TADS and local am-dram productions while sending off the occasional play to the Royal Court Theatre.

"I turn down work from other amateur groups nowadays though. If you're not careful, you end up writing, directing, doing the lights and organizing the tickets."

"And what about going forward?" asked Sarah.

"I suppose the next thing is to write a sitcom or create a sketch show. Seeing as I'm in the department twice a week."

"That would make sense, although cracking the sitcom is the biggie."

"I've tried writing a sitcom half a dozen times but I never seem to get anywhere. I will this time though. I have to."

Sarah's flat-mate came in at half-ten. Soon after, Erin was settling down on the sofa for the night. Not only was it more comfy than the one at the grotto, it didn't smell of beer and sweat either. Within a few minutes, she was fast asleep.

Erin and Sarah were up at seven and walking along Cambridge Heath Road by eight-fifteen. Erin had decided to start writing some scenes for her box factory sitcom. Then, after lunch, she would get a train down to Beckenham before the rush hour got under way.

Descending the stairs into Bethnal Green station, she recalled Sarah's account of the wartime disaster. It gave her the shivers.

Down on the busy, stuffy platform, the temperature bore little relation to the cold January day in the world above and Erin wasn't the only one to groan when the train pulling in was full. As it was, the doors slid open to reveal enough room for two small pixies to board. That being the case, she was alarmed to find herself propelled into the carriage where those inside clearly viewed her as the head of an invading force.

The doors closed. She turned.

"Wait for me at Oxford Circus!" Sarah seemed to be yelling from the wrong side of the glass.

The train lurched, a woman's paperback raked Erin's cheek, and her hand shot up to grab the overhead handrail. How could anyone read *Bridget Jones's Diary* standing on a crowded train? Obviously, the whole business of evolution needed updating. Londoners were adapting.

At Liverpool Street station, more people squeezed aboard. It raised another evolutionary question: were armpits necessary? For Erin, it was a question of increasing importance thanks to a particularly sweaty example radiating noxious gasses three inches from her nose.

Reaching Bank station, she prayed that Radioactive Armpit Man would get off. He didn't.

"Mind the gap," announced an automaton's voice over the station's loudspeaker.

Erin sighed. The train was packed tighter than a tin of sardines that had been opened, had the contents of three other tins squashed in and been resealed.

"Mind the gap."

Stuff mind the gap. *Mind the bloody armpit.*

The doors closed and train jolted forward, throwing

Erin's face into said armpit. Its owner glanced at her before returning to his own problem: namely, staring at the back of someone's greasy head while clinging to the overhead handrail for dear life.

At Oxford Circus, Erin gratefully disembarked and waited by the escalator for Sarah – who arrived two minutes later looking surprisingly unfazed. It was time to ask her for one final indulgence.

"You don't mind if I use your address, do you...?"

Ten minutes later, she phoned her dad at work and explained her predicament. Ralph was worried but not surprised to receive the call at the office rather than at home where Jenny would overhear and go into meltdown.

"Can you get down to the bank, Dad, and explain the situation. I need a new cheque book sent care of my friend Sarah's address. I also need you to do the same when my bank card arrives in the post there. I'll also give you the details of the local branch here so I can get some cash."

Erin went on to tell Ralph what she was wearing so he could give the Taunton branch a description for them to confirm with the branch near Broadcasting House. It was a complete pantomime, but Erin soon had two hundred pounds in cash.

Back at Broadcasting House, Erin paid Sarah back and launched into a morning's work writing up more scenarios and bits of dialogue for her box factory sitcom. Then, before lunch, she nipped into an empty office and phoned the grotto. It would be worth trying to get hold of Trish's new number.

"Hello?" said a hesitant male voice.

"Who is this?" asked Erin. "Actually, never mind. Do you know if anyone there has a new number for Trish, please?"

"She's right here. Shall I pass you over?"

"What? … Yes please!"

"Hello?"

Hearing Trish's voice was a truly wonderful thing.

"Oh Trish."

"Erin! How's life in Taunton?"

Arghhh!

Erin calmed herself and explained the situation.

"Beckenham?" said Trish. "Great. Although the loft room's free if you want. Jack, who just moved in, has just moved out again and—"

"Yes please!"

Erin was elated. She'd be back with Trish. Maybe things were looking up at last.

24. DEEPER INTO THE ENTERTAINMENT WORLD

It was Monday lunchtime and Erin, alone at the grotto, was enjoying a fried egg sandwich while listening to the news on the radio. It had been a good catch-up weekend. Friday had seen Trish evict all excess occupants and Erin joined her in a mammoth clean up. They had accepted the lame excuses of Frances and Mitch, and to a lesser degree, Lucy, and life was much as it had been before Christmas.

Saturday had been a more relaxed affair. Erin even found time to enjoy the tape of Friday's *INTU*; in particular, a sketch about Tony Blair's ever more robotic cabinet. The credits hadn't sounded too bad either.

It seemed daft, but hearing her name on the radio made her feel completely different about the entire course of her life. She was glad for Paul, too. He deserved to make it this time around.

Just as she finished her egg, the communal payphone rang. Unlike some at the grotto, she was happy to answer it.

"Hello?"

"Erin?"

"Paul?"

"Hi, I would've phoned your mobile but I didn't want to spend all the *seedcorn money I got for Buck House!*"

"Oh brilliant! Now you make sure you keep going, Paul Fielding. There are lots of people who believe in you."

"You're one of them, aren't you."

"Yes, I am."

Along with Amorous Alice and Smoking Woman on Balcony.

"Thanks Erin. You're a very important person to me."

Her heart beat a little faster.

"That's nice of you to say, Paul."

"So how did your weekend go?"

"Great. I had a good catch-up with Trish and my jaw's only just recovering. How about you and Alice?"

Erin noted a slight hesitation.

"Yes, it's good, thanks. We're going out for a meal tonight. A nice quiet restaurant. What about you? Any plans?"

"Er…" *Do Not Lie To Paul.* "I'm seeing ICT. We're going to a comedy gig."

"Yes, I saw him on Thursday. He said something about Camden."

"Paul…"

"I have to go. Don't let anyone dictate to you, Erin. At least keep that in mind."

"Well, obviously—"

The line went dead.

Hey, I haven't explained the Ian situation! What was it with men and their little strops? You didn't catch women acting like that!

*

Later, setting off for Ian's place, Erin found herself leaving the grotto alongside Mitch. What's more, he had a cab waiting to take him up to Golders Green, which meant he'd pass through Erin's West Hampstead destination. She wasn't too keen on arriving at Ian's place early, but as it was cold, dark, Monday evening…

The cab driver described West Hampstead as a show-off address. It sounded great because it had the word Hampstead in it, but it would be less confusing and more accurate to rename it East Kilburn. Still, the block itself was a neat low-rise affair, possibly dating back to the 1950s.

When Ian answered the door, he was surprised – and not properly dressed.

"You're early," he said. "Um, take a seat. I won't be long."

As he disappeared upstairs, Erin looked around. It wasn't too bad inside. A neat two-level apartment that probably looked great around 1985 but now needed freshening up.

In the lounge, she found a tank with three bored goldfish. Taking a closer look, the little fellas came straight to her. Was that right? Was Ian feeding them properly? She looked around for fish food. There wasn't any to hand so she tried the kitchen.

Fish food, fish food…

"Ah-ha."

There was a large pot of fish flakes on the end of a shelf. She took it, only to guess that it also served as a bookend to prevent envelopes and takeaway leaflets from falling to the floor – as they did. Picking them up, she couldn't help but notice the Lloyds Bank paying-in book and the NatWest cheque that had fallen out of it. Was this a BBC payment for Ian's services? No, it was a cheque from his mum. Why was Ian's mum sending him two hundred pounds? Was it his birthday? No, that was in the summer. And who sent that kind of money as a gift? Was she helping him out? No, Ian was a successful writer. Successful writers didn't need money from their parents, did they?

Erin fed the fish and restored the pot to its rightful place. Just as she took a seat in the lounge, Ian came down.

"Right, the show starts at eight-thirty. That gives us an hour or so before we have to leave."

Erin didn't like the way he said it, or the way he appeared to be sweating. Was that hurried-dressing sweat or pervert sweat?

"I don't mind getting there early. We could have a drink."

"Yes, exactly what I was thinking. Get there early, have a drink. That said, I do have some really nice wine in the fridge."

He returned with a chilled bottle of Liebfraumilch.

"You'll love it."

Sweet wine? Not likely.

Despite her lack of enthusiasm, he poured them a glass each.

"Did you have any thoughts about Jane?" he asked.

"Jane?" She didn't like being seated while he stood. "Jane Clearwater?"

"No, sitcom Jane."

"Oh." *Sitcom Jane, the girl obsessed by sex.* "Yes, I have a few thoughts. Maybe she shouldn't be obsessed by sex."

"That would take a lot out of the equation."

"Sex isn't an equation."

"It is when you're plotting and planning."

"Yes, I know, but this woman needs to find some self-respect. Otherwise she's out of some bad seventies sexploitation film."

"That's silly."

Why's he standing over me? Why can't he sit down like a normal person?

"Couldn't you give her doubts and uncertainties, Ian? Make her unsure of the way forward but keen to press on anyway. Maybe she's always accepting bad advice or..."

He turned the side lamp on. In Erin's opinion, it was too bright and it dazzled her eyes.

"Erin, I've got this half-formed scene where I need to know what a sex-starved, sex-crazed woman would be feeling and thinking when she meets this hunky guy who shows an interest. In your own time."

"You want me to describe her sex fantasies?"

"Yes, it's called writing."

"They won't end up in the script."

"They might."

"Me being here doesn't feel right, Ian."

"I'm being friendly. Don't you like friendly?"

"Yes, but not Nazi interrogation friendly."

"Don't be silly. We have wine."

Erin stood up.

"How about we head out early?"

"This is a big opportunity for you. You don't have to go back to Taunton a failure. Did you know I'm being considered as the new script editor on *INTU*?"

"What?"

"As you know, I love to champion those writers who are prepared to go the extra mile."

No-ooo. Erin felt sick. Trapped. There was no way forward.

"I'm sure you'll get sketches galore on," he said. "You'll be a commissioned writer before you know it."

"Ian, I hate to break the mood, but isn't there a comedy club we're meant to be visiting?"

"Yes, of course. I was only trying to be helpful."

Two hours later, Erin was cringing alongside a laughing Ian. The new acts open mic show was an all-male affair, with recurring themes of bad sex, fantasy sex, taking drugs and... no, it was just those three. Seeking refuge in successive bottles of Budweiser, she wondered – was Paul having as much fun with Alice?

Prior to Wednesday's show meeting, Erin was studying the notice board in the LE reception area, dreading the thought of Ian taking over from Gavin. A young man called Michael Holbrook was smiling at anyone who was interested. He'd started after Erin, possibly around November, but had already scored a few sketches on the show. Of course, Erin had congratulated him, but she didn't want to hear a breakdown of his writing method.

Paul and Simon Driver came in. Simon was looking particularly pleased with life.

"Is it me or is *It's News To Us* the best show in the history of radio?"

"No, that's *Newslines*," said the producer of *Newslines*, coming out of the admin office.

They waited for him to disappear into the LE inner sanctum.

"How many sketches did you get on?" Erin asked

"Two," said Simon, "and they came to just over three minutes."

"Ooh, lucky."

Erin did the arithmetic. Just over three minutes meant

getting paid for four. Four times £36 meant…

"144 quid. Lucky indeed."

"168 quid, actually. I'm not on the basic money."

"The rate goes up," said Paul. "If you're successful."

"Oh right," said Erin.

"It's still a mile behind TV money," said Simon. "So let's not lose our long-term focus."

Erin thought about asking Paul how he got on, but she wasn't the one who had put the phone down abruptly.

Gavin emerged from the inner sanctum and popped into the admin office. *Lovely Gavin.* But what of Ian taking over? She waited until he came out again.

"Could I have a quick word, Gav?" She inclined her head towards the door to the outer corridor. Gavin obliged.

"I've heard we might have a new script editor on *It's News To Us.* Any truth in it?"

Gavin seemed surprised.

"It's news to me, if you'll pardon the pun. No, I've got a contract with the BBC. Who told you?"

"I'd better not say. It wasn't any kind of a senior source though."

"Yes, well, let's forget it, Erin. We have a show to do."

She followed him back into the LE reception, where she took a seat while he continued through to the inner sanctum for the commissioned writers meeting. Paul meanwhile said something about getting a coffee and left. Erin decided to go after him.

"You're not following me, are you?" he said halfway up the stairs to the second floor.

"Are we still friends?"

Paul stopped.

"Sorry I put the phone down. It was childish."

"Yes, it was… but we all do stupid things. Let's forget

it."

"You're very generous. Are you going to the canteen after the meeting?"

"No, I want to get a lot done this afternoon."

"Right. Good. Very commendable."

"Paul, it's early in the run but we're neck and neck for a commission. It's my aim to leave you trailing in my wake."

"Spoken like a true writer."

Back at her room in the grotto, apart from cups of tea and a plate of beans on toast, Erin barely stopped. Then, around eight p.m., she stretched, yawned and headed for the kitchen. Trish was there reading the evening paper. There was an empty tea mug in front of her.

"Mitch is hogging the TV," she explained. "You don't fancy half a lager in the pub, do you?"

Erin wasn't sure. That said, she'd been at it for over six hours.

"Half a lager, then."

It was good to get away from sketch-writing for a while. Erin was true to her word though. They had half a lager – followed by a glass of chardonnay. Trish had lots of news about her teacher-training course and her latest placement. Erin was pleased for her – she seemed to be getting on fantastically well.

The following morning, Erin was up at eight and polishing her sketches by half-past. At eleven, she set off for Broadcasting House.

Once she had handed her stuff to Gavin, Sarah invited her in for a chat. If Erin's radar was up to much, it was detecting a bee in Sarah's bonnet.

"Just to be sure, you did three Edinburghs?"

"Is this an interview?"

"I'm just making myself aware of the talent we have. It's part of my job."

"Yes, of course. Okay, I wrote three shows for Edinburgh, plus I've done numerous local am-dram productions."

"But you're not keen on working for more church panto outfits because they'd have you selling tickets?"

"That's not the half of it. One group asked me to sell the snacks and soft drinks too."

That evening, Erin and Trish went to a comedy club North London. It was to see comedian Joe Reece, who Erin had seen with Ian in a South London pub a while back.

Entering a half-filled room to the booming sound of "All Around The World" by Oasis, Erin coughed. Annoyingly, there were a lot of smokers in and the room was thick with smog.

The compere, a tall, angular man, opened with observations on the way women use their vaginas to wield power. Erin tried not to laugh as a point of principle, but the rest of the small crowd were well up for it. Five excruciating minutes later, the first act to be introduced was a nervous female comic. Erin prayed she would do a set about how men's willies controlled them. She didn't. Instead, it was five minutes about how sticking with horrendous dieting regimes led to bodily consequences. Unfortunately, she spoke too fast and rushed on from her punchlines as if fleeing the scene of a crime.

Following a second session from the compere – this time a fantasy concerning cocaine and porn stars – it was Joe's turn on stage. He opened with his New Year resolutions and how he'd failed to keep them. Erin found him funny in a warm way.

After the show, she made sure she got to him.

"Great set, Joe."

"Thanks."

"I was wondering if you've heard of a radio show called *It's News To Us*?"

"No, can't say I have."

Erin told him about the show and how it gave non-commissioned comedy people a chance to meet producers.

"It sounds like a good opportunity," he said. "I wonder why I didn't know about it. I only live across the park from Portland Place."

"Well, you know about it now."

He gave her his business card and jotted a few notes into the back of his gig diary.

"Thanks," he said. "I'll try to come along."

As he headed off, Trish nudged Erin.

"You do realize what you've done?"

"Invited someone to be another rival for the very thing I want?"

"I was going to say 'been really nice' but, yeah, that."

Friday morning, Erin was up at seven. Powered by coffee and choc chip cookies, she wrote up ideas for the upcoming potential *Comedy UK* slot. Then, after a toasted cheese sandwich lunch, she treated herself to walk around the Trafalgar Square area and a visit to the National Gallery. For the first time, she began to feel that London had room for her. That it didn't mind her presence. That it had something to offer her personally.

The evening saw her in the King's Arms with Trish,

Frances, Lucy and Mitch. It was a good night; friendly, with a fair bit of chatting with the other regulars. Of course, at ten to eleven, she had to rush off to set the tape running, and then rush back for a last drink.

Later, around one a.m., she listened to the end of the show.

"It's News To Us was performed by Brian Grainger, Hannah Dobson, Anne Garston-Green and Ben Tidy. It was written by Gavin Gould, Martin Dobbs, Shaun Donoghue, Simon Driver, Josh Steinman, Colleen Nicholls, Dave Singer, Erin Goodleigh, Jamie Strand, Paul Fielding, and Michael Holbrook. The producer was Toby Lock."

Was this really happening? Was she actually on her way to becoming a commissioned writer?

25. UNOFFICIAL

Erin arrived for the weekly non-comms meeting with a spring in her step. She hoped she wasn't being a show-off but it was hard not to smile when you'd had a sketch on the previous week's show.

Paul was in Sarah's office discussing something. He looked pleased too.

"All hail the successful writer," he said in a cod-Roman manner.

"I don't fraternize with rivals," said Erin, failing to hide her smile.

"Sarah's just told me the next commissions might be the end of March."

"Around that time," said Sarah. "Don't rely on early April to boost your minutes."

The end of March…

It bounced around in Erin's thoughts all the way to the writers' room.

"Hey, good to see you." The voice came from behind a body of writers.

"Joe, you came. Brilliant."

Erin was thrilled to have introduced stand-up comedian Joe Reece to the process. She only hoped he wouldn't have a miserable experience and hate her for the rest of his life.

Filing out after the meeting, Paul caught up with her.

"Lunch?"

"No, I'm off home to work."

"Okay. Are you here tomorrow?"

"Yes, why?"

"I might have something you'll be interested in. Can't say any more at this point. Waiting for someone to get back to me."

"Okay."

Later, at the grotto, Erin worked on her sketches until nine and then flopped onto the sofa beside Trish to watch TV. She was in bed by ten and asleep by five-past.

The following day, she was up early and worked on polishing her sketches until twelve. Up at Broadcasting House, she handed them in and went to lunch in the BBC canteen with Paul.

Sitting down to Mexican fajitas and chips, he seemed excitable.

"Right, so, I was waiting for Giles Sebright to get back to me. And he has."

"Great. Who's Giles Sebright?"

"Don't you listen to the radio?"

"Well…"

"He's in a sitcom called… it doesn't matter. The point is he said yes."

"Yes to what?"

"Honest opinion, Erin. Would you be interested, horrified or indifferent if I asked you to write for a pilot I'm making?"

Erin wasn't a hundred percent sure what he meant.

"When you say making…?"

"I mean we're recording a sketch show."

"Wow, sounds exciting."

"It's called *Real Britannia*. It's a kind of look at Britain without being strictly topical. More a spirit of the age kind of approach. The thing is I need more material. I can't guarantee it'll be used and there's no money even if it is, but... well, what do you think?"

"You mean everyone else has turned you down?"

"Bloody cheek. I'm fighting them off."

"Is there a deadline?"

"Yes, we're recording on Monday."

"Monday?" It didn't leave much time. Still... "Yes, I'd love to help. I'm not sure I can give you what you want, but I'd love to be involved. Thanks for asking."

"Great. I'll let you have a copy of what we've got so far."

"Okay to join you?" It was Sarah with a salad on a tray and a document folder tucked under her arm.

"Of course," said Erin. "Paul's got some exciting news."

"No," said Paul. "Sorry, Sarah, it's a state secret."

"No problem," said Sarah.

Erin didn't get it. Was Paul joking? If so, it wasn't very funny. But no, he wasn't joking. This annoyed her. Why couldn't Sarah be told about the pilot?

"Ever thought of applying for a trainee producer's job?" Sarah said to Erin.

"A what?"

Sarah recapped what she knew of Erin: her Edinburgh productions, her years of writing for am-dram groups...

"You forgot to mention directing, doing the lighting, marketing, producing flyers and selling the tickets and snacks."

"Then why not apply?" said Sarah, proffering a typed document. "The ad goes out next week."

Trainee Producer Role

We are offering a 12-month Trainee Producer contract to work in radio comedy production. You will work with established producers and have an understanding of comedy. You will be expected to take the initiative in spotting opportunities and making the most of your time with us. This is a creative role, so we are looking for someone to generate ideas and turn them into reality. There is no guarantee of a producer job at the end of the contract but, if successful, we will extend your stay with a view to a permanent contract.

Responsibilities

You will:
Attend production meetings and radio recordings, both to observe and assist.
Generate ideas and suggest comedy talent.
Learn editorial guidelines.
Learn to record radio and edit the content.
Learn about budgets, rights clearance and contracts

Erin was in a whirl. She had to stay focused.

"I can't, Sarah. I have to concentrate on writing. That's why I'm here. Besides, let's be honest, I haven't got that great a CV. Too long between the Edinburghs and *INTU*."

"Fair enough," said Sarah.

Paul's mobile phone rang.

"Hello?"

Erin ate while Paul seemed to be rearranging his life on the phone. When he'd finished, he looked agitated.

"The thing I was telling you about? It's not Monday, it's tomorrow. Can we talk later?"

"Okay."

After lunch, Paul gave Erin a photocopy of the script.

"A couple of sketches would be great. Just bring them along tomorrow night. We're meeting at six in the Crown & Sceptre."

"Okay."

That seemed odd. Surely, it would be wise to avoid the pub prior to recording a pilot.

The following day, just before six, Erin was bowling along Langham Street feeling very positive. She was about to be involved in the recording of a radio pilot. She still thought it a bit odd to meet in the pub though. Why weren't they meeting in Broadcasting House?

Reaching the doorway of the Crown & Sceptre, she peered inside. It looked quiet, except...

"Oh."

Erin had been wondering whether Paul & Alice would last, but it no longer mattered. Paul & Balcony Smoker Woman was definitely on.

What a rubbish time to for a reworking of Romeo and Juliet.

Well, he could stick his stupid pilot. *Erin Goodleigh has pride!* She began walking back to the Tube. Trish had said she'd spend the evening in front of the TV and record *INTU* for her, but that would have to change. She'd get Trish down the pub. She didn't need to be around a writer who openly behaved like a sewer rat.

She stopped. Wasn't she a writer too? It was hard to get away from that. And despite what Paul was up to, this was still an opportunity to learn something. Besides, it wasn't as if she'd returned to London because of Paul Fielding. She came back to make it as a writer. Paul was a mere footnote. She would do the pilot because her name would be in the credits as a writer. That was the business she was in. There was no room for sentiment.

She entered the pub and made straight for Paul and Balcony Smoker Woman. It was difficult to deny that she was very attractive.

"Erin hi! This is Sandy. She's our studio manager."

"Hi," said Sandy.

"Hello," said Erin, suspecting that she might have misread the situation.

"What can I get you?" said Paul.

"I'll have a sandy – *shandy*."

She smiled at Sandy. "So… have you known Paul long?"

"We met at the LE Christmas party. He said he was trying to get a pilot recorded and, well, here we are."

"Great," said Erin. It still didn't make sense though. If they were about to make a pilot for the BBC, what were they doing in the pub?

Sandy finished her drink.

"Right, I'll call you," she told Paul.

With that, she departed. Now Erin *really* didn't get it.

"It's okay," said Paul. "Sandy has to get a few things ready. No need for us to be there. Did you bring any sketches?"

"Three," said Erin.

Paul seemed happy with her efforts, but it was still a long half-hour before his phone rang. Ten minutes later, Sandy met them at the main reception and signed them in. They took the lift to an upper floor and strolled down an unfamiliar corridor.

"Here we are," said Sandy, showing them into a small control room. On the other side of the thick glass, a man and a woman sat chatting. Erin couldn't hear them and guessed it had to be a soundproofed room.

"So," said Erin, checking the front of her script. "Giles Sebright, Robin Storey and Karen Calder." She peered through the glass. They seemed to be one short.

Paul was on his mobile, looking concerned. A moment later, he put his phone away.

"Robin's been held up at a read-through in Teddington."

Sandy's sharp intake of breath didn't auger well. Erin didn't know Teddington but it sounded far enough away to be a problem. Still, she was impressed that Paul had got well-known radio performers. It felt like another world to find herself in a BBC control booth, script in hand, with professional actors on the other side of the glass.

"That's why we had to shift the recording date," said Paul. "Giles is busy on Monday."

Erin was surprised by that.

"Don't they sign a contract to commit to the show?"

Paul looked at her as if she'd suggested they all take their clothes off.

"It's off the record. Unofficial. On the quiet."

"I see," said Erin, wishing she could get a clearer picture of what was actually going on.

"Even their agents don't know, otherwise I'd have to shell out money. It's not easy doing a pilot for free."

"Well, almost free." Erin glanced around the room. "This can't be cheap."

Had she not known Paul, she would have said the smile that formed on his face was condescending.

"Erin, we're not paying for the studio."

"Oh, so the BBC lets out free studios. That's brilliant."

She understood it all now but couldn't work out why Paul's latest expression brought to mind someone having trouble training a chimp.

Then the penny dropped.

"Ohh... you mean the studio is unofficial too?"

"Bingo."

Erin was shocked. "You mean we're doing this at night because we don't have permission to use BBC property or equipment. Won't security find out?"

"No, he's reading a novel."

Erin felt uncomfortable. She also felt excited.

"We might be able to record some of it," said Paul. "While Robin's on the way."

"Where is he now?" asked Sandy.

"He hasn't actually left Teddington."

Sandy puffed out her cheeks. Paul looked crestfallen.

Just then, an idea began to form in Erin's mind.

"I've got the number of a good stand-up. Joe Reece."

"Get him," said Paul.

"Well, I don't know if he'll... but..."

She took her phone out, scrolled through to Joe's stored number and rang him.

"Joe? I wonder if you could help me..."

Twenty minutes later, Sandy brought Joe up from the main reception.

"I can't stay too long," he said. "I'm onstage in Camden at half-nine."

"No problem," said Sandy. "We'll have you back outside the building by half-eight."

"With taxi money," said Erin eyeing her bag.

"So," said Giles Sebright, "are we ready, London?"

"Are you ready, Britain?" said Karen Calder. "I worry about Chesterfield. Never ready."

Joe took his seat beside them in the studio, adjusted his microphone and eyed Erin through the glass.

"Are you a whirlwind in *everyone's* lives?" he asked.

Erin smiled but it didn't last. For some reason the performers kept chattering. Why couldn't they shut up while Sandy sorted out the equipment?

"Keep talking, guys," Sandy told them. "Still getting my levels."

"How *are* your levels?" said Karen.

"I've heard there are people one can see to boost one's levels," said Giles.

"Don't they have a place somewhere off Carnaby Street?" said Karen.

"See the writers for details," said Joe. "They're all members."

"And we're good to go, people," said Sandy.

She looked to Paul.

"Okay, guys," said Paul. "From the top, please."

"Liz, Liz, do the marines wear purple uniforms?" said Prince Phillip – or at least Giles Sebright said it, sounding uncannily like him.

"Phillip, one mustn't pry into one's son's clothing catalogues."

Erin laughed. Karen Calder *was* Queen Elizabeth the Second.

The recording went brilliantly and they were back in the pub by half-eight.

"That's a lot of effort, Sandy," said Erin over a drink. "For free, I mean."

"Not really. You guys are making a pilot for the BBC. So why not help?"

"Fair enough. It's just that the BBC didn't ask for a

pilot."

"If you wait around for the BBC to ask you, you'll never get anywhere. It's all about pitching. Not just to the BBC, but to everyone. Seriously, never stop pitching."

"Thanks, I'll take that on board."

"Best not go around telling everyone I worked for free though."

"No, of course not."

"We'll do the edit on Monday," Sandy added. "You should come up for that too."

"If Paul doesn't mind, I'd love to."

Erin left the pub at a quarter to eleven and got a train from Oxford Circus. While she daydreamed of a successful series, an elderly woman getting off at Baker Street discarded a paperback. Curious to know what an elderly woman would read – seeing as she'd be one herself someday – she tucked *The Cold Captain* into her bag.

Reaching the grotto at twenty-five past, she found that Trish had gone to bed. Up in the loft room, the cassette was recording. *Thanks Trish.* She increased the volume to catch a sketch about the royal family – quite funny. How many months would it be before her heart didn't thump so hard at such moments?

A minute later, the sketch ended and the credits theme tune came up.

Come on, Erin.

"It's News To Us was performed by Brian Grainger, Hannah Dobson, Anne Garston-Green and Ben Tidy. It was written by Gavin Gould, Shaun Donoghue, Paul Fielding, Martin Dobbs, Oliver Goldman and Joe Harrington, Colleen Nicholls, Michael Holbrook, Jamie

Strand, Simon Driver, Erin Goodleigh, Dave Singer, and Joe Reece. The producer was Toby Lock.'

Wow. She started to laugh aloud but stopped abruptly. She didn't want to sound like a gibbering idiot.

Later, in bed, attempting to calm her thoughts, she flicked through *The Cold Captain*. Lady Samantha Fanthorne, it seemed, was a lovely lass being constrained by the demands of her privileged life. The aloof Captain Stansbrook was definitely not the man to win her heart. Or so it appeared – because the captain's coldness was actually down to the loss of his fiancée to a wealthy London merchant while he was in France fighting Napoleon.

Erin imagined Paul as Captain Stansbrook. Yes, go on Paul... seduce Lady Sam. No, that wouldn't be right. She couldn't have Paul being unfaithful. Unless...

Erin became Lady Sam. *Now back to the story*. She read on for ten minutes. God, it was slow. She flipped to the end – happy together, good... she flipped back a chapter... and another. *Ah, the juicy bit.*

'Her eyes were limpid pools that reflected his passion. She could hold back no more. At last, she received what her entire being had long craved. His kiss was heaven.'

Kiss? Come on, Stansbrook, you're a bloody soldier. Get stuck in, man.

'I hope I haven't exceeded my welcome, my lady.'

'Captain Stansbrook, you will never exceed your welcome, because it comes from my heart.'

'Then I shall speak with your father and ask for your hand in marriage.'

Sam swooned, and so did Erin a bit. Could a woman ever ask for more? A true and great love had united the Fanthornes and Stansbrooks, and the workers on the estate would keep their jobs and homes. Erin turned the light off and settled down for the night. Lady Sam and Captain Stansbrook… Lady Erin and Captain Paul…

Maybe she wouldn't go straight to sleep.

26. A KIND OF DATE

It was just after nine on Sunday morning and Erin was trying to enjoy a lay-in. With the communal phone ringing down in the hall, she prayed it was for someone else and that they *would bloody well answer it.*

Someone answered it.

"Erin," yelled Trish. "Phone…"

"Great…" Erin got up, pulled on her dressing gown and headed down to the hall.

"Hello Erin, it's Mum. I didn't get you up, did I?"

"No, of course not."

"Now listen, I don't want you to overreact to bad news…"

Erin feared the worst. "No need to turn it into a drama, Mum. Just tell me."

"I've decided to hand the rest of your duties to Sharon."

"Is that all?"

"Is that all? That's your career we're talking about."

The call went on for a few minutes with Jenny trying to persuade her daughter that it wasn't too late if she acted swiftly and decisively.

"Well, thanks for letting me know, Mum. I'm glad you're well. I have to get dressed now."

"Alright, keep well. And think about what I've said."

A few moments later, back in the loft room, Erin flopped onto the bed and closed her eyes. There was something about a Sunday morning that—

The communal phone rang again.

Please God, not Mum again.

A moment later, Trish was calling up again.

"Erin, phone."

"Oh, for God's sake."

She went down to the hall and grabbed the phone.

"Hello?"

"Hello," said a familiar male voice.

"Paul?"

"I was wondering if you fancied coming out with the gang? We're going to a comedy pub not far from you."

"Sounds fun."

"We're meeting at five in Covent Garden, then it's up to Little Venice near you later."

"Okay, count me in."

"Great."

For some reason, the rest of the day passed at a glacial pace. Finally, at four, Erin grabbed a shower and a change of clothes. Then she tried to do something with her hair. Something weekend-ish that wouldn't look like she'd gone to a schoolgirl crush level of trouble. In the end, she was ready far too early, but walked very slowly to the station and let the first train go.

Just before five, outside Covent Garden station, she met Paul, Colleen Nicholls, Simon Driver, Shaun Donoghue and his girlfriend Lizzie. They went straight to a wine bar that gave Paul his usual problem. He was a two pints of lager kind of guy, so, seeing as they didn't sell draught beer, it was straight on to the stronger bottled stuff – except Erin intervened and persuaded him to drink chardonnay with her. Not being a wine drinker,

Paul was dubious – but he obliged.

"That's a first," said Colleen. "I've been trying to get him onto wine for ages."

"You don't get a beer gut with wine," said Shaun, patting his far-from-trim waistline. "Oh this? That's all pies and cheeseburgers."

The general chatter got noisier as they steamed through the first couple of bottles. By then, Erin wondered how things stood with Paul.

"So how's Alice?"

"Oh, you know. Gone."

Play it cool, girl. Do NOT make an idiot of yourself.

"Gone – as in gone?"

"Yes, how's Ian?"

"Oh, you know – never there in the first place."

"Right…"

Erin began formulating a plan along the lines of: *Do NOT be a desperate, instant Alice-replacement.*

The Covent Garden part of the evening continued to go well. Erin dipped in and out of conversations with the others, but kept a focus on Paul. And in those moments, they talked and talked and talked. She had never felt so comfortable with a man. Unlike Phil and Charles, Paul left spaces in the conversation and sought her opinions, thoughts and feelings. Before she knew it, it was half-nine and they were all drinking more wine in a comedy club above a pub in Little Venice.

"Having a good time?" asked Paul.

"You bet." And she wasn't referring to the comedy.

They left at half-eleven and headed for the little bridge over the canal. Erin loved the beautifully painted narrow boats that moored around the edge of the wide basin.

"It's so lovely here," said Colleen.

"It certainly is," said Erin. "What do you think, Paul?"

"I think… I shouldn't drink wine. It's strong, isn't it."

"Best not to drink it like lager," said Shaun. "Oh, too late."

Erin sighed. Paul was definitely drunk.

Just then, the others spotted a taxi and decided to go off somewhere in Soho. Erin thought it best to avoid that at all costs.

"I think Paul needs a walk," she said.

They all waved and yelled their goodbyes and then… silence.

"Come on," said Erin, leading him down the street.

"Are we going somewhere?" asked Paul.

"It's best if you keep walking. Trust me, I know."

They were leaving the rather nice Little Venice area behind and things were starting to look a little less inviting. It was the back end of Paddington and there was an elevated motorway above them. From somewhere nearby came the sound of a train and, just as she was thinking of turning back, the sound of a taxi coming up an unlikely slip road.

Could it be?

Another taxi came round and headed down the same slip road.

"You know what you need, don't you," she said.

"Oh I do, I do."

"A fried egg sandwich."

"Is that a euphemism?"

"No, it's a snack."

They walked down the gloomy slip road towards the railway.

"Actually, I really could eat a fried egg sandwich," said Paul.

"Good."

Erin tried to ignore the rubble piled up on either side

of the rough road surface. She just hoped they didn't see any rats.

"You did say a fried egg sandwich?" said Paul.

"Just keep walking."

It had to be right and yet it was beginning to look like a mistake. Had she got this wrong? Then, up ahead… a cab was coming along. They stood aside as it passed them on its way out.

"Not far now."

They soon reached it, just short of Royal Oak station, the cabbies' cafeteria by the tracks.

Erin gave a little "ta-dah".

Paul was amazed.

"How did you even know this place existed? This is like top, top secret London. Insiders only."

"I'm not fresh up from the country, you know."

There were only a couple of drivers inside, sitting over in the far corner. The man behind the counter explained quietly that it was for cab drivers only but Erin smiled pleadingly and he shrugged.

A few minutes later, they were enjoying steaming mugs of tea and hot sandwiches.

"It's been a lovely day," said Erin. "The conversation, the comedy, the company, the chardonnay."

"Please don't mention that last one."

"Just keep eating."

"You're right though. We need to do this more often. What are you doing tomorrow night?"

"Editing a radio pilot with some dopey writer."

"Oh yeah."

When they were ready to leave, one of the cabbies also got up. It was soon arranged that he would drop Erin off at the grotto and take Paul home to North Acton.

"I think I fancy you," Paul whispered as they neared

Erin's destination.

"We're too tired and it wasn't even a proper first date."

"I'm happy to tear up the rule book."

"Captain Stansbrook would never behave like this with Lady Sam."

"Who?"

"Oh, you're so uncultured."

"Don't you fancy me?"

"No, you're hideously horrible."

"What about we go out again. A nice candlelit dinner, very little alcohol…"

"That might be acceptable."

The cab pulled up at the grotto.

"Sorry I overdid it," said Paul. "I don't normally drink wine. Unless it's you I'm intoxicated with."

"Goodnight Paul."

She kissed him on the cheek and left. A few minutes later, she was in bed, falling asleep, very tired and very happy.

Monday was a quiet day. Lucy unexpectedly moved out of the grotto – she'd privately been waiting on a possible flat-share in Notting Hill to materialize – and it had. After Erin helped put her stuff into a mini-cab, she used the rest of the day to write up some ideas for *Comedy UK* and to mull over her Sunday with Paul. What exactly did the future have up its sleeve?

Around five, she headed into town. As arranged, she waited in the main reception to meet Paul and Sandy. As it was, only Sandy showed up.

"Paul's not coming," she said. "He was in an accident."

"What?" Erin felt an icy chill. "Is he okay?"

"A nurse phoned me. Paul says we should carry on without him. Do you want to edit?"

"No, of course not!"

27. OUT OF THE GAME

Having learned that Paul was in St Mary's Hospital in Paddington, Erin headed straight for the Tube. All the way there, a flurry of images assailed her. How badly was he hurt? How long might he be in hospital? The whole time, her anxiety was increasing.

At the hospital, with directions from a receptionist, she took a lift to an upper floor. She was soon standing at the foot of a bed containing The Mummy.

"How are you, Paul?"

Stupid question.

"Erin... hi."

"So, what have you been up to? Apart from playing the twit on a bike?"

"Bike?"

"Oh, I assumed..."

"Blimey, Erin. I had a massive hangover. No way would I ride a bike."

"Oh."

"No, I popped out this morning for some fresh air and I walked into a reversing van."

"Bloody hell."

"I remembered to look the correct way when attempting to cross the street... only I didn't think of a van reversing from the other direction into a parking space. All I could do was put my hands out."

"To stop it like the Hulk?"

"Yes, except it smashed both my wrists, whacked my head, knocked me over and cracked a couple of my ribs. But apart from that, yes, it was exactly like the Hulk."

"Not like the Hulk at all then, really."

"Well, I'll give you that I looked a bit green from all that wine."

"It's all my fault. I shouldn't have let you drink so much."

"I'm thirty-seven, Erin. I think we can agree it was my fault."

"So how long might you be here?"

"It's twenty-four hours observation for the head knock. Then I can go home."

Erin studied his plastered wrists. The casing went down to his knuckles meaning it would difficult for him to do anything with his hands, such as type his sketches.

"There's one obvious hand-related problem that springs to mind," she said.

"Yes, well, I've already spoken to my mum. She's ready to resume where she left off thirty-five years ago. I'm told I should be able to deal with matters myself soon enough."

"That wasn't the problem that sprang to mind. Although now it has, it won't go away."

"Right, so now that I've put you off your dinner...?"

"I meant writing. You can't use a keyboard."

"No, well... I'll be going back to Huntingdon for a few weeks, so..."

"You're not going to let it slide, Paul?"

"There are at least a couple of writers ahead of me and they'll probably only commission two."

"You don't know that."

"Don't worry about it. It's not important."

"Of course it's important."

"The pilot's more important. You should have edited the recording with Sandy. She's away for a few days now. Take her number off my phone. We need to put a tape into the next PDG."

As Erin did so, she wondered about March and whether Paul would return. Might they not see each other again?

"Hello darling," called a voice from the ward entrance. "What have you done to yourself?"

"Hello Mum," said Paul.

Erin turned to see a short, stocky woman in sensible clothing.

"How are you feeling, son? Is there pain?"

"I'm fine, Mum. I'm already full to the brim with pills."

"Hello love," said Paul's mum, finally noticing Erin standing twelve inches away from her.

"Hello."

"This is Erin, Mum. A fellow writer."

"Hello, Erin. So you're doing the same daft thing as him then, eh?"

"Um, yes, I guess so."

On the Wednesday, Erin arrived at Broadcasting House early for the writers' meeting. She had planned to check the list of leading non-comms while it was quiet but, annoyingly, Ian was in the LE reception area reading a newspaper. As soon as he saw her, his face lit up.

"Sitcom," he yelped. "Come on, let's walk and talk."

She followed him out into the main corridor.

"Shame about Evel Knievel," he said.

That infuriated her. "Paul wasn't actually on his bike and it's not funny to compare him to some crackpot stunt rider. Now what do you want?"

"Our sitcom. Any further thoughts about our female character and her peccadillos?"

"Look, to be honest…"

"This is a big opportunity for you. You don't have to go back to Taunton a failure."

"No, I could stay here and get my mum to send me money to keep me going."

His eyes – a flash of recognition!

"Being a writer has its up and downs, Erin. We can't all be writing for the top shows. But I'm on my way. I dispensed with parental support ages ago."

Bloody liar.

"Okay, Ian, I've got it. The perfect way to play it. You see, you've been getting it all wrong. You need to change the character. Make her someone different."

"Someone different?"

"Yes, there's a really juicy way of doing this."

"Yes…?"

"One that will be funny and so raunchy you'll have trouble controlling the contents of your pants."

"Seriously?"

"Yes, seriously."

"Go on then. Tell."

"Tell? Why would I tell you when I'm planning to co-write it with Evel Knievel?"

She headed back into LE. *Co-writing with Paul? Maybe I should have checked with him first.* She went straight to Sarah's office. Sarah wasn't about so she checked through the accumulated minutes. Michael Holbrook was first, Jamie Strand second and Paul third. Erin was fourth but only by thirty seconds.

After the meeting, Colleen asked Erin what she intended to do about *Comedy UK.*

"Not sure. I was meant to come up with some ideas with Paul."

"Why don't you team up with Simon and me? Paul can sit this one out."

"Um…"

"Give me your ideas tomorrow. I'll send them over to Callum with ours. They don't have to be polished. Callum just wants to be sure we have something worth working on."

"Right… okay."

Sorry Paul.

Erin went home and set herself a target of six sketches for *INTU*. Six *good* sketches. Nothing less would do. She got to bed at half-one in the morning.

Six hours later, she was up and polishing the sketches. Aided by tea, coffee, toast and chocolate hobnobs, she was finished before lunchtime. The final thing to do was type Paul's name at the top of two of them.

Monday the second of February was freezing. Erin's mum had phoned on the Sunday to warn her to wrap up warm, so Erin avoided the bikini and flip-flops her mum obviously thought she'd wear and went for three layers and a parka.

The failure to get anything on *INTU* had largely receded, fading slowly like a bad hangover. Paul had failed too, the twit.

She met Sandy in the main reception at Broadcasting House at half-six and they were soon ensconced in a warm editing suite listening to the recording. It sounded weird to be listening to something that had taken place under such different circumstances.

"Paul's original idea was for twenty-two minutes," said Sandy. "We've got thirty. What do you think?"

"Twenty-two."

"Right, well, this bit of waffle can go."

Erin loved how the technology had reduced the pilot show to a series of squiggly soundwaves on a timeline of 0-30 minutes on the top half of a computer screen. Sandy copied a small section of soundwaves near the start, dropped it into the bottom half of the screen and pressed 'play'. Now they were listening to a snippet of the show that they could mess around with.

Boring bits, delays and mistakes were thereby cut before the chunk was returned, slimmed down, to the main line at the top. They continued like this, gradually shortening the pilot, until they reached the end.

"Just over twenty-six minutes," said Sandy, pointing to the timeline.

They went through it again – but at twenty-five minutes, it was still too long.

"We need to cut a couple of sketches," said Sandy.

Erin had listened to the whole show a few times now. Her two sketches weren't the strongest.

"Take out my Buckingham Palace loft conversion."

Sandy did the necessary.

"Twenty three, just over."

"That's fine," said Erin. "Let's go with that."

I'm not cutting my other bloody sketch.

Sandy pressed some buttons and put a blank cassette tape into a machine.

"Can I say how nice it is to work with you, Erin."

"You too, Sandy."

Once done, Sandy retrieved the recorded cassette tape and wrote something on the label before handing it to

Erin. It read: Real Britannia – produced by Paul Fielding and Erin Goodleigh.

Erin felt ten feet tall… and slightly worried that Paul would think she was overstepping the mark.

It was eleven o'clock Tuesday morning and Erin was stepping off the train at Huntingdon station wondering how Paul was managing with his fractured wrists. The smallest room scenario reared its ugly head again.

Getting into a cab, the driver changed the cassette in his player. As the Bee Gees kicked off, Erin thought of the cassette tape in her bag. She had made copies on the multi-tape machine in the LE admin office but she was giving Paul the one Sandy had made. That way, if Paul got angry about her producer credit, she could point out that it wasn't her idea, or handwriting.

The cab soon dropped her at an unimaginative concrete block of 70s council flats that overlooked a large car parking area.

Ringing the bell of a fourth floor flat, Erin was struck by the sign screwed to the wall next to it: Home Is Where The Heart Is.

Paul's mum opened the door and smiled.

"Come in, love. He's just through there."

"Thanks."

"I'll put the kettle on."

Erin went through to a largish room, where Paul was on the sofa watching daytime TV.

"Erin, hi."

"Hello Paul. Feeling any better?"

"Yeah, not too bad. Good journey?"

"No trouble at all. I got a cab from the station."

"So what do you think of Huntingdon?"

"Er…"

"Yes, it is, isn't it? From here you get a good view of the midnight motorbike skidding championships."

Erin glanced out over the car park.

"Is that where you learned to ride?"

"No, we had a little house in Cambridge – until Mum and Dad split up. I came here with Mum when I was twenty." He lowered his voice. "And moved to London when I was twenty-one."

Erin guessed that Paul's mum didn't send him money.

"Right, well, anyway – the tape." She handed him the cassette, which he could just about hold. They could deal with any unpleasantness first. "You'll see the names on it."

As it was, he wasn't annoyed at all – he laughed.

"Yes, why not," he said.

"Tea or coffee?" came the call from the kitchen.

"Tea please," Erin called back.

Erin took the cassette and placed it on the coffee table. She then opened the "Get Well Soon" card she'd got and held it for Paul to read.

"That's very thoughtful."

"Shame about last week's *INTU*," she said, standing the card on the table. "Thinking about this week – are you planning to submit anything?"

"I don't think so."

"Have you got a cassette recorder? You could speak your sketches onto a tape. I don't mind typing them up for you."

"I'm really not bothered. Besides, I missed last week."

No, you didn't. Although you might as well have.

"Think about it," she said.

"I'll start again in April. Hopefully, they'll commission again in early July."

"No, you're good enough for March but you can't afford to miss any more weeks."

"No, really, it's impossible to think straight and I haven't kept up with the news."

Paul's mum returned with a tray of tea and biscuits. Erin was slightly disappointed to see three cups. The important stuff would have to wait for another time.

The following day, Erin went up to Broadcasting House for the weekly meeting. Before they got under way, she asked Sarah if it would be okay for Paul to e-mail his sketches in. Sarah was fine about it. She would personally print them off and hand them to Gavin. She said it was good practice as, after the next computer upgrade, it might be that all writers would be able to e-mail their sketches. Erin was wary. Non-comms needed to come in to the building.

After the meeting, she used Sarah's office phone to call Paul and tell him the news. Paul's mum helpfully held the phone for him.

"Thanks for that, Erin. Until the plaster comes off though, I really can't type anything up."

"I told you – I can type for you."

"Erin, no, it's not on. Get your own stuff on. That's your priority."

On Thursday, Erin found Gavin in a small office and handed him five sketches.

"Three from me and two from Paul."

"Great. How is he?"

"He's switching to lightweight casts next week. Almost back to normal."

"Fab. If there are any minor tweaks needed, I'll do them for him."

"Thanks, Gav."

Leaving the building, Erin walked up to Regent's Park. All the while, a question was burning into her brain. Why was she helping Paul? This was her dream. She had left a perfectly good life and career in Taunton for this opportunity. Had someone put it to her last April, before she first came up, that she would risk her future in order to help someone else achieve their dream, she would have laughed.

Late on Friday night, in the pub with Trish, she agonized over whether to listen to the show. But, at a quarter to eleven, she slipped away, put a cassette in the machine and returned to the pub.

Later, around one a.m., sitting on the end of her bed, she found the end credits.

"It's News To Us was performed by Brian Grainger, Hannah Dobson, Anne Garston-Green and Ben Tidy. It was written by Gavin Gould, Martin Dobbs, Josh Steinman, Phil Holston and Nick Ferris, Dave Singer, Oliver Goldman and Joe Harrington, Colleen Nicholls, Paul Fielding, Michael Holbrook, Joe Reece, Shaun Donoghue, and Simon Driver. The producer was Caroline Felby."

Erin was thunderstruck.

What have I done?

28. LOST VOICES

It was Monday morning and Erin was in the reception area at Television Centre in Wood Lane chatting with Simon and Colleen. At least a dozen other writers were loitering and every few minutes another one would come in and greet those they knew. The chatter between them was more subdued than normal, possibly due to the fascination with the large wall-mounted TV screens showing off the BBC's brand new 24-hour news channel. To Erin, it seemed weird that you could watch the news at any time of the day or night.

Before long, TV producer Callum Court came to collect them. They duly followed him upstairs and along a long circular corridor. She could see across an open space to the other side of the ring of offices.

"We call it the Concrete Doughnut," said Callum, indicating the design. "Whichever bit you're in, on whatever floor, it always looks exactly the same. New visitors have been known to go round several times and end up dizzy and lost."

They were soon seated in a large office, with Callum and two men standing at the front.

"Right," he said. "I'll give you the talk and we'll put you into a schedule for your location and studio time. Dave here is your camera operator, Sanjiv your soundman. Listen to them when you're filming. They know more about their business than you or I do. You won't meet the actors until nearer the time, but they're bright, they're young and they're prepared to work hard."

Callum went on to explain the health & safety rules that would apply and recommended retakes of anything that felt shaky. Dave and Sanjiv would be within their rights to call a halt at two takes if they thought it was without hope. Next, he drew up a schedule. Gavin Gould and Martin Dobbs would get first dibs. *What a surprise.* Erin, Simon and Colleen were allocated some location time the following Tuesday. That gave them scope to polish their ideas.

After the meeting, with Simon and Colleen heading back to Central London, Erin decided to do a location recce in Hammersmith. It wasn't far from TV Centre – as per the guidelines – and it felt like the kind of day to explore her roots once more. The gods must have agreed, as the weather was unseasonably warm for February, with the cold spell over and the temperature heading into the mid-teens centigrade.

She emerged from the Tube at Hammersmith with notes and sketches in her pad and a thought of popping in to see Elsie Haddon again.

At Brook Green, she found a bench and sat down to study the *Comedy UK* material she had been writing over the past month. Perhaps her barrister sketch might work on location, rather than in a studio. When you watched TV dramas, people often talked in the street or outside a relevant building.

She began reading her 'Lawyer' sketch.

LAWYER:
As an experienced lawyer, I can only suggest you brace yourself and prepare for the worst.

ACCUSED:
I see. So, I'm looking at fifteen to twenty then?

LAWYER:
Somewhere in that region. I can only advise that you try not to dwell on it during every waking hour. It'll be easier to bear in the long run.

ACCUSED:
Yeah... okay... okay.

LAWYER:
Good, that's my fee agreed then. Now, let's discuss your case...

Yes, that could take place outside a police station. *What else?*

She flicked back a few pages and found her summer music festival idea.

DAWN:
Apparently, it's visible from the Moon.

TINA:
What is? The Great Wall of China?

DAWN:
No, this queue for the ladies' loo.

Erin wasn't sure. How could they recreate a festival?

She flicked to the end of the sketch, where, after six hours of agony, Dawn and Tina find they're in the line for the burger van.

Erin put her notepad away and took out the *A to Z* map book. Five minutes later, she was with Elsie Haddon. She was keen to learn more of the Wednesday Club. Fortunately, it was a topic Elsie would have gladly talked about all day.

"What did you sound like?" Erin asked. "Are there any recordings?"

"No, but if you've ever listened to the Andrews Sisters…?"

Erin had to stretch her memory, but could recall some old black & white footage of the Andrews Sisters singing with Bing Crosby.

"Chatanooga-Choo-Choo, sort of thing?"

"Exactly that," said Elsie. She then launched into singing it for Erin. In fairness, she still sounded pretty good. It made Erin wonder what the other Wednesday Club singers sounded like.

On the Wednesday, Erin was up at Broadcasting House for the *INTU* meeting. While the commissioned writers were with the producer, she sat in the LE reception area thinking about the lost voices known as the Wednesday Club. Her thoughts were interrupted though – by Kirsty Gray coming in with Sarah.

"…writing and generally helping me," Kirsty was saying, "and of course they'll get a TV credit into the bargain."

Erin smiled. Kirsty hadn't been around in a while. Something to do with TV work.

"You know most of the regular writers here," said

Sarah as they headed into the inner sanctum.

Was this an opportunity being discussed? She followed and arrived at Sarah's office door just as they sat down.

"I couldn't help overhearing," she said.

"Hi," said Kirsty. "I remember you from the Christmas party. "Disco 2000" wasn't it?"

"Um, yes, it's Erin Goodleigh. I'm not recommending me though. I was wondering if you'd thought of Paul Fielding."

"Paul? Yes… Paul's good."

"I know there's a room full of commissioned writers over there, but Paul's as good as any of them. And he's off the bike for a few weeks."

Sarah explained Paul's predicament. Erin could sense sympathy in Kirsty.

"Paul… maybe… the thing is my dream job has turned into a bit of a nightmare. I just need someone to help me. The money's not great, which might put off some of the comms, but Paul… if he's off work anyway. Thanks Erin, I'll ask Paul."

"I've got his number," said Sarah. She handed the phone to Kirsty and flicked through her phone book.

As Kirsty made the call, Sarah addressed Erin.

"I wonder if he'll be up for working in Scotland."

"Scotland?" said Erin, an octave higher than normal.

"We're based in Edinburgh," said Kirsty.

Crap…

"Hello," said Kirsty into the phone. "Could I speak to Paul, please? Oh… oh right, no problem. I'll call back in ten minutes. It's Kirsty Gray calling from Broadcasting House. He'll know me. Thanks."

Kirsty put the phone down.

"He's just finishing up in the bath."

Just then, the commissioned mob came out of the

writers' room. In ten minutes, Erin would be in the non-comms meeting unable to listen in.

Grrr.

Twenty minutes later, Erin hurried out of the meeting and went straight to Sarah's office. She wasn't there. Neither was Kirsty. A quick check of all the other offices failed to locate either of them. Had Kirsty spoken to Paul? Had Paul said no? Was Kirsty now having an early lunch with another writer? What was going on?

"You coming to this?" asked Simon Driver, approaching.

Erin was standing outside producer Leanne Fuller's office where there appeared to be a meeting about to start. It was larger than Sarah's office, although having Leanne and eight writers inside tested its capacity.

"Coming to what?" said Erin.

"Just follow me."

Erin did so.

"Okay," said Leanne as Simon closed the door, "we have a new cast, but it's the same as usual on the writing front..."

As far as Erin could tell, she appeared to be in a show meeting. *INTU* heavyweight Martin Dobbs was there, as were Shaun Donoghue and Josh Steinman. There were some *Newslines* writers too.

"Martin will be script-editing, so feel free to run any ideas past him. Apart from Messrs Donoghue, Gordon and Carlin, I'll allocate any commissions based on how you do. Now can I rely on you guys? I need a commitment."

There was a firm muttering of commitment and Erin joined in, promising to give her all for whatever it was they were committing to.

"I want lots of funny sketches, okay?"

Okay.

"Okay," said Martin. "If I don't know you, see me with your details. Essentially, the first show goes out on Saturday week, so we're going with a Thursday five p.m. deadline. There won't be any feedback because it's quicker for myself and Jay Carlin to tweak as we go. Credit stays with you, the writer, of course. Sadly, there's no repeat fee but that's life. Are we all still aboard?"

"Yes," was the reply.

Yes, definitely, maybe. This ought to have been great – a taste of what it felt like to be a professional radio writer, even if you had no idea what anyone was talking about. But how could she fit it all in?

As the short meeting broke up, Erin gave her details to Martin Dobbs. She resisted the temptation to ask him what show she was signing up for as that probably wouldn't impress him on the commitment front. Instead, she waited until she was in the LE reception area with Simon.

"Have I just signed up for a satanic coven?"

"Kind of. It's *Game On.*"

Erin raised an eyebrow. Obviously, she wanted *Game On* to be the most famous radio show in the world, but right now, she couldn't quite recall having heard of it.

"It's a Radio Five sketch show."

"Er…?"

"Saturday lunchtimes?"

"Um…?"

"You mean you're serious about writing for a show you've never heard of?"

"Er…?"

"Welcome to the world of professional freelance writing."

"Is that right, we could get a commission?"

Simon brought her up to speed – explaining how it was a comedy sketch show based on the newspapers' back pages. Erin could foresee a slight problem in that she didn't really follow sport. Still…

Or would it make more sense to drop it and stick with *INTU*? After all, was she good enough to cover two shows with quality sketches written in the same 24-hour period? Well, at least she had a week to think it over.

The following morning, having been up until midnight writing for *INTU* until midnight, Erin spent a few hours polishing sketches. Then it was back to Broadcasting House.

There she found Sarah who confirmed that Paul was travelling to Scotland with Kirsty.

Great. I've helped them elope.

"Paul's also e-mailed some sketches in. He was curious to know how he got one on last week, when he hadn't submitted anything."

"Oh, um…"

Erin made her excuses and left.

Why do I always have to interfere!

She sneaked into Toby Lock's office and used his computer to gain access to the internet. Logging on to her e-mail account, she found one from Paul.

> Hi Erin
> Thanks very much for shunting me in Kirsty's direction. I owe you one. I'll be in touch again when I've found my feet.
> Cheers
> Paul

She replied with a simple 'no problem' then logged out and left the office. A moment later, as she pushed through the LE doors into the main corridor, Ian was coming down the stairs.

"Erin, have you heard? They're ending the show."

"What show?"

He stopped right in front of her.

"Your show. *It's News To Us.* They're killing it off. Interesting, eh?"

"Ian?"

"Yes?"

"Fuck off."

Before he could say another word, Erin stormed off. Not in anger, but in search of Sarah. She found her by the LE photocopier.

"Just an idea, Sarah, but are we completely limited to comedy here?"

"What's the idea?"

"I was wondering about a short documentary. Maybe a kind of 'Lost Voices of the BBC'.

"What kind of lost voices?"

"I'm in touch with a singing group called the Wednesday Club. They sang for the BBC during the War. From this building, in fact. They still meet and I thought it might be fun to do something."

"Talk to a producer of factual entertainment. They're around if you look. The canteen's a good place. Just ask around."

As it was lunchtime, she went up to combine work with a hot lunch. Joining the queue, she asked a few people if there were any factual people in. She was soon talking to a broadcast assistant, but it only showed Erin how little she had thought it out. Being asked what the Wednesday Club sounded like *now*, not fifty years earlier, made the idea seem amateur.

Eating alone, she thought about that. Was she basically still an amateur? Did she really have a chance to make it as a professional writer? Or would she be trapped in a hell of earning a bit of money here and there, a sketch on this show, a gag on that? It didn't sound much of a career.

The idea still resonated though. Whether she, Erin Goodleigh, stayed or not, this was a chance to capture something of the BBC's heritage. She'd already taken part in a guerilla recording with Paul and Sandy. She knew what to do. The time was coming when Broadcasting House would be closed for extensive renovation, or possibly even be knocked down and rebuilt.

She took out her mobile phone and called Sandy.

"Hi Erin, how's things?"

"Would you be up for another guerilla recording?"

"I'm not at Broadcasting House."

"Oh…?"

"I mean I'm still employed there, but I've been sent to TV Centre."

"Ah right, I didn't know. Sounds exciting."

"It is. We should catch up sometime soon."

"Definitely. And you don't get back to Broadcasting House ever?"

"Well… I didn't say ever."

29. CITY TO CITY

At the grotto, having made a cup of tea, Erin took to the lounge and fired up her laptop. There was rubbish on the table. The new guy – Giles – who had moved into the ground floor bedroom a few days ago was a man of mystery. Sleep and work. That was it. You only knew he'd been around by the rubbish he left in the lounge.

As Erin checked her e-mails, Frances came in.

"What do you reckon?" She was holding a smart woolly blue jumper and black leggings against her body.

Frances hadn't planned to do anything big for her thirtieth birthday, so her parents had stepped in with a family do at their place in Watford.

"It's perfect, Frances. Don't spill champers over it."

"Champers? We'll be lucky to have shandy. They're non-drinkers."

"Oh, right. Still, I'm sure it'll be a lot of fun."

"I've decided to have a massive booze-up tomorrow to make up for it. King's Arms lunchtime to oblivion. You up for it?"

"Now *that* does sound fun."

The grotto's phone rang. Erin went into the hall to answer.

"A fiver says it's for Mitch." His breathy new girlfriend had taken to calling hourly. No wonder he'd gone to a football match.

"Hello?"

"Erin? It's Paul."

"Paul, hi. Happy Valentine's Day."

"What? Oh…"

"So, what's on your mind? Apart from Valentine's Day."

"I didn't know if you'd seen my e-mail. Anyway, I just wanted to say thanks in person – well, via the phone. Did you know the job was in Scotland?"

"You must think I'm a complete twit. Yes, I knew the job was in Scotland. It's only for two or three weeks. Isn't it?"

"It's looking more like seven or eight."

Arghh!

"That long? Oh well."

"Yes, and we'll be hard at it the whole time. Work, work, work. Seven days a week. Madness, eh?"

"Yes… so where are you staying?"

"With Kirsty. She's got a flat in Gorgie."

Bow locks!

"It sounds lovely, Paul."

"It is – if you like it damp and dirty."

The flat or Kirsty?

"Clean is best, Paul. Clean and dry."

"Oh, it's not too bad. Kirsty's only just moved in and it needs a bit of TLC. It's not too bad for work either. The offices are in George Street, so we can walk it in half an hour. Bit of a nuisance having to pay rent on two places, mind, but I can't give up my flat in North Acton for a temporary job."

"I'm assuming it's two bedrooms?"

"What, here? Yes, it's two bedrooms. Otherwise, I'd be on the sofa – obviously."

Erin wondered about that.

The following morning, at around nine o'clock, Erin found herself at King's Cross Station.

This doesn't mean I'm going up there. That would be stupid. And a bit desperate.

She went to a ticket office window.

"Purely for information purposes – how much is a ticket to Edinburgh?"

"I can do you a forty-two pound fifty return."

"Wow, pricey. How long is the journey?"

"You're looking at about five hours."

"Five hours? That's a lot of looking out of the window."

"It certainly is."

"Still, I expect there's a lot of lovely countryside to see."

"Do you want a ticket or not?"

"Yes – why else would I be standing here?"

Erin bought a return ticket and boarded a train bound for Edinburgh Waverley. She would arrive there at 2.30 p.m. That gave her plenty of time to work out what she was playing at. It also gave her time to make serious inroads into the *Sunday Times* and think about life. Of course, she felt bad for missing Frances' birthday – the grotto's membership would be at the King's Arms as soon as it opened until somebody threw them out. *Lucky so-and-so's.*

Arriving in Edinburgh, Erin bought a cheap tourist map. She'd been a summer regular for three years but now it seemed a strange place.

Crossing Princes Street, she set off for Kirsty and Paul's office in George Street. In her heart lived a hope that a brilliant reason for being there would occur to her on the way.

Arriving, two choices cropped up: a) ring the doorbell or b), see if there was a back entrance with windows she could spy in through.

She eventually found a narrow little lane that ran behind the building. Paul said they were working seven days a week. If they were in there, she would...

Of course, she had no idea what she was doing, either in the lane or in Scotland generally. If ringing the front doorbell would be embarrassing, where did skulking in a back alley rank? No, this was madness. She would just have to go to the front door and pretend she'd come up to see an old friend or to scout out accommodation for a week at the Fringe in August or...

Her phone rang.

It was Paul's number.

"Hello? Paul?"

"Erin, we're in the same city."

She dropped the phone. It smacked onto her big toe then skidded into a shallow puddle – forcing her to kick it free before the water got in.

She chased after it, yelling.

"Paul, are you still there?"

She retrieved the phone and wiped it.

"Paul?"

"What the hell's going on?"

How...

Horribly...

Embarrassing!

"Okay, have your fun. All poke your heads out of the window and laugh."

"What? Look, I'm in London to get some of my stuff from the flat. I went up to Scotland direct from my mum's, so… anyway, I thought we could have lunch."

"Lunch?"

"Yes, lunch."

"No, we can't."

"We can't?"

"No. Sorry."

She ended the call and headed back to the station. This would take a bit of explaining. Either that or she could avoid the entire subject for the rest of her life.

30. INFORMATION

The first half of Monday morning seemed to have extra gravity. Yes, it was a time that traditionally bore down on people, but today it felt particularly onerous. It didn't help that Erin hadn't slept well, with scenarios of varying levels of awkwardness preventing her getting more than four hours. Maybe Paul had slept badly too. There were modern technological ways to find out, of course – assuming you weren't too embarrassed to phone or e-mail.

At eleven, she travelled up from Kilburn Park to meet with Simon and Colleen at Simon's flat-share in Willesden Green. With Colleen based in Neasden, Simon's place was pretty much the midway point. There they went through their material for Tuesday and Erin was pleased to get their approval for her summer festival sketch.

Later, back at the grotto, she shared with Trish her disappointment that Paul hadn't been in touch.

"I thought he might have e-mailed."

"What, to laugh at you for going to Edinburgh while he was in London?"

"No, he would never do that."

"What, not even a little bit?"

"Not even a little bit – although that would be because he doesn't know I was in Edinburgh."

"I thought you spoke to him on the phone. You said he asked you to lunch."

"Yes, but I said no and ended the call. I couldn't have him seeing me as desperate."

"Going to Edinburgh isn't desperate. Well, not *completely* desperate. Just e-mail him and say you'd love to see him."

"I can't. He's back in Edinburgh. It's not like I can go up there."

"But you already have."

"Yes, but he doesn't know that."

Trish puffed out her cheeks. "I give up."

The following day, Erin, Simon and Colleen met up with Dave the camera operator, sound guy Sanjiv and four young, aspiring actors at the BBC in White City. Producer Callum Court was also there to give them a quick pep talk before he waved off their BBC van.

"Remember, I want *your* take on comedy, okay?"

Then it was off to Brook Green in Hammersmith to shoot a few sketches.

The filming went too quickly and Erin worried that some of it was lost in the rush. Still, her festival sketch went well, with the open side door of the BBC van dressed with painted cardboard signs and a cardboard serving hatch to look a bit like a burger van. With a decent edit, it might yet be brilliant. One thing she loved was making decisions with Colleen and Simon. She half expected her mum to pop out of a bush with an authoritative *don't do it like that, do it like this*. Instead, a nod of approval generally greeted her suggestions.

Later, Dave, Sanjiv and the actors returned to TV Centre, while Colleen and Simon had a drink planned with friends in Soho. They invited Erin, but she wasn't in a drinking mood. Instead, she wanted to stay on in Brook Green and see Elsie to arrange the next Wednesday Club get-together as a rehearsal for a return to the BBC. Assuming they would be interested.

Later, at the grotto, Erin opened an e-mail.

Hi Erin,

Sorry about the no-notice lunch offer. I was in London and thought it might be fun to meet up. I'm stuck in Edinburgh now. They've seriously overloaded the schedule and are relying on a handful of low-paid people to deliver the whole bloody series. I'm currently a writer / runner / assistant producer / VT editor. Not really complaining. We're all in it to get our names on TV and because the series was half Kirsty's idea. Anyway, it's only another six or seven weeks.

Have fun,
Paul

She was pleased he'd got in touch. It was hardly Byron though and he'd failed to put an x after his name. Why was that? Was Kirsty getting those? No, that was uncalled for. She was just feeling frustrated that their relationship had stalled. Well, not stalled. You couldn't call a relationship stalled if it hadn't started.

She typed a reply.

Hi Paul

Regarding you asking me to lunch and me saying no. These situations often occur when a woman is dissatisfied with a man's tone or disposition or assumptions. However, it occurred to me (and Trish at least five times) that, on this occasion, it might be worth letting you know that when you phoned me in London I was in Edinburgh hoping to surprise you.

Yours sincerely
Erin x

Ps – You'd better not be laughing.

Thirty seconds later, she received a reply.

Hi Erin

Ha-ha-ha-ha-ha-ha-ha-ha-ha-ha-ha!!!!!!!
xx

*

Entering the LE reception area on Wednesday, Erin found Joe Reece with a large envelope.

"Ah Erin – just the person. I wonder if you'd might reading a sitcom for me."

"Me?"

"I'm looking for opinions from one or two people so I can polish it before I approach a producer."

"Joe, I'd love to. Thanks for asking."

Erin eventually attended two meetings: *INTU* and, straight after, *Game On*. Afterwards, she popped in to see

Sarah.

"Hi Sarah. Busy?"

"Afraid so. A ton of paperwork. You couldn't spare me a minute, could you? There's a fax coming through for me and I'm expecting a phone call. I need the fax for the call, but if I move…"

"The phone will ring. No problem."

In the admin office, Erin found the fax machine being used by Jodie, PA to Roy Dixon, the Head of Light Entertainment Radio. The heading on the top sheet of A4 tucked under Jodie's arm jumped out: 'Not For Circulation'.

Interesting.

A sudden need to reach for a new biro off the shelf along with a surreptitious head tilt enabled Erin to appear to be choosing between a blue and a black while taking in: 'This is to update Heads of Radio Departments and senior staff …' *something, something* … 'future of Broadcasting House.'

Very interesting.

With Jodie putting the document down to feed something into the machine, Erin got a further flash of words. In particular, 'Regarding new writers'.

"I don't suppose a fax came through for Sarah?" she asked.

"Yes, it's just there."

Erin picked it up.

"Thanks."

Wondering whether any of this would affect her own future, she raced to Sarah, handed her the fax, and then went back to spy on Jodie. A moment later, she ducked down by the photocopier as Jodie came along… and then followed her to Toby Lock's office. Along with Jane Clearwater, he was the most senior producer in LE.

Jonathan went straight in and came straight out again.

Once she had gone, Erin ambled by Toby's office. What would she say? Hi Toby? Did Jodie leave you a copy of a report just now? And did you know I work for a special BBC advisory body and need to approve the contents before you can read it?

Or maybe asking for a chat about sitcoms would be better.

She knocked on the door and waited.

There was no answer.

She went in.

And there it was.

This has to be quick...

Not For Circulation

This is to update Heads of Radio Departments and senior staff as to ongoing initial thoughts regarding the future of Broadcasting House.

The likelihood of extensive renovation works has moved a step closer and you should now factor in the closure of the Radio Theatre for a period of two to three years. Departments may have to be dispersed to other buildings, such as Henry Wood House and Great Portland Street while BH is closed. This means an end to series having 39-week runs, as currently enjoyed by *It's New To Us* and *Newslines*. This is all still under discussion, of course, but it is highly likely that twice-yearly six or eight week runs will be more practical for open-door shows.

Regarding new writers: It might be that the
new arrangements for e-mail submissions
could take over, with non-comms submitting
remotely. With recent IRA terrorist activity,
security is an ongoing concern. There are
early thoughts to installing reinforced glass
security screens during the renovations, with
pass-holder-only entry. With this in mind,
there is an idea being proposed to take new
writer access away from departments and
lodge it within a new postal and e-mail only
writing initiative.

Voices. Outside. Erin left the office, nodded to Sarah
talking to Jodie and nipped into the empty writers' room.
Were all the current non-comms effectively fighting over
a final opportunity for a commission? Was this a genuine
last chance? Like so many others, Erin had walked in off
the street; a complete no-hoper. There was no test to
pass, no exam to make sure you were the right quality, no
requirement to have a promising sitcom script that had
already been vetted. You just came in, mingled with
producers and tried to make some headway. How could
you do that by posting stuff in or sending an e-mail?

She didn't hang around. Instead, she bought a
sandwich and took it up to Regent's Park. Sitting on a
bench, she munched and wondered if she should e-mail
Paul with news of the confidential memo. But didn't MI5
monitor e-mails? What if they alerted the BBC? Would
that happen? Or was she confusing life with James Bond
movies?

Life…

What if she took an admin job in the West End or the
City? Her experience at GPL would stand her in good

stead. It wouldn't be too bad. She would continue to see Trish. And Paul, of course. She would have failed as a writer but she would be happy-ish. And who knows what the future would bring. She could continue writing as a hobby. And that might lead somewhere.

But wasn't that ridiculous? If she couldn't make it as a writer, there was a career waiting for her in Taunton.

Later, she e-mailed Paul with news that the show might be coming to a permanent end. He e-mailed back with a string of ungentlemanly words that would have made the secret service people blush.

With him in mind, she could see what was bugging her. If she wanted to stay on in London, she'd have to get a job outside of writing for radio and TV. A job with British Telecom, for example – a good employer with plenty of opportunities to climb the corporate ladder.

And if she worked for BT and stayed with Paul…?

If he succeeded, he would be living the life she came to live. And she would be right there, by his side, watching him live it.

Was that something she could accept?

31. WE'LL MEET AGAIN

Erin failed to get anything on *INTU* or *Game On,* but was pleased to hear Paul's name in the *INTU* credits. She could only imagine the hours he was working to keep everything going. It wasn't all bad for Erin, though – she spent the Monday in a BBC studio doing some *Comedy UK* stuff – and it was great to have Callum Court there watching her directing.

Also, Paul had posted her a first draft of a new sitcom he was writing with a request for her to give him feedback. She'd spent the day reading it repeatedly and her view was that it lacked a personality. Yes, it was very well structured and funny in places, but it felt a bit stilted, a bit forced. But how could she tell him? And yet, how could she not?

The weirdest thing was she really enjoyed the bits between readings, where she imagined being his co-writer... in Tuscany... soaking up the culture while injecting life into his characters. They would argue gently and then fall into each other's arms. And there would be romantic sunsets and Italian wine as they wrote a sitcom about a South London council worker who dealt with blocked drains.

Joe Reece, on the other hand, had written a dog's breakfast of a sitcom about a corporate events team. The structure was all over the place, but the main character was hilarious. With Joe, there were no dreams between readings. Just the nagging feeling that he and Paul might make a great writing team.

She talked to Joe after the *INTU* meeting and gave him his script back with a page of notes, although she left out the idea of him teaming up with Paul. He seemed genuinely thrilled that someone had taken time to give proper feedback. The other reader, whoever it was, had commented: 'it's great.'

No, Joe, it's not great. But it could be.

On Thursday evening, Erin arrived at the address in Chiswick Elsie had given her. It was a lovely detached house, possibly late Victorian, on a leafy street near the river. The lights were on in the downstairs bay window and she could hear the tinkle of a piano.

A thin, sprightly white-haired woman of Elsie's age answered the door.

"Florrie?"

"Yes, and you must be Erin," she said in a sing-song voice.

"I hope I'm not late?"

"No, bang on time, Erin. Do come in – Elsie and Davina are here."

Erin was shown into the lounge, where she was greeted by Elsie and an elderly woman at an upright piano.

"This is Erin," Elsie explained to Davina.

"Oh right. Hello."

Erin had been appraised of Davina's failing memory, but by all accounts she never forgot the music or words to a song.

"Well, I suppose we ought—" but Erin was cut off by Davina launching into 'We'll Meet Again'. She supposed Elsie or Florrie would bring her to a halt, but no – they joined in.

Erin felt odd. They sang beautifully, but it all seemed a bit strange.

Then she reminded herself this was their show.

The evening went well. Erin especially liked their renditions of 'Winter Wonderland' and 'Underneath the Arches', although all fifteen songs had charm.

At the end of the session, she wondered if they might forget the BBC and instead hire some recording equipment to set up at Florrie's. She was about to suggest it when Elsie interrupted the thought.

"We're more grateful than you will ever know, Erin. The thought of going back to the BBC to record some songs… it's energized us. Hasn't it, ladies."

There was an enthusiastic consensus.

"Well, that's fab, ladies," said Erin. "The BBC it is."

32. SERIOUSLY

A week later, Erin was having a good Wednesday. Having got a sketch on both *INTU* and *Game On* the previous week, and enjoyed a second rehearsal with the Wednesday Club, she entered the BBC as if she'd be working there for the next twenty years.

Sitting in the LE reception, skimming through a newspaper, she tried to filter out the noise of one newbie lecturing another about the terrible situation in Serbia.

The recipient of the broadside nodded politely, while Erin resisted the urge to state that *INTU* was a comedy show.

"We need to be more vocal," the newbie went on. "Summary executions, innocent people dying, more to come. I was thinking *It's News To Us* could do a special, you know, looking at the whole post-Yugoslavia situation."

Erin cringed. *Seriously?*

"You should raise it in the meeting," she suggested.

After the meeting, in which Gavin expertly derailed the idea of a post-Yugoslavia half-hour special, Erin checked the writers' league table. She was fifth. Paul was third.

*

The following Wednesday, Erin was humming Madonna's "Frozen". Having got a sketch on *INTU* the previous week, she was in a good mood.

Sitting in the LE reception, skimming through a newspaper, she nodded to a new female face.

"First time?" Erin asked.

"Yes."

Erin wanted to give support and tips, but she just couldn't raise the energy required. She wasn't going through all that with every writer who showed up – not unless they showed some backbone and toughed it out for a few weeks.

Still...

"Whatever happens this week," she found herself saying, "make sure you come back next week. It's all about staying power. This show may or may not be here in the future, so try to connect with a producer and hang on."

"Thanks, I will."

After the meeting, she grabbed Joe Reece for a quick catch-up.

"How's the sitcom going?"

"Oh, not so good. I've tried moving scenes around but..."

"You know Paul Fielding who did the pilot you starred in?"

"Yes, he's working on a TV show in Scotland – which is clever, because he still gets his name in the *INTU* credits most weeks."

"He is clever. He's also very good at sitcom structure. If you like, I could have a word with him. He might say no, but I think you should consider co-writing with him."

"Seriously? I don't know... I mean I'll think about it. Thanks, Erin."

The following day, after Erin had handed in sketches for *INTU* and *Game On*, she popped in to see Sarah.

"Hi Erin. How's it going?"

"Oh, you know… I'm getting stuff on but I can't see me getting a commission."

"Never say never."

Shaun Donoghue appeared in the doorway.

"Erin? Fancy a gig tomorrow? No guarantee of being paid but I'm short of a Colleen Nicholls for *It's Not Who You Know.*"

"Seriously?"

"She's unavoidably busy and we're close to getting aboard the commissioned team. It's just for one week but it won't do you any harm."

Erin was delighted. It was a chance to write gags for popular entertainer Bob Coates' ITV show.

Erin met up with Shaun the following morning outside a glass-fronted office building off Tottenham Court Road. He signed her in then they waited for a lift.

"There's an area at the top of the atrium where the smokers go. Bob spends most of his time up there."

The lift whisked them to the top of the building, where they stepped out onto a terrace under the huge glass roof. Bob Coates was pacing up and down, smoking and looking nervous.

"I think something bad has happened," said Erin.

"No, he always looks like that. He hates performing to an audience. It makes him sick."

"But he's really good at it."

"I know. Now shush. Bob! Hi! I've brought Erin

Goodleigh along. Colleen's working with Hat Trick today."

Bob mumbled something and lit a cigarette.

"Go and see Jimbo," he said. "I need gags."

They returned to the lift and headed down a few floors.

"You're in," said Shaun. "He can't have anyone strange in the office during the meeting. He gets twitchy."

Fifteen minutes later, they had a show meeting. Erin felt at home, as it was just like an *INTU* or *Game On* meeting, with a script editor telling them what was required. Only here, you didn't go away afterwards to write. You stayed.

After the meeting, with script editor Jimbo's guidance fresh in mind, Erin sat beside Shaun at a desk in a corner. Bob Coates wanted topical gags to launch the show. They would spend the day providing them.

Just as they got started, Jimbo came over to ask if Erin was okay.

"Yes thanks."

Jimbo smiled and leaned in close.

"Don't trouble yourself too much," he said.

Erin didn't get it. What did he mean? Was he requesting her to look crap in front of everyone so that she wouldn't be invited back? She was only there for one bloody show.

"He's a ladder up man," said Shaun, once Jimbo had gone. "Hates the thought of other people getting a chance to nick some of his airtime."

"Bloody cheek."

That night, Erin went out and partied with Trish, Frances and Mitch plus his new girlfriend. They ended up in the

West End so she missed the chance to record *INTU*.

On Saturday morning, nursing a slight headache, she tried to take stock of the situation. If she was honest, Paul was the only factor keeping her in London and they had no actual relationship. Yes, he'd be back soon but she would be a non-comm in a world where non-comms struggled to get access to anything. Firing up the laptop, she checked her e-mails.

> Hi Erin
>
> Fancy lunch on Sunday? My treat, and I'll do all the travelling. All you have to do is say yes.
>
> Yours
> Paul in Scotland x

She replied straightaway.

> Hi Paul
>
> Yes.
>
> Yours
> Erin in England xx

At twelve, she listened to *Game On*, where she scored a sketch, then, at one, *INTU*, where she scored another. *Double-bloody-yes!* Later, she watched the opening of Bob's ITV show, where she and Shaun scored two gags.

Was she actually going to make it as a writer? Or just go insane?

*

On Sunday, she met Paul at King's Cross Station. He looked tired.

"I thought we'd get a cab up to Hampstead. If that's okay with you?"

"Isn't the BBC canteen open?"

"Seriously?"

"No, not seriously."

"Good, because I was thinking more a nice little pub. Just two friends having Sunday lunch."

"Hang on, you mean we'll be going somewhere without loads of other people coming with us. Sounds a bit like a date."

"Yes, it does, doesn't it."

Twenty minutes later, they were sitting at the bar in The Spaniard's Inn.

"It's lovely, Paul. It seems really old."

"It is – sixteenth century. It's mentioned by Dickens in *The Pickwick Papers* and Keats wrote *Ode to a Nightingale* here."

"You certainly know your history."

"It's written on that sign behind you."

Erin laughed. "It's really lovely. Thanks for bringing me."

"I just thought it would be nice. You know, two writers trying to make it in the big city. Well, different cities."

Erin looked around. "Unlike the good folk of Hampstead who don't seem to be struggling at all."

"It's one of the most expensive parts of Britain. It's like living in the Cotswolds but you're only a short cab ride from Central London."

"Will we see Hampstead Heath?"

"We're on top of it right now, but if we walk a little way, there's a really good place to look out over the whole of London. You'll love it."

They enjoyed a good pub lunch and talked about writing, hopes and ambitions. Then, half an hour after they'd eaten, they ventured outside. It was only a short walk to reach the green heath and its breath-taking views over the capital.

"Can we see Hammersmith from here?"

"Not really – it's a fair way over there," said Paul, pointing to the right. "Didn't you do the *Comedy UK* shoot there?"

"Yes, I've been there a few times, looking for memories."

"Did you find any?

"A few. The first time I went, I found my old primary school."

"That must have been weird."

"It's funny looking through the gates into the playground. It's like imagining ghosts still playing there. *I am the Lady of the Lake; these are the actions I must take*."

"Sounds like an old skipping song. I bet you can't remember the rest."

"Salute to the General; Bow to the King…" Erin felt warmth surge through her veins. *"Kiss my true love; Wear his ring."*

High on the heath, in the breeze, she felt like an ancient Olympian looking down over the metropolis. She just hoped she wasn't blushing.

"Oh, I'm also going to do a guerilla recording," she said.

"Really?"

She told him of Elsie and the Wednesday Club. He laughed, but in a nice way.

*

Later, at the grotto, Erin reported to Trish.

"It was really nice. We had a lovely lunch and a stroll to the heath. Then, back at the station, we had a little hug and I got a kiss. What do you think it means?"

"Well, Erin – there's a guy who spends five hours on a train, has lunch with you, then spends another five hours on a train going back. That's his entire day devoted to having lunch with you. *What the hell do you think it means!*"

"Seriously, Trish – I'm thirty, not thirteen. I just don't want it to go wrong, that's all."

"It won't."

33. ADVICE

Erin entered Broadcasting House on the Wednesday humming Celine Dion's "My Heart Will Go On". Reaching LE, she was disappointed to find that none of the newbies had stayed the course. Naturally, there were a few *new*-newbies – they would continue coming through the doors for one or two shows until the Universe ended. Or at least until they closed Broadcasting House.

She checked the non-comm writer standings. Her sketch had been short, meaning she was still off the pace in the race for a commission.

Oh well.

The commissioned writers' meeting finished and Shaun Donoghue and Colleen Nicholls came along.

"Thanks for last week," said Shaun.

"No problem, I loved it. Well, sort of liked it."

"Spend it wisely," said Colleen.

Erin supposed she could make those sorts of contacts, given time. The word was that Shaun had been on the case for over a year. He deserved a TV commission where you could start to earn real money. Erin hadn't enjoyed it at all. It was a bunch of men trying to out-gag each other to please Jimbo. Colleen must have grown used to it.

After the non-comms meeting, Erin came across Ian

in the LE reception area.

"I hear you got some gags on Bob's show," he said.

"Well, two gags, co-written with Shaun. Listen, my little outburst that time…"

"All forgotten, Erin."

"Well, it shouldn't be. Not the rudeness, but… Ian, I don't speak for all women, but some of us would like you to take a step back. You know, to give us room to breathe."

"I wasn't aware…"

"Don't say anything. This may only be me, but I get the impression you crowd in on women. I have to tell you it's a deeply unattractive trait. Just stand back a bit, try to listen and, well, who knows, it might change your life. It would certainly improve things for any woman working with you."

"Right. That's um…"

"It's called advice, Ian. Try taking it."

Later, back at the grotto, she checked her e-mails. There was nothing new, so she read Paul's e-mail from late on Sunday again – for the umpteenth time. And her reply to him.

Hi Erin

It was great to see you earlier. I hope you had a lovely time. You seemed to be enjoying yourself. We should do it again.

Yours from the North
Paul xx

Hi Paul

Thanks for getting in touch. You must be
tired after all the travelling. Yes, I had a really
lovely time and would definitely love to do it
again.

Yours from the South
Erin xx

They were two lovely e-mails. If only she didn't have a
nagging doubt about which way her future should be
going. On the plus side, he was offering another date. On
the minus side, she had come to London to be a
successful writer and it looked as if that wasn't going to
happen. Could she stay as a bits and pieces writer? Paul
was doing well enough to get a commission. Would that
be the thin end of a wedge between them?

The following Wednesday, having failed to get anything
on *It's New To Us* or *Game On*, Erin sloped into
Broadcasting House wondering when they would knock
the bloody place down and put everyone out of their
misery.

In the meeting, Erin got the distinct impression that
Titanic winning a million Oscars would lead to an
explosion of spoof sketches. She thought better of
attempting one. Why compete with thirty others?

That evening she wrote three sketches for *It's New To
Us* and three for the final show of the current series of
Game On.

The following day, as she handed her sketches in,
Game On producer Leanne Fuller came over.

"Well done this series, Erin. Sorry I couldn't give you

a commission. It was ever so close. Do try again next series. I'm sure you'll crack it."

"Thanks Leanne. That's really encouraging. When is it?"

"October."

"Right… great. Thanks."

October… six months away.

As she watched Leanne disappear down the corridor, Joe Reece caught up with her. He was waving a script.

"Me and Paul have been e-mailing."

"Oh?"

"It's the opening of a radio sitcom. See what you think."

"Okay."

Erin took a seat in the writers' room and had a look.

NEW IMPROVED RADIO
PAUL FIELDING & JOE REECE

GRAMS: "Dies Irie" from MOZART'S
REQUIEM.

NARRATOR:
The place, Broadcasting House. The time, several years into the future… and if you're listening to this on a cassette tape several years after the original broadcast, it's still set several years into the future otherwise this episode doesn't work. Now, if I'm not mistaken that's young Chris Junkin, staff writer, entering the building.

GRAMS: OUT
F/X: ATMOS. BUSY RECEPTION AREA.

CHRIS:
Mornin' Fred.

FRED:
Oh, mornin', Mr er... erm...?

NARRATOR:
Yes, popular, well-known Chris makes his way to
Light Entertainment, which has been tasked with
making the middle classes laugh into their tofu.

Erin read on… and quite liked it. Especially when the
characters learn Radio Four is to be rebranded Four Play.
Yes, it needed polishing, and yes it needed a few extra
gags, but it had a good structure, good pacing and
characters you could follow in a radio comedy. Maybe
this wasn't the worst place in the world to get involved as
a writer.

It also crystallized her own take on writing sitcoms.
Maybe she too needed a co-writer. She loved sitcoms, no
doubt about that, but writing them solo…?

A bit later, instead of giving feedback, Gavin alerted
her to the fact that producer Toby Lock hadn't picked
any of her sketches.

Oh well, no need to listen to INTU then – like, EVER!

She bustled out of the building and came to a halt.
Watching the heavy traffic crawling by, she tried to make
sense of her situation. Maybe she would get something on
the final *Game On*. But did that matter? Would that
change anything? Unless you became a TV regular, being
a paid writer was a giant-sized pain in the backside and
she'd had enough of it.

Back at the grotto, she phoned Dad. It was his
birthday and probably the one time of the year Mum

wouldn't grab the phone off him.

"Hi Dad. Happy birthday. The doctor says you're in perfect shape for a man of seventy. Shame you're only fifty-eight."

"Very true, Erin. How are you?"

"Oh, not so bad. It's all the usual stuff this end. What about you?"

"I'm just back from a trade fair in Birmingham. I've heard through the grapevine about an American firm that sells books and CDs online. Amazon, they're called. It's starting to boost the packaging industry over there. Whether it catches on over here, of course... I'm not sure I see people abandoning bookshops and record stores."

"You never know, Goodleigh Packaging could become a huge multi-national."

"I doubt it, but I'm putting plans in place so that we move ahead of the competition if anything develops."

"You're a wise man, Dad."

"So how's the writing going? Any more TV work?"

"No, although there are other shows that accept gags. It's just a worrying way to make a living. You must have had that back in London, when Mum was acting."

"True."

"Just tell me this one thing – how good was Mum when she was a young actress? I mean really. Like, not what you always say, but the truth?"

"What's that, Erin? There's some crackling on the line. I can't quite hear you."

You should join TADS. You're the best actor of them all.

"Mum's a lucky woman, Dad."

Later, in the pub, Trish was talking of the future. She was getting good signals from the school where she was placed as part of her training course – but taking a permanent job there once she qualified would mean leaving the grotto. That said, she had already made enquiries about renting a two-bedroom flat in Neasden that was currently being refurbished.

Erin was also wondering about the future. Only she couldn't see which way it was leading.

"What do you think I should do, Trish?"

"Tough question. You seem to want a career that's just out of reach. What you do have is the chance of a good relationship with Paul. He'll be back from Scotland next week."

"If I stay in London I'll have to get a job outside of entertainment. I know I could write amateur drama and non-commissioned novels, but that's not why I left Taunton."

"Yes, but you'd be with Paul."

Erin coughed. There were too many smokers in the pub tonight. Her clothes and hair would pong.

"Madonna's new stuff is good, isn't it," she said. The CD player was halfway through the *Ray of Light* album. "I read somewhere she's working with William Orbit."

"Erin, just wait till Paul gets back and you two can have a nice long chat."

"That's the problem. If I see him I'll want to stay – which is nuts because we've only had one proper date."

"Go on another one then."

"Trish, as it stands, I've got no job and I can't afford to live in London. That's why I'm acting like a clueless teen student, not because of Paul."

"You'd be fine if you got some office work."

"Look, if I stay here, and if Paul turns out to be the man I know he is… I'll be in a relationship with someone who is constantly meeting up with producers and successful writers. It will be in my face, day after day, reminding me that I'm a failure."

"You're not a failure."

"I am. I came to London to achieve one thing and I failed."

"There must be a way out," said Trish, seemingly looking around for one. "I mean Paul's not going to relocate to Taunton, is he."

"Of course not. He's on his way to commissions and contracts. He'll probably get an agent soon."

"What are you saying then? That you'll forget about Paul and go back to Taunton?"

"I really don't know, Trish. I wish I did."

34. THE RECORDING

In Portland Place, outside the side entrance to Broadcasting House, Erin held the taxi door open and helped the Wednesday Club singers get out. She supposed it would have been a more dignified exit back in their heyday, but no matter. They were here now – albeit forty minutes late. For some reason, they were dressed extravagantly, as if they might be about to step onto a West End stage.

"Sorry we're so late," Elsie began, but Erin was more concerned with getting them to the door where Sandy was waiting and checking her watch.

"We seem to have pulled up short," said Florrie. "The main entrance is a little farther on."

"We're not going in through the main entrance," said Erin.

"Are you sure?" said Elsie. "It took us three hours to get ready."

"Yes, we're dressed for the main entrance," said Florrie.

"Sorry ladies, this is strictly a side door operation," said Erin, aware of Sandy's growing frustration.

"Is this where bombs fell?" said Davina.

"You're quiet safe," said Elsie.

"I really have to go in five," said Sandy, approaching

with a pained expression.

Erin thanked her and kept the introductions brief. Having spent an age waiting with her, Erin was aware that Sandy was assisting with a recording at a Soho studio half a mile away and had only slipped out for half an hour to help Erin. She had also made it known that she had to be up early the following morning for a recording in Manchester.

"I'll just set you up, then it's over to you," she insisted.

Erin was in no position to argue. She could see she had asked too much of Sandy, and had stretched their friendship too far.

Up in the studio, Sandy set up the equipment and established the recording levels for each microphone.

"Okay, it's all yours," she said. "Have fun."

"Thanks Sandy. I owe you big-time."

Once things had settled down on the other side of the glass, Erin began the recording with a brief recorded introduction.

"This is recording number one. The Wednesday Club Singers produced by Erin Goodleigh."

"You'll have to do better than that, Erin," said Florrie. "It was hardly Bruce Forsyth introducing someone at the London Palladium."

"It's just a studio recording," Erin insisted, before nudging the singers into action.

With Florrie at the piano, they began with 'Boogie-Woogie Bugle Boy'. After that, Erin relaxed. These ladies knew their stuff.

With five songs recorded and one to go, there was a knock at the door. Erin tensed up. Although… maybe Sandy had come back.

She opened the door to a man in security attire.

"Sorry to interrupt," he said, "But I don't have any

evening studio use on my list."

Erin stared at him with her best expression of innocence.

"List?"

"Yes, we've had a growing number of unauthorized recordings – hence the evening usage list. Only, there are no studious booked out for this evening."

"Ah right, I think there's been a mix-up." Erin fought to put some words onto her tongue. "Um, this was meant to be booked for a few weeks' time, only we had to change it at the last minute."

"The best I can do is ask you to phone the Head of Studio Services and get them to phone me with authorization. There's a phone there you can use. I don't mind waiting."

Erin turned to the phone at the back of the control booth and felt the game was probably up.

"Let's not worry about that," she said. "We're pretty much done here. I'll book another slot if we need to do more."

Switching the equipment off, she wondered how she'd get access to the master recording so that she could edit and produce some cassette tapes. After all, the ladies would want one each, and she'd need to hand one to a factual entertainment producer along with the pitch for a radio documentary.

The following day, Erin was in Broadcasting House for *It's New To Us*, and to wander up to the recording studios. Only, there were men in overalls at work.

Erin tried to take it in. Equipment was being taken out.

"What's going on?" she asked.

"Speak to your boss," one of the men suggested. "The notice went round a couple of days ago."

"Where's the equipment going?"

"Into storage, for now. There'll be some re-use at Great Portland Street and Henry Wood House."

It seemed that, gradually, the closure of Broadcasting House was already underway.

Erin used a BBC phone to call Sandy's mobile.

"Hi Erin, did it go alright?"

"Yes and no. Did you know they were going to move equipment out? The studio we used is practically empty."

"No… no, I didn't. To be honest, I've been so busy at TV Centre and in Soho… and I'll be in Manchester for six weeks."

"What about the recording?"

"They'll probably wipe everything. Sorry."

"Ohhh… it's my fault, Sandy. Too pushy. Oh well."

"Maybe you could hire a private studio?"

"Maybe – but I think the BBC was a big thing for them."

Erin phoned Elsie. Before she could get to the point, she learned that Davina had been taken ill. Too much excitement seemed to be the consensus.

"Thank God you captured it all, Erin," said Elsie.

35. A LAST DITCH PLAN

Erin wondered if it really was a Friday, because she certainly wasn't getting any of that Friday feeling. She'd had better Mondays with root canal treatment thrown in. Having bid everyone at the grotto the heartiest of farewells, she was making her way to the Tube hoping she'd soon feel better.

The only people she hadn't contacted were Elsie and Sarah, the latter being on assignment at TV Centre in White City. Erin worried that Sarah might make her re-examine her decision, so had decided to give her a call from Taunton. As for Elsie, she too would receive a phone call from Taunton, as Erin simply couldn't face seeing her in person with bad news.

As she reached the station at Kilburn Park, her phone rang.

"Hello?"

"Erin, it's Sarah Bryce."

"Hi Sarah. I was just thinking of you."

"Fancy lunch?"

"No, I'm travelling today."

"Paul said you were going back to Taunton. Is that happening as we speak?"

"Yes, I thought it best to e-mail him. You know, in case he had the police dragging the Regent's Canal for a body, kind of thing."

"He's asked me to stop you."

"Sarah, the whole thing… it's been a great ride, but I've run out of rocket fuel. I particularly wanted to say thank you to you. You've been completely brilliant."

"Oh Erin…"

"Say thanks to all the producers I worked with and to Gavin too, bless him."

"Look, why don't you pop over for lunch? We could catch-up and maybe find a way—"

"No, I need to get going."

"I'm at TV Centre all day. If you want to talk, just come over and ask for me at reception."

"Thanks for everything, Sarah. You're a star."

While Erin waited on the platform, her phone rang again.

"Paul?"

"Where exactly are you?"

"I'm getting the Tube to Paddington."

"I want to see you again."

"I'm going home, Paul. You know that."

"Plans can change, Erin. For example, I swore I'd never call someone's mobile phone at a pound a minute."

"Paul…"

"I'm stuck in final editing. There are four of us putting together a whole bloody series. I can't leave yet. I can't let them down. We'll be done on Monday. We have to be. That's the Channel 4 deadline. I'll be back on Tuesday. At least stay until then."

"I'm sorry, Paul."

Erin ended the call and boarded a Bakerloo line train.

At Paddington, for some inexplicable reason, she failed to get off. She carried on until Baker Street, where she switched to the Circle Line for King's Cross. It felt as if she might get a train up to Edinburgh, although the logic of it escaped her.

Somewhere between Great Portland Street and Euston Square, things clarified once again. Paul would be working flat out to get the show finished. It wasn't the right time or place for a long chat about the future.

Crap…

Sitting opposite was a young man in a smart outfit. She had seen him before somewhere… On Day One, a whole year ago. The advertising interview guy. Or had she dreamed that?

Eye contact.

She looked at the floor. What an adventure it had been. She'd come to the big city to be a successful writer. She'd risked her stable life for something she had wanted so badly. And now?

And now she had failed.

She got off and crossed over to the opposite platform. A few minutes later, she was on a Circle Line train heading back to Paddington. Taking a seat, time seemed to stand still as a myriad of scenarios flared and faded. Yes, she could have stayed and got an office job. That would have helped Paul. Assuming she and Paul were living together. But the other option, to go back to Taunton and have a settled life, surely that won hands-down. If Paul wanted to be with her, he'd come down to Taunton. Okay, so he'd be compromising his writing career, but he could carry on creating sitcoms and sending them off to London. Moneywise, he could take a job at Goodleigh Packaging and… no, he would never leave London.

The thoughts continued to tumble, over and over…

Oh crap!

She'd missed her stop.

She sat there, somewhat defeated.

Death take me.

She read the stations on the map above the seats opposite. The next stop was Royal Oak. As the train slowed, it passed alongside the cabbies' retreat. She recalled a midnight sandwich there with Paul. God, had he not been so drunk that night…

If she stayed on the train, she'd reach Hammersmith. Childhood memories stirred. A skipping game. Silly songs in the playground. And stories by a fireside with a soothing voice reading *Winnie The Pooh*. Elsie's voice.

No, the past was gone. The here and now was all that mattered. She would write to Elsie, to make friends from a distance. There was no option to make any more of it than that. Elsie was the source of Erin's love of stories, but what could you do from the other side of the country other than send letters and cards. At least they'd had a laugh putting the old team back together for one last hurrah.

She wasn't far from Shepherd's Bush – which was a short walk from Television Centre in White City. She wrestled with it while they passed through another station.

Oh for God's sake…

At Shepherd's Bush, she hauled her suitcase out to the street and asked a passing elderly couple for directions. Leaving Shepherd's Bush Green by Wood Lane, she decided to make it a friendly farewell lunch. There would be no going back on her decision to leave though.

She stopped halfway up Wood Lane to catch her breath. Opposite was the old Wood Lane station, long since shut down through a lack of interest. *Closed stations. Ghosts stations. What a great setting for a story.* Maybe she'd write a novel. Or perhaps a play.

There was a phone box just ahead, which triggered something else she needed to do.

She phoned Elsie and confessed to the failure of the recording session. Elsie was philosophical.

"That's showbiz," she said.

"Perhaps you could do it again sometime?"

"No, we've been pushing our luck for a fair while. Davina's actually quite ill. She's just been able to hide it quite well until now. I'm afraid the lost voices shall remain lost. Maybe the gods of radio decided that a long time ago."

Erin felt sick.

"I'm so sorry, Elsie."

"Nonsense, it wasn't your fault. Besides, we had fun, Erin. Thank you for a great adventure."

Erin smiled and felt a little better.

She arrived at Television Centre and asked for Sarah. Five minutes later, her friend came down to reception and eyed the suitcase.

"You meant it then."

"Yes, I'm going home – via here, obviously."

"Let's have some lunch."

Erin followed Sarah up to the canteen, where they were soon sitting down to pizza and salad.

"Are you sure you're giving up?"

"It's time I grew up. Playing a female Peter Pan isn't working for me."

"Oh, I think you've grown up. No doubt about it. You've learned a lot."

"Well, I know I'm not completely rubbish at writing. The problem is I'm only in the 'reasonably good' category, which isn't good enough."

"I think you'd be a brilliant asset for the BBC."

"As a writer? Are you serious?"

"No, Erin, as a producer."

Erin was a little surprised.

"Are you just being nice?"

"Maybe you should have gone for one of the trainee producer jobs. I know it's only a one-year contract, but it's sixteen grand, which isn't too bad if you're prepared to live cheap while you go for it like a mad woman."

"If I remember rightly, the deadline passed an age ago."

"An age and a bit ago, to be exact."

"Well, there you are then. Too late. And, for what it's worth, I'm not the sort of person they're looking for."

"You're right about it being too late, but you're wrong about the sort of person they're looking for. Would you be up for a spot of time-travelling?"

Erin laughed. "I know they make *Dr Who* here, but… you haven't got the keys to the Tardis, have you?"

"No, but I do have an idea. If you want to become a trainee producer, I mean."

Erin couldn't get her head straight.

"Sarah, what are you talking about? I mean *exactly*?"

"Let me phone the admin office."

Sarah called a Broadcasting House number stored in her mobile phone.

"Carol? It's Sarah. Yes, I'm at TVC. Do you know if the trainee producer applications are still in with Roy Dixon? … Thanks." She put her hand over the phone. "She's just checking with Jodie."

Erin didn't understand at all. Roy Dixon was Head of Light Entertainment Radio. What was Sarah playing at?

"Yes, Carol? Yes, I just want to know if he's read them yet. They won't be there if he has."

Sarah smiled. "She won't be long."

Erin felt numb. She was due to get a train back to Taunton. What did it matter whether the Head of Light Entertainment Radio had or hadn't read the applications?

Sarah nodded. "Yes… yes… okay. Thanks, Carol."

She ended the call.

"Okay, Erin. How do you feel about applying?"

"What?"

"They're on his desk, unread, but he's due to read them because Personnel want a list of names for interviews."

"But aren't they logged into a system somewhere?"

"Yes, it's a system called 'Everything's On Roy's Desk.' If we add your application to the pile and he likes what he sees, he'll hand it to Personnel and… look, what I'm saying is we can do something to help you. When they eventually upgrade the computers, everything will be logged electronically and we won't be able to do what we're about to do."

"I see. So what *are* we about to do?"

"Roy's in a meeting with all the producers. We've probably got an hour. Come on, I can skip this afternoon. We're meant to be researching for a film shoot."

"What, right now?"

Five minutes later, they were outside hailing a cab.

"Broadcasting House, please," said Sarah.

They were soon on the Westway doing fifty miles an hour along the elevated section, over Notting Hill, over Westbourne Park, over the cabbie's café… mercifully, the Marylebone flyover was clear and a cut-through somewhere around Harley Street soon had them at their destination in Portland Place.

Sarah rushed into the building. Erin and her suitcase followed as best they could.

"Are you sure about this, Sarah?"

Up in LE, Sarah got Erin a blank job application form. "Right, let's do this."

Erin's head was in a spin.

"Name," said Sarah. "Write your name down."

"Name, yes, er…"

"Erin Goodleigh."

"Yes, that's it. Thanks Sarah."

It took thirty minutes to fill in the form. The stuff about why she thought she was suited to the job was a killer. One trick Sarah introduced was to suggest that Erin's slowly crumbling three Edinburgh shows were in fact deliberate reductions in the number of performers, from eight to two, in order to give the audience a more intimate experience. Erin thought Sarah was far better suited to applying for the job.

"Now sign it."

"Isn't this a kind of fraud or something?"

She signed it anyway – then they took it to the Head of Light Entertainment's office, where Sarah slid it into the pile while Erin waited outside in the LE reception area.

Just as Sarah emerged, Roy Dixon came in from the main corridor with Jodie and a couple of producers.

"Right, I'm getting my coat and I'm off home," said Roy.

"You haven't read the trainee producer applications," said Jodie.

"I'll take them with me. Tell Personnel I'll give them a list on Monday."

Erin and Sarah snuck away to Sarah's office.

"Job done," said Sarah.

"Honest opinion," said Erin. "My application and CV? Good enough?"

"Honest opinion? It's not bad."

"Not bad? As in not good enough?"

"I've seen the others, so... I thought it might have looked stronger on the page."

"Right. Well. Thanks for trying. I really appreciate it."

"You really are the right sort of person, Erin. I do mean that. It's a shame we couldn't beef up your CV in some way."

Erin's mobile phone rang.

"Erin, it's me. Are you in London or not?"

"I'm at Broadcasting House, Paul."

"Good. Stay there till Tuesday. I'll be in at lunchtime."

"I can't stay here till Tuesday."

"Well, stay in London then. I want to see you face-to-face. Then I'll know where we stand. For someone I've only been on one date with, you've made my life seem very complicated. Please don't go anywhere. You're a very important person to me."

Paul ended the call and Erin's choices stared her in the face. Could you fall in love with someone via e-mail, mobile phone calls and a single date? Okay, so she and Paul had been out many times as part of a group, and she'd got drunk and lusted after him, and he'd got drunk and lusted after her, and they had been friendly ever since she trod on his foot in a meeting a year earlier...

"So now what?" asked Sarah.

"Oh, that's easy. I either hurry off to Paddington or I wait till Tuesday for Paul and let him persuade me to stay."

"And the decision is...?"

36. FINALLY

Four Days Later…

Listening to the mid-morning Pop Quiz on Radio 2, Erin unpacked the last of her things from the suitcase. It was now a matter of having a coffee, having a think and having the courage to get through the rest of the day.

Moving out of the grotto had felt strange. Although it had never been a real home, she had got used to its atmosphere. It was nice to have a change of scenery though.

She checked her e-mails. Nothing. She re-read the last one she'd sent.

> Hi Paul
>
> I hope you have a pleasant, trouble-free journey and I look forward to seeing you at Broadcasting House.
>
> Yours
> Erin xxx

He had yet to reply, although there was a good reason for that. You couldn't reply if you were on a train. Assuming he was on a train. Or had he missed it?

No, of course he hasn't missed it!

It had been kind of Trish to invite her to share the new place in Neasden. She was glad she'd accepted. It was so freshly refurbished you could still smell the paint and new carpets.

She was also glad she'd be with Paul when he received his radio writing commission – which was happening today, although that was strictly unofficial as Jane Clearwater had told him in an off-the-record way. He deserved it. And he'd done a great job for Kirsty too – who was now teaming up with her Scottish producer-boyfriend to form their own independent production company. With Channel 4 already showing interest in their latest ideas, it was all incredibly exciting.

She tucked the letter from BT into her bag. An interview for an admin job in a fortnight. That was promising. She would step into the corporate world and do her best. She'd also get in touch with Elsie Haddon to arrange afternoon tea, even though Elsie would be disappointed to see Erin fall short of her dream. The main thing would be supporting Paul. If he got anywhere, his earnings would still be precarious for a while. On the downside…

Yes, the downside…

Could she be happy living close to – or possibly, at some point, *with* – someone who was doing what she had wanted her whole life? Wouldn't that drive her mad?

No.

She was facing the facts. She had tried and fallen short. She had been up there with the leading non-comms, but had just lacked that tiny missing piece that got people over the line and into the world of the successful writer. But in her heart, she knew how she felt about Paul.

An hour later, she arrived at Broadcasting House. This was it – the big lunchtime booze-up for the newly commissioned and those who were moving on. Erin would keep her upcoming interview to herself. This was their day, not one for her to drag everyone down with talk of jumping ship. Some of these people would go on to write on the biggest shows in Britain, possibly even the world. Twenty years from now, one or two of them might have a New York or Hollywood office, or be putting together the BBC's top-rated shows. It just wouldn't be Erin Goodleigh, and that's what hurt.

Still…

Up on the first floor, the gang had gathered. Paul was the only one missing: last reported leaving King's Cross Station. She checked the notice board where Sarah had left a neat handwritten note:

Dear all

Thanks for the lovely best wishes. Looking forward to my new job at TV Centre. Good luck to all of you. And those moving on to pastures new – do keep in touch!

Love and hugs
Sarah xxx

Next to Sarah's note was a drab, official statement announcing that *It's News To Us* and *Newslines* would both have six-week runs after Easter and then be cancelled permanently. In their place would be new shows with eight-week runs beginning in September. Non-comms were advised to contact the shows via a new information e-mail address.

Erin looked around. Ian was there, soon to be off to

Manchester to script edit a TV series. Colleen Nicholls and Simon Driver were there, freshly signed with a top TV writers' agent and soon to be working for the presenter of a very popular satirical panel show. Colleen would also be co-writing with Shaun Donoghue for Bob Coates on ITV with a whole series commission.

Joe Reece was there, too – soon to be writing for the presenter of a long-running music-based panel show. He'd met the producer through studio manager Sandy. Also, a Channel 4 daily breakfast show was looking for writers with a commissioned background. Shaun Donoghue would soon be starting a two-week trial at a thousand pounds a week and had promised to put in a word for Paul, who would see out the final editions of *INTU* as a commissioned writer.

Jane Clearwater and Gavin Gould came out to gather them.

"Okay, everyone here?"

Paul burst in from the main corridor.

"Hello London!"

Erin gave him a hug. Not a full-on one; that would have been embarrassing.

"Ahem," said Jane. "The commissioned writers for the final *INTU* shows are Paul Fielding, Michael Holbrook, Jamie Strand and Joe Reece. Congratulations all."

"Yes, congratulations," said Gavin. "I'll be checking to make sure your wallets are full before I march you to the pub."

"You are coming, Erin?" said Paul. He leaned in close. "It wouldn't be the same without the woman I—"

She pulled away.

"Yes, I just need…" …*a minute.*

Erin left the building by the main entrance and stood watching the traffic trundle by. Those heading south would hit Oxford Circus and Piccadilly Circus. North looked a better prospect. Those drivers would soon be up to Park Crescent with the prospect of driving into Regent's Park where they could get out and sit on a bench for a couple of hours, thinking about things.

No place for regrets, Erin. You gave it everything.

She took a deep breath – and coughed out the fumes. Yes, she would vent her writing passion in am-dram while supporting Paul a million percent. Everything was going to be just fine. Brilliant, even, if tinged slightly with sadness for what might have been. She would always be grateful to the BBC though. Their open doors had changed her life. And what's more…

"Ahem."

She'd know that ahem anywhere.

"You left in a hurry," said Paul, slightly out of puff from running. "Roy came out to say well done to everyone just as you went. He's asking to see you."

"What for?"

"It seems, over the past few days, Sarah and I… well, this morning Sarah told Roy you're exactly what the department needs and I phoned him to say how you edited and co-produced my pilot. Oh, and Joe Reece told him how you talent-spotted him and matched him with me to write sitcoms, Kirsty told him how you found her the ideal back-up writer for an urgent TV production, Sandy told him how you found her a last-minute talent replacement for a recording, Ian told him how you straightened out his approach to working with female talent, Callum Court told him you were incredibly professional to work with… phew, I'm out of breath."

"You and Sarah arranged all that?"

"We weren't sure if it would work, but…"

Erin's mobile phone rang. She pulled it out and stared

at it. Unknown number.

"It could be Roy."

She answered. "Erin Goodleigh speaking."

"Hello Erin, it's Roy Dixon, head of the department. I'd like you to work with us as a trainee producer. I think you'll do very well."

"You mean… wow…"

"There'll be an interview, but you have my personal recommendation. I've asked for you, Erin, so please say yes."

"Um, well, yes!"

"Excellent! Come and see me tomorrow at one for lunch. I'll tell you what I'm expecting of you."

"Yes. I will. Yes. Thank you, Roy!"

She ended the call, tucked the phone away and looked up at Paul through blurry eyes.

"Must be the pollution," he said. "It's making your eyes stream."

"Yes, well, I can't stand here all day."

"Look, seeing as you're going to be a producer…"

"Trainee producer," she said brushing away a tear.

"It's just that I've got a new idea for a sketch show and wondered if I could discuss it with you."

Erin's heart fired up. "Yes, well, it's certainly going to be part of my job to work with newly-commissioned writers."

"Perhaps we should have a meeting?" Paul suggested.

"I'll have to check my diary. Being a soon-to-be trainee producer, I might be busy – I'm already booked to meet the Head of Light Entertainment Radio for lunch tomorrow. Although, I *might* be able to see you…" she checked her watch "…in the Crown & Sceptre about now-ish?"

Paul drew her in close and kissed her on the lips. She

allowed it to go on for around ten seconds before pulling away.

"So that's about now-ish in the pub," she said, wanting to dance with him all the way down to Oxford Circus and back.

"I love you, Erin Goodleigh."

"Yes, well, right. It's Paul, isn't it?"

"Yes, Paul Fielding."

"Yes, well, I love you too, Paul Fielding."

"Great."

She leaned up and kissed him. Then, as they set off for the pub, she pulled her phone out again. Her parents and Elsie Haddon would be keen to learn her news – but first, Sarah and Trish had to be told how she was madly in love and about to begin a brilliant new career.

Before she tapped in the first number, she looked up at Paul and smiled.

"If I'm still talking when we get to the pub, mine's a large chardonnay."

37. THE TOP FLOOR

The present day.

The lift came to a halt on the top floor.

"Here we are," said Jonathan.

Erin followed him out and a short way along the corridor.

"If you could just wait one moment."

Jonathan knocked and entered. But even before Erin was summoned within, she could hear a sound that took her back a couple of decades. It was all in the email, of course, how the recordings Erin made had been unearthed by an audio archivist. The Wednesday Club Singers had been found and would form a small part of a radio documentary looking back at the history of Broadcasting House and the names, big and small, that had made its reputation.

As a producer with fifteen years' television experience alongside her five years in radio, Erin wanted to turn it into a multimedia experience, with a TV and radio documentary alongside interactive online content.

Sometimes things get lost, but it doesn't mean they can't been found again. Whether it was Paul and Erin telling their daughter Sophie not to fret over a missing earring as they got ready for an awards ceremony, or an unauthorized studio recording of three lovely old ladies singing their hearts out – never giving up hope, that was the main thing.

THE END

To keep up to date with all my new releases, simply pop over to my website where all the latest news is waiting for you.

www.markdaydy.co.uk

Many Thanks,

Mark

Printed in Great Britain
by Amazon